Inno

"Those who are [...] [...] [...] d for use in the Temple," Carpen said.

"Where I may be, in time, converted?" Bulinga sneered.

"I have told you . . . I cannot permit myself to be diverted from a plan which will give to the Temple that which belongs to it."

"You will have to use force," Bulinga said, and knew his answer long before he gave it.

"I will use force if necessary," Carpen said.

Bulinga ran to the doorway. For one wild moment of hope and triumph she thought she was away. She gained the passageway. Then Carpen's hand was around her waist and his other hand on the back of her neck forced her body over; forced her to fold. The pressure was cruel. She struggled and fought—Carpen held her easily, impassively.

"Let me go!" she stormed. "How dare you lay your hands on my body! I will not be used in the Temple!"

He pulled her back, her heels sliding over the plank floor.

"You will come to no harm," he said. . . . "You will be taught, and you will learn. . . ."

Books by Jane Gaskell

THE ATLAN SAGA
    The Serpent
    The Dragon
    Atlan
    The City
    Some Summer Lands

King's Daughter
Strange Evil

Published by POCKET BOOKS

Jane Gaskell —

KING'S
DAUGHTER

PUBLISHED BY POCKET BOOKS NEW YORK

POCKET BOOKS, a Simon & Schuster division of
GULF & WESTERN CORPORATION
1230 Avenue of the Americas, New York, N.Y. 10020

ISBN: 0-671-82165-2

First Pocket Books printing August, 1979

10 9 8 7 6 5 4 3 2 1

Trademarks registered in the United States and other countries.

Printed in the U.S.A.

Preface

When, after much debate and with some reservations, we published Jane Gaskell's first novel, *Strange Evil,* written when she was fourteen, we were naturally influenced in our decision by a careful consideration of her second book, which she wrote a very short while afterward and brought in to us at the same time. Reading the two books together convinced us that her talent was a sturdy growth, and would not, as some critics have feared, fade through early exposure. She has, in fact, in revising this book, derived much benefit from the wealth of advice and criticism the publication of *Strange Evil* has brought her; and she has emerged from the inevitable plethora of publicity with dignity, grace and charm, and with writing still as her main interest in life.

Her début has, strangely enough, coincided with the appearance of an increasing number of other child writers, and this would be a disadvantage if her writing depended for interest upon its curiosity. The reception of *Strange Evil* has shown that it does not. Her talent is, and will clearly remain, a highly individual one, and response to it will therefore inevitably be diverse. But *King's Daughter,* like *Strange Evil,* while intriguing as a *tour de force,* can be read with delight by all those who are still sensitive to imaginative writing. In it she departs from the supernatural world, and, as she explains in her own prefatory note, chooses a setting remote in pre-history, when, according to the Hoerbiger Theory, the world was without a moon. The civilization she conjures up is visualized and described with complete consistency, and she draws for her many exotic details sometimes upon her own imagination, and sometimes upon the reading she has done about this period. Her story is one of adventure and search, most thrilling at its climax, and quietly moving at its unexpected close. Much of its strength lies in the variety and scope of her inventiveness, but she shows a marked advance in the handling of sustained narrative and a refreshingly objective interest in character.

King's Daughter is an original and ambitious book, and it has, of course, its youthful idiosyncrasies. These, combined as they are with an often astonishing maturity of thought and expression, and the latent poetry which is characteristic of her writing, add to it a curious and attractive flavor. Her imagination is so robust and her visual sense so clear-cut that she can project us into her world and make us accept it on her own terms.

Author's Note

The civilization written of in *King's Daughter* is that of a time on earth when there was no moon.

It is a widely held theory that the small dead planet which is our present moon was captured about fifteen thousand years ago by the gravitational power of our earth; that before then, between then and a much earlier period prior to the disintegration of a previous, much smaller, moon, the earth enjoyed a moonless era, a longer day, and a climate much different from that which we know. It is held that in this time famed Atlantis and legendary Mu between them ruled a world which perished and whose continental masses were radically altered by the cataclysms accompanying the capture of our present moon.

Mu is supposed to have lain in the Pacific area and the action of this story is placed on a land approximately where Indo-China is today.

1

It was on the third night of the trader's stay that Bulinga decided she must leave Grood.

One of the palace servants lurched toward her, dexterously coping with a tray of the small fruit pies. He had almost tripped over one of the large cats which prowled and played and purred about the hall.

Bulinga waved him away.

"I do not want any," she said, and he picked his way irritably among the cats and offered the cakes to the other ladies.

Jura, Bulinga's aunt, took fifteen. She chose carefully, counting them and carefully placing them, almost surreptitiously, in a little heap beside her. Her wish to appear dignified was quite unequal to the controlling of her greed. Already this evening she had had many dozens between courses. The eternal excuse reached Bulinga's ear.

"They are so very small . . ."

Jura's daughter Egfra bridled self-consciously when the tray was held before her. She swept a pile to the table and pursed her mouth affectedly, considering her action.

"Aren't I greedy?" she giggled, and, suddenly imperious, ordered the man from her.

From her seat—safely afar from them—Bulinga regarded them with scorn.

Egfra delighted in being more of a princess than her cousin. She had decided years before that the rank was more hers, and no one objected. Bulinga, with the help of her mother's blood, scorned to. Jura had no objection. The only other who could object, Rugul, said nothing. He never saw anything but the goblet in front of him.

Egfra felt she was born to command. She had, she thought, the manner, and she considered herself the rightful Princess by descent. All her blood was royal, she had informed her associates. As indeed it was. On both sides she was descended from the Royal House of Grood—and who knew what Bulinga's mother had been before she became Rugul's captive slave and then Queen? Anything can be said of an alien when nothing can be proved and it would be like Rugul to insist that his Queen was of importance in the world outside.

Bulinga, from the Princess's seat, regarded Egfra's imperiousness and made her a mental gift. She could have it all, soon.

One of the biggest cats looked up with a snarl. It was hungry. It placed its paws on Jura's lap.

Jura laughed shrilly and threw it a fruit pie.

"Nice catty," she said. "Dear animals," she informed her admiring sycophants.

The women chattered, squealed, and laughed in little coteries around the broad low braziers on which were huge indeterminate animals roasting whole. Jura and her court shrilled and lorded from the circlet of little tables round the great pillar.

The men were separate—but no quieter. Their noise was more of a bass undertone.

At the tables the men sat—and drank.

Not for the men the small breathlessly sweet fruit pies between courses. The men drank a liquid which had something of the quality of flames. They drank amidst a continuous battering, a not entirely unmusical pounding of a myriad unmatched drums, the sound of pot after pot being pounded on the table, the signal for the pitcher to be passed along. This particular part of the noise hurt the great savage cats and they slunk past the tables with folded ears.

At the corner of the great dais, alone except for the attendance of her own slave, Bulinga brooded. This seat had been her mother's. It was for the reigning queen—a tradition Bulinga had broken. It gave her some peace from Jura and the others to sit here, for the seat was hedged invisibly but surely. Only Bulinga had dared to break the petty taboos with which they had bound themselves.

Rugul had made no objection. When appealed to by Jura he had merely laughed into his goblet.

Rugul was laughing into his goblet now.

Both arms and one booted leg spread over the royal table, he lounged in the Great Seat; for the twentieth time he pushed back the thick hangings which always swung to enfold him; for the twentieth time he cursed by the Moon that was Gone and sprawled forward over the table again, drank deep and pounded for the pitcher—unnecessarily, for there was a special pitcher, and a special servant for the pitcher, always beside him.

The trader and his men came into the hall late.

They paused in the entrance, were seen, and their entrance applauded by a shout. There were more shouts, a pause in the appalling din, the welcome grew, they were welcomed vociferously.

Rugul, with a kick, dispatched his pitcher servant as a messenger to the trader.

There was a dignity, unmatched in Grood, in the trader's easy path to the Great Table where Rugul was with his noblest, and a condescension unnoticed save by Bulinga, in his easy acceptance of the seat of honor on Rugul's right. He had all the grace of a young man; too young, some would have thought, to have been elected leader of the traders. A small smile glimmered satirically in his eyes. These crude people amused him even while they paid him many gold parings for the goods he brought them, and he was vastly entertained by them while they thought they honored him by seating him at their Great Table for Rugul to speak with nearly as an equal and to fill his cup for him.

Rugul, the King, pounded for more drink.

"A cup for Emalf," bawled the King.

There was bustle. Ridiculous, boring, stupid, redundant bustle, thought Bulinga with scorn. But Emalf got his cup. And it was filled, from Rugul's own pitcher, and Emalf drank a toast to Rugul and to Grood and to the Princess Bulinga, to which Bulinga nodded regally, and to the nobles and the people and the history and the future of Grood. And after that there was more pounding on the tables and while Bulinga picked delicately with her silvered skewers at the dish in her lap, Rugul her father emptied his goblet to the success and long life of Emalf and his friends and his men. For these three nights of feasting, of which this was the last, were in honor of the traders and of the things they brought, including news from the world beyond the great forest which hemmed in Grood and protected Grood from the world and protected the world from the rude good-humored brutality of Grood.

"My last night here," thought Bulinga.

Bulinga saw Emalf's eyes glint a little in the torchlight.

He had looked, again, across at her.

When this night was over he would be gone and with his going the impossible dreariness would return. The three brief days of feasting and bartering and listening to the strange songs and the stories of his men would be over till another whole year had ceased to exist. During that time, if she stayed here, her new clothes would have palled on her; the ornaments she had bought yesterday and which at the moment seemed so novel, so magnificent—she knew that by the traders' next visit, when another whole year had dragged past its slow weight, she would hate the sight of them. If she stayed here.

During the past three days it had come to her gradually but more strongly than ever before that for the rest of her life, between the visits of the traders, she would be immured with these stupid proud people.

Soon the life, the individuality, would be stifled within her.

Whom would she wed?

But it would be one of them. It must be.

Emalf, a trader when abroad, was courtly in Grood, like a king among barbarians; and he was only a trader.

She must clear all the issues in her mind.

Was she to spend all the numberless years until her death doing nothing but trying to hold her mind clear and safe from anesthesia?

She would escape now because she must.

It was a duty to her soul, to her self.

She could not let her self be erased, and what was left be smudged, by the dreary stagnation here. There was so much of dreariness here, and tonight, dull as it was, was a gala night in Grood. Her everyday existence was so dull, with the monotonous dreary deadening death of morphia, that she knew much more of it would be fatal. And even the fatality would be without excitement.

She glanced round the enormous wooden hall, her face unfriendly and aloof from the clatter and din, from the cacophony of laughter and stupid shouting and the drunken bawling of monotonous droning drinking songs. She looked from one to the others of the traders trying to judge, to guess, to decide whose help she would be most likely to enlist—and her glance met the glance of Emalf—and she felt that, perhaps, he was the best, perhaps the only one.

Emalf's eyes widened.

Rugul filled his cup for him.

Bulinga planned the details of flight.

It must of course be tonight.

It was exciting.

But it was cold excitement.

Here was none of that joy in escaping. This was duty.

True at the end of it all there was Nipsirc, Dejanira, perhaps Atlan!

Emalf smiled. His gaze left Bulinga's face which

had been star-pale compared to the brown faces of all others in the hall.

"You leave us tomorrow," Rugul boistered. "And all we've had from you is women's talk—sleeves and —and the Moon alone knows what, for I don't. Man, there are men here. Is there nothing that matters happening out there? A new fashion in clubs, a new way of wearing handspikes, eh?" he laughed. His wit pleased him. It pleased those near him too. There was even more babble.

Emalf rose and the King pounded with his goblet and the server hastened to his duty and was thrust back so that he fell and drenched himself. Other servers brought in the eighth course, a bison roasted in spice.

"Give me peace. Peace," bawled Rugul.

The noise in the hall rose to a pitch, stilled a little and then rose clangorously as everyone settled to listen.

Emalf spoke of warring, of revolts, battle. He spoke of Rutas-Mu, the great country far to the East whose peaks could be seen, if you traveled to the coast, on the wet horizon: and Bulinga leaned forward to catch his words and learn all she could of the outer world.

He described the wonderful cities and the people and the wrestling for power of a new religion, but spoke lightly of the latter for it quickly became obvious that no one was interested and instead he spoke of the queerness of the land—of how half of the great islands of Rutas-Mu were more savage and more terrible than was any other place on earth; of the great saurians—of the cruel and brutish giants who lived in the fastnesses of its poisonous forests. But against that was the good half, he reminded them, less civilized only than the colossal and great northern continent of Atlan, although more corrupt.

Atlan! Her mother's land. Was it too much to hope for? The traders reached everywhere. And if a mother could come from there surely a daughter could go back.

Except that her mother had come as a slave. There must be eternities full of barbarous tribes between Grod and Atlan.

She must first go where the traders would take her —and she knew they were bound for Nipsirc. For where but Nipsirc, the great trading center of this side of Tellur, could a trader make for—after Grood?

It would be fortunate that there were no horses in Grood.

She would be gone, gone from Grood, for ever and ever. No coming back, no smallest chance of being brought back, for Bulinga knew that horses could travel faster and farther than could man. And the men of Grood had not been designed for speed of movement.

Bulinga's hand, as always when she was deep in thought, went to her throat.

The little silver pangolin there, on its fine chain of orialc, had been her mother's. Bulinga thought of it as being still her mother's. And when in thought, or in need of her mother's counsel, her fingers fondled it, the only thing purely of her mother's she possessed. It was a beautiful piece of jeweler's art, from some distant Northern Kingdom. The pangolin, twisting its body, so that the representation had just the requisite touch of comicality. The expression on the face of the little silver animal was purely animal but of almost human astonishment. So pangolins looked, in reality, as Bulinga knew, for there had been two in the palace grounds when she was a little girl and they were so exactly like her jewel except that the jeweler had made of it an albino and the tiny rubies which had been its eyes had long since fallen from their settings and been lost.

"Not," the trader was explaining fairmindedly, "that the people of Dejanira lead a licentious life, but from what we hear of the people of Atlan none of at least their ruling caste has ever done a base action, much less thought a base thought, in the whole of their lives."

"Yes. Oh, yes. We've heard of Dejanira and of the islands of Rutas-Mu," agreed Rugul. "But how often has their ruler with his bare hands broken a boar across his knee?"

There was a hoarse, quickly stifled, laugh from somewhere, and much murmured appreciation of this question of Rugul's. The King could do this. He'd done it once, seventeen years before.

Emalf had known this would be mentioned. It always was.

He eased himself into his chair. He'd had a long day. On his feet since dawn. And everything to be checked and packed before they came to the feast tonight, for they would be off before the next dawn. There would be no sleep for him tonight. Not that he minded that, though. He could sleep as he traveled, tomorrow. But that didn't alter his tiredness of now.

Break a boar over his knee.

His eyes flicked to Rugul and away. As on previous occasions, year after year, he granted it could be true.

And a man like this had a daughter—like that one over there!

Emalf found this less credible.

Rugul was turning to him again, his mouth open to speak.

Emalf forgot Rugul's royalty and spoke first.

"That boar wasn't your only great deed. You begot a wondrously beautiful daughter."

Rugul, almost in a rage, was diverted and chuckled. "Bulinga? That one! Is that something else Dejanira can't better?" He stared across at his daughter and some of his drunkenness left him.

"It was for that beauty I raised her mother, who was a slave, to be my Queen." Rugul turned more to his guest, leaning his elbow on the thick baulks of the table, cupping his granite chin in his huge thick-fingered hand, looking less than before a possible father to Bulinga. His broad back turned to his court, shut them off. He was alone with Emalf.

Meshed in a trap of minute red lines, overhung by

the great bony ridges and the tangled white wire brows of the ape in him, his small protuberant eyes bored with unwonted kingliness into Emalf's.

"She was a princess of Atlan—before she was my slave."

Emalf conceded the kingliness in Rugul.

Surely he'd never noted that quality, here, before.

Though it was hardly the kingliness of more civilized courts.

Perhaps it was the fieriness of the liquid of Grood on a tired mind that worked on Emalf, but he found his tongue venturing further impertinence.

"There is no doubt in my mind, Most Estimable Liege, but that her mother, your Queen, was a princess of Atlan. Doubtless she thus gets her beauty."

He thought that would pass; but it didn't.

There was no narrowing of Rugul's eyes, nor did they widen, but the smile, the hint of a smile in them retreated and became distant and Emalf knew that his, Rugul's, eyes had not dilated one jot but they seemed now to be so big that Emalf could see nothing else, and Rugul's eyes which were ordinarily blue-gray had become—but for that merest hint of a smile—had become the expressionless colorless coldly contemplative eyes of the animal on the verge of the kill.

Emalf spoke warily.

"Her blood shows in her."

For what to Emalf seemed long minutes Rugul regarded him fixedly, then with a muttered appeal to the Moon that was Gone he belched, and relaxed.

"Traders do not speak to Kings of Grood like that, my friend," he said almost softly. "Have your cup filled and think of other things."

A small tightness eased inside Emalf. The King's hand beckoned and the cups were filled. They raised them and drank, without speech, and Rugul turned away and Emalf saw he must now excuse himself and leave.

Who would have thought the old ape could have summoned all that presence, mused the trader. He regarded Rugul's monumental form with new-found appreciation. "So that's why he is King," he thought. And then he remembered the daughter. Of the House of Atlan, was she, and her sire . . . Even in his mind the sentence was left unfinished, but there lingered in his memory those great eyes of the Princess, the largest he'd ever seen, the fantastic beauty of her, and he knew now from where had come at least a large share of the regality her every movement betokened.

He smiled a little ruefully.

It was a pity she was a princess.

And what, anyway, had been the stifled message in her eyes when they'd met his, this evening?

Well, whatever it was, he could do without learning it.

He was a trader, no boar to be broken by those great hands.

2

Emalf's long sleeve was caught and he whirled about, a long broad black blade ready in his hand, his arm drawn back for the slicing thrust that was peculiar to the forest-bred men of Guanche.

Even by the miserly light of the stars he saw at once it was a girl, and the blade disappeared as magically as it had happened. Bulinga was interested in this. Traders were not supposed to wear weapons within a town, and moreover Emalf had just left her father's hall, and, in fact, the King's presence. There had been about him no sign of a weapon, or keen eyes would have discerned it.

"Where," she asked, "is it sheathed?"

Emalf grinned ruefully in the darkness.

This wasn't one of his lucky nights.

First the father and now the daughter.

But his mind was slow. Very slow tonight.

The non-existent Moon alone knew why he was so honored, or perhaps if he asked the lady would tell him.

Emalf, almost master of himself again, bowed to the Princess Bulinga and waited for her to speak. He grinned to himself again. He'd learned tonight to respect this family.

"We shall go over into the shadows," said Bulinga.

"As you wish," agreed Emalf and meekly followed her to the pitch-black shelter of one of the terrific buttresses, formed of the whole trunks of trees, which at regular intervals supported the high walls.

He was intrigued, but only a little.

Something of the traders' wares which she desired and which was beyond her purse, he supposed, would be the reason for this waylaying. And, he fancied, she gave sufficient thought before acting. He wasn't being led to the buttresses near the door, where they were so liable to be interrupted by those from the hall whose desire to urinate was too urgent to permit them a long walk. She brought him well round the side of the building and practically opposite the porch to another typically Groodian edifice, doubtless to give her quick recourse to where her own rooms lay. What she hadn't considered was the danger in which he stood if he were found leaving this quarter.

So far, all had gone well. They were paid no attention.

Of course, it was dark. The Groodians bothered not at all about light. Once it was dark it was dark. But when it was time for him to leave it might be another matter. Nobles in constant numbers were now leaving the hall, for the shelter of the buttresses which must be noisome. And each noble was accompanied by at least one, sometimes by two, of the great savage hunting cats. There was much talking and song now near the hall doors.

She turned and faced him: close, so that he could almost see her.

"I desire that you take me to Dejanira, in Rutas-Mu," she said.

That startled Emalf from his placidity.

"I—will pay you well," she added.

There was a little silence.

"Does your father know of this?" and "Do you realize what you ask of me?" he said. "We leave, the most of us, in about three hours' time; is that enough to prepare for such a journey? And I have no such facilities as you would require. Traders' parties such as mine are unaccustomed to traveling with royalty."

She had waited for him to finish, impatiently, for he heard her foot tapping the ground.

"These questions are superfluous," she told him. "I am running away. But I want you to take me. Do you expect me to go on foot?"

The trader was rubbing his chin.

Dreams, that her beauty had brought, of selling her in Nipsirc for the figure her figure would fetch, returned to him amply reinforced by promise of reality. But, whether that was or wasn't the outcome, Emalf couldn't now be sure of his later decisions in this matter. If he could get her away . . .

His quick mind agreed that Grood was a place to run from. It never occurred to him to question the wisdom of her desire. But how wise would he be to help her? And *could* he help her?

"My lady," he said quietly. "You must understand that for me to help you to leave here, against the wishes of your estimable father the King, is to expect much of me. I do good remunerative trade in my yearly visits here. I could never return. For us to leave at the same time would be sufficient for Rugul." He smiled grimly. "If I help you it must be more subtly than that."

"This is your last year here," Bulinga reminded him.

"Is it so? And who told you of that, Regality?"

"No matter. I know."

He looked at where the girl's eyes should be—and there was there the merest glimmer of white.

"Who told you?" he asked.

Bulinga smiled thinly.

"I myself heard you remark of it to one other. Yesterday when I looked at cloths. Because I was at your stall there was no other there. But I kept the fact. It seemed to me you might more easily help me."

"Yes," he agreed. "You have me there."

His mind shifted again.

Why shouldn't he? For a jewel like this, with her slim rich beauty, her evident breeding, those superbly lovely purple eyes, and, moreover, that particular utter fairness—for her hair was the white of a priceless milk-white foal from Urga—for all this her price in Nipsirc's market would be fabulous indeed. He almost heard the bidding now. It would be easy to trick her there. He had only to get her away. She was young, virgin he'd swear.

Emalf leant back against the timbering.

He disliked doing business in darkness. He liked to see as he dealt. He was a trader. Had chosen this calling years before—or had it chosen him? Anyway he was a trader and to be one was lucrative enough. And would be more so if he could get this morsel away, and the pith of it was she'd be coming willingly. And why not? Even if she meant now to be other than a slave, she herself would be rich before the year was out, if she used her charm to that end, and what woman wouldn't? No woman was fit for more than a man's pleasure, but when they had royal blood they were at their best, having inherited worthy characteristics, so that men should bow to such, and he'd give her the opportunity to collect many bows, to her advantage.

"Give me a few moments for thought, Your Tranquilness," he suggested; and, without really caring how she felt about that rather brusque treatment, settled himself to consider thoroughly.

If she were willing to go, she could. It was as simple as that. Doubtless if she were running away she would accept suggestions which would help to keep her departure unknown until the traders had time to get well away. He must warn Carpen about that. Carpen intended to wait his departure until later. He'd better not. But that was by the way. He could get her away all right—and as she came willingly she'd stay with him willingly, until Nipsirc. He could cope with that end, too, easily enough. But his cavalcade would take some time to reach Nipsirc and he didn't quite like the thought of her in his possession until then, during all the stops he must make and among his ruffians of men. For he could not risk damaging such goods as this by keeping her enclosed in a prison all day; he must let her walk upon the ground between the men each day when she was tired of her litter so that she could exercise: he must let her know nothing of what he purposed for her until the actual crisis came.

If he could tell from what he had heard before and learned of her just now, she was obstinate and of more fire than reason; such people were unpleasant to provoke; she'd have to be in ignorance until the very last, but specious tales and arguments could keep her mollified and within his will.

Surely all that could be done, and care kept.

By the Yolk of the Egg of the Serpent, let anyone else just so much as lay a finger on her and the party would be fewer, by a trader or two, when they finished up at Nipsirc's canopied bazaars.

He looked through the darkness to her.

The emotions penned up in Bulinga found their outlet and tumbled out in a disdain of traders.

"Well, trader," she demanded, "I have waited. Have you counted what you dare do?"

He could feel her haughtiness.

"Your Tranquilness," he began gravely in a tone

suggesting he wished to mollify her. "You must, to begin with, understand that my taking you to Rutas-Mu would put me in danger with your father. None knows what may come to a man. It might easily be that I should later return. And that I must put from me, whatever it may ultimately cost me."

She brushed aside his danger, not seeing what it might cost her.

"You will take me then?" she asked eagerly, all her soul in her voice.

The trader in him ignored her soul. She'd come all right and at his price. But still he mustn't seem too keen to help her.

"You will give me gold in advance?" He used a wary tone.

"You may have forty full-weight gold parings in advance," she answered, "for a safe journey."

His hands spread themselves in the darkness: his astonishment was not even feigned.

"Your Tranquilness," he expostulated. "Two hundred parings is the least I should ask for a journey to as far as Rutas-Mu, and even after that we might travel many days to reach the island on which Dejanira yet grows. And it must then be enough for me to return to the mainland, for I have no other business to be in Rutas-Mu. Mainland traders such as I are not welcome there. In Rutas-Mu they have their own guilds."

"Forty parings is all I can spare," insisted Bulinga.

"It would take twenty more to cover the cost of your food and journeying to Nipsirc," cried Emalf. Of course she had more wealth than that. It was reasonable that she'd keep some back, for spending in Dejanira when she reached there.

"Surely a princess can pay more than that to someone who will help her to escape, against all loyalty to her family."

"*You* owe no loyalty to my family and you are in no danger, for we both know you will not be here again. I see no reason for extra price. I can eat what there happens to be and I can sleep on the ground. I had no thought to travel as royalty journeying."

He thought she had a small knowledge of the world if she did not know what would come to her if she slept on the ground among the men. Great Yolk, it would really be expensive to him to provide the necessary guards and the wage big enough to keep the guards honest.

"But," he said, "you are a princess."

"I am not allowed money, except when you come," she flared. "And of what I had most was spent on the ornaments and gowns I have bought from you in the past three days. I am afraid I cannot offer them back to you. It—it happens that my aunt puts my things away with her own for me."

"Your Tranquilness, I find this not fully to be believed . . ."

"You are impertinent," she flashed.

Well, it probably was true, he conceded mentally, but he must not give in too soon. He was afraid of awakening her suspicions. She might notice nothing now but would be likely to retrace this evening in her mind—when she was clear of Grood and she met her first discomforts.

"You think me grasping," he told her quietly, "but indeed the cost of a rodent's food for that time would be more than forty parings . . ." He left the sentence unfinished so that he could spread his hands toward her in a pleading way. His gaze was demure as it met her stormy one.

Bulinga began to feel desperate.

Soon they would be seen. Now they could see each other. The feasting had reached the stage when the women left and only the stalwarts remained with Rugul to drink the dawn in.

This light!

This huckster before her!

She had, in reality, if he would only believe her, no more than she said. She had cut herself down to retaining just less than ten parings for her own use when she reached Dejanira and had, she saw now, made the mistake of offering, at the very beginning, the maximum payment she could make.

She made a last despairing appeal.

"If you will not . . ."

"So you are seeing sense at last," he broke in. "You would be miserly indeed if you did not give me at least a hundred parings, my dear Princess; my *very* dear Princess."

Bulinga looked at him. Her lip trembled. She thought she saw he was adamant and fury grew within her. So her hope was gone. She could not leave with the traders' cavalcade.

"I will not be so spoken to!" she cried violently. "You want too much money! You insist on more than you know I have, and you don't in the least need it for such service as I asked! Very well, you can do without my forty parings, small sum though you say it is. For I'm not going with you!"

She turned away and ran.

A quick glance about assured him that none had yet perceived them or considered them of interest. He pursued her.

She was breathing unevenly as he caught her and turned her round to him. He saw wonderingly that she was crying; she must be at once poorer and more desperate than he had believed. Her face was wild with anger.

"Leave me now!" she cried.

"Your Tranquilness," Emalf said humbly, "I would not let you think me unwilling to help you—I'll . . ."

"Never, never, never!" she cried, and stamped her foot like a naughty child that throws its chance away for anger. "I would not take passage with you were I allowed to pay *nothing* for it! I will show all of you what I am capable of! I will *walk* to Dejanira!"

He laughed briefly.

He'd lost a fortune. A man can be many times a fool in the space of a short life. He was sorry for

what he'd done to her, too. So cruel a destiny, for
such a girl, to be born into Grood.

He said:

"I advise you, however, Your Tranquilness, not to
adventure that road in the clothes of a princess. And
find yourself a dagger, my girl. You'll need more than
woman's wits to get you to Rutas-Mu, but you'll probably take my advice only when you leave Grood. And
that's unlikely, isn't it?"

3

Emalf spat out the remnants of the plug of seasoned
bison meat he'd been chewing. It fell short of the dying
fire and he pushed it forward with the toe of his boot
and kicked it so that it landed sizzling among the
embers.

"At this stage of a journey I always prefer caravan-
ning up into the deserts, Carpen," he said. "You can
load camels and leave them loaded for hours. They'll
sit perfectly contented till you want them. Horses you
can't do till the last moment."

The man to whom he spoke was lean, older and
solemn.

He didn't laugh sympathetically as he should have
done. He accepted the remark as a statement and
silently considered it.

Emalf knew what was happening.

"My friend," he thought, "I'd think you a fool if
I didn't know you weren't. But that religion of yours
is taking too much of you. A man's religion is something to brighten his hopes, and encourage him to
better actions, but you make of it a whipping stool.

And it deadens your common sense. You'll land in trouble yet. In half an hour's time you'll tell me you don't really agree with me and why." He wouldn't wait for that though. In two hours it would be getting light. There were still some not returned from the feast. They could leave with friend Carpen and see how they enjoyed that. Though why Carpen wanted to go directly back through the Jilvassian forests to Nipsirc when there was much trading to be done yet on the roundabout open route was beyond his comprehension. He supposed it was again something to do with religion.

Religion. Pah.

He'd tasted a dozen.

The forests were no place for a trader.

Though if he'd had that girl he might look himself for a more direct route.

Carpen was a fool.

Antagonizing too many people. Becoming more of a bore as he aged.

Emalf grunted something indistinguishable which Carpen could take as he liked, moved away to the piles of merchandise, sat himself alone on a wide pack saddle and looked about.

There were only three fires left in the yard behind the palace. The others had died and been dug over into the earth so no sparks could be fanned by a rising wind; though, he thought as he sniffed the air, it smelt like a fine day coming. Camels were better. He'd miss all this, in Nipsirc, and wish himself back on the trading routes. But he'd enough wealth now to live a more comfortable life than was possible eternally trudging from one to another of the little uncivilized kingdoms.

Two yawning figures, staggering somewhat, loomed up out of the darkness, ignored Emalf, and, grumbling, set about locating their own saddles.

Emalf smiled. If he hadn't upset Rugul's befuddled pride, he might himself be suffering from too much of Rugul's sak.

A snarl like a hoarse cough made him stand still.

One of those brutes of hunting cats. Surely it couldn't be that one of his had got loose! No. There was the animal that had made the noise, lying, belly down, guarding its drunken master, one of Grood's picturesque pot stalwarts.

May everyone's gods combine and keep safely within their cages the two cats he'd bought. They'd cost enough. There was nothing else a trader could take from Grood. But what a price they'd been to buy.

And what was this? A horse loose!

"Stop, you fool! Stop!" he shouted, and under his breath: "All right, you drunken fool, I'll stop you."

Running swiftly Emalf caught the bridle, dug his heels into the tough earth and pulled the pony's head hard down and down and in practically the same moment grasped the ankle of the mounted Groodian and pulled. There was a squeal of pain and surprise and rider, saddle and very nearly horse as well fell in a heap on the ground.

The two fumblers from the saddle heap came running over.

"Thieving a horse, eh!" shouted one.

There was no sound from the figure at his feet, but Emalf had a handful of long loose hair.

"All right, I can handle this," he asserted. "You two get on with loading up."

He waited till their retreating figures were dim blurs in the fading light of the dying fires.

"Now, Your Regality," he said, almost grimly, "what do you think you're doing? That way would take you back into Grood."

He released her hair and, shifting his grip to her arm, helped her up, in fact pulled her up.

"Yes, it's you all right," he said. "Now what am I to do with you? Were you here to join us after all, or were things as they seem and were you making off on your own with one of my horses?"

Bulinga, handled so for the first time in her life, didn't like it. She endeavored to wriggle her arm away.

He seemed not to notice the movement. She was still held.

Coldly she said:

"Take your hand away."

"I'm not sure that I should," replied Emalf. "Oh, lose the impression that you can command now. I shall never be back here to have your vengeance wreaked on me. And, on your own, away from Grood, you really cease to command the privileges of royalty. To me, at the moment, you're no more than a chit of a girl in boy's clothes who has been caught trying to steal a horse. You must see that, you know," he continued, in a much less bantering tone, "if you *are* going to escape, and it appears you mean to.

"It's a blow to your pride, isn't it?" he said, even more kindly, "but you'll get used to it. And what made you try to ride off on a horse without first tightening the bridle and girths?" He picked up the saddle with knack and easy strength and fastened it again on the horse's back.

Bulinga watched him moodily.

All he said was very true and, hard though it was, after the initial shock she knew it was so. But she was seething inwardly with rage, and resentment.

Danger after danger she had circumvented and now he had stopped her, just as she was finally getting away, and stopped her with comparatively little effort, and treated her like a naughty child.

Her eyes blazed at his back. If she'd had a weapon, she felt she would have plunged it into him.

She couldn't trust herself to speak.

He finished. More slowly than he need have, for he was sorting his own emotions.

When he turned to her, the reins loose in his fingers for the horse was quite quiet, there was admiration and liking in his eyes and his voice.

"Why not just come with us, lady? We could be friends, and you'll need them, you know. We'll be away in a very short time now. Come as my guest; I'll not charge you a single link of metal." He paused.

"You could learn to be a trader on the way," he laughed. "There's a good living in it, Tranquilness, and I like your courage . . ."

He broke off.

"Hey, you!"

A figure shambled forward.

Emalf's tone became rough.

"So it's you, Patta—can't you ever leave the barrels alone? I told you at the tables before I left tonight, we're nearly due gone and there's little done. Are the others coming? Finished, is it? Well, hurry with things: I must be well away by light-come. I've reason, more than before, and find Carpen and ask him to see me on an urgent matter. . . ."

His voice was fainter to Bulinga for she was stepping backward, and farther back, and turning and hurrying away, her cap in her hand, her belongings tightly clasped in a bundle against her. Hot tears welled in her eyes and crawled in scalding lines down her cheeks. Her knees shook as she walked.

She would never go with him, never, never, never. "Oh mother, help, help, help."

"Oh!"

She was on top of the cat before she was aware it was there.

And the fire had flared. She should have seen it.

It crouched, ears back, tail slowly swinging its stiff length. Ears back, nose wrinkled and teeth bared, snarling gutturally—on the very point of springing.

Bulinga stumbled back.

This was a menace she'd always feared to face.

She knew only too well what would happen, had seen it all so often, when she was in safety and some hapless animal the victim.

The great cat-eyes were yellow, baleful horrible yellow.

It swayed back on its leg muscles.

And then Emalf and another had it by the collar, she heard the snap of the jaws, but there was nothing between them. Another man with ropes was hovering about, a running noose ready in his hand. The group was a tangle of legs and grunts and snarls and strong outlandish oaths.

There were some clothes torn, and they were all of them scratched and hot and dirty and surprised to find themselves all whole, when the beast was tied up.

But of Bulinga there was nothing to be seen.

"She may have gone back to her palace, or anywhere," said Emalf out loud, but to himself: "No, it won't be to her palace. By the Yolk of the Egg of the Serpent, but she *is* a princess.

"Yolar, get things moving. We must get away from here, fast."

He looked round at the little crowd.

"You seem to be all here now. Bartin, check up, and if there's anyone missing find him. Leave the Groodian sot here. Wrap that animal in a double bundle with its head out and a bar tied between its jaws, we'll take it with us. And all of you hurry. Hurry, I tell you. Eosh, get me Carpen."

Emalf stood, satisfied. All knew what to do and they were doing it, competently.

Carpen came up.

Emalf dodged as sparks flew when the last fire was kicked apart.

Over in the paddock Bulinga was stealing another horse.

She cautiously dropped over the low fence into the enclosure. As she knew, they were tethered in a long line and she made for the end of the line. She could hear the hubbub in the camp and guessed fairly accurately what was happening, so she must hurry. She was grateful to Emalf for rescuing her from the cat, but she was, too, grateful to the cat for rescuing her from Emalf. For though she conceded to herself that she was maybe being too confident in her own powers, yet she had so far managed on her own. And although it was no more than a vague feeling, perhaps born of inadequate knowledge of the ways of men such as Emalf, still she didn't quite trust Emalf. She was furious with him, still, in any case. In spite of her rescue from the cat.

Silently she approached the end horse. It seemed to her inexperienced eye to be very friendly. It tried to move toward her. She patted its face and stroked its mane, carefully. The horse whinnied and thrust its nose into her hand. She could feel in her cupped palm the movement of the sensitive nostrils.

She bent and untied the tethering, held the reins, led it a little way over the springy turf. She wasn't making the same mistake twice and she soon found the buckles and fastened the straps round its belly as she had seen Emalf do.

She mounted, very awkwardly, for the horse was already moving off.

A very few minutes later she slid thankfully from the back of the horse to the firm ground.

Only utter ignorance had made her believe having a horse would help her get away. She couldn't make it obey. She must go without the horse or not go at all.

The horse looked at her and moved off. It paused to crop the grass and moved off again. She couldn't see it now.

Bulinga sat on the soft friendly turf.

She'd only ridden long enough to clear the traders' camp, cross the river and reach the road but it was evident to her that she must, as she originally intended, escape on foot.

Though she'd thought she had been unwise in going back for another horse, perhaps she had been wiser than she knew. Surely they would soon see the hoof marks through those clay pans beside the river. They'd see that the tracks led to the ancient road and think she had gone on in that direction.

The horse could roam where it would. May it go far so they had a long way to follow it.

Now she would skirt back, behind the palace, through the newer quarter of Grood where the nobles mostly lived and where the sight of a page late at night wouldn't cause comment; and then she could reach the old road again and go on in the opposite direction.

It was a good plan.

4

The road left Grood in a broad sweep, and ran between trees tall and tangled in the roots and twigs and branches of their neighbors. These trees all seemed very black and there came to her mind stories of dangerous animals and men who lived in these forests: but surely there would be none so near to the town as this.

She had never left the town before. Never before had she been out so late at night. In this one night she had achieved two ambitions. She felt that she could never again know such ecstasy as she had felt when she passed quietly through the lightless streets of Grood. The grim high walls of the palace had watched her pass, but she felt they had not accepted the fact that she was going forever. The thick high houses of Grood had seen her pass; the rough high trees before the house of the priest had seen her go, but, as all things in Grood, they had been without intelligence and perception and, without understanding that she would never return, they had let her go.

High had been the stone thick walls of Grood around her all her life, high had been the traditions and the taboos, harsh had been the rules of Jura; but now all this was stayed, she had outwitted the taboos and she had slipped out from almost below the high walls, while they thought they kept her from within.

Gone she was from the halls of Grood, she had left

the stifling life which had held her a captive for so long, never more would she see the faces of the fools about her, the face of her father intent in his goblet, the face of her aunt with disapproval plastered upon it, the sharp spite in the faces of her cousins.

Slipping stealthy as a snake beneath the lightless walls of Grood, she had felt free and bold as a new-born goddess; the windows of the tall houses on either side of her had not perceived her, neither had the dark cobbles down between them betrayed her steps. The dark streets had been lightless and without the sound of any; the leaves of the creepers on the walls had not touched her, nor had they rustled at her passing; no bird had flown up from her feet, no cat had come at her from the shadows, its gold eyes burning in its yellow face, no dog had barked at her going; her heart had beat silent and strong as the wings of an eagle which reigns the sky, but her steps had been lighter than the steps of a thief who searches for a chink in the wall that he may gain ingress, her strides had been smoother than a stream which flows without fear into the bosom of the enormous river. The stars in the sky so high above the high black houses of Grood had not sought her out, Grood had been aloof in the night and she had fled from Grood while the night was purple in the sky.

The shadows beneath the trees offered themselves silently to the feet of her who had left Grood.

5

Layne, the innwoman, sat in her small kitchen and cursed because Vathok was in the house and Vathok sat in the ground floor's other room and cursed.

Vathok had a great fund of curses and he used them all freely, not to give pith to his remarks but merely as a habit. It had helped to impress the more impressionable of his companions when he was younger and so contributed in no small degree to his position. But it was his undoubted ability to plan well, his instant grasp of essentials and his undoubted courage which had given him, for so many years, undisputed sway over all the masterless men of the forest. They followed him, when they wanted to, because it paid to do so.

The inn room was bare and unfriendly. The walls were shored up, inside and out, by rough tree trunks; the hurdled, mud-plastered walls gaped and bulged. There were so many holes, small holes, that when there was a light in the room at night to anyone outside it seemed a minor heaven; bright, strong-beamed stars shining by the thousand from its walls. But it wasn't a minor heaven. It was an inn because the other hovels in the hamlet were too small to accommodate guests. Everyone had now forgotten, if they ever knew, why this house had been built so big and with two floors.

The little village consisted of Groodians who had been thrust from the community for minor wrongdoing. Men, and some women, who were too timid, too weak, or too conventional in outlook to join the forest bands.

But they still gave allegiance to Vathok, in their case because it was unhealthy not to do so.

Vathok wasn't drinking. He was alone and he got no value from drinking alone. He wished he'd brought his son after all. When the slab door was pushed open on its leather hinges Vathok looked up—with relief and a welcome—no matter who entered they were very welcome.

And because Vathok was a big man for a portion of a moment he saw no one come in—then he adjusted his focus and regarded the little man in almost benign amusement.

"Drink," bellowed Vathok, so that the innwoman would hear, but the little man straddled a hole in the floor and glowered up at him. Vathok stared at him realizing he was not after all one of the villagers, taking in his ragged finery and trying to guess what was in the two leather dans on which the man had seated himself.

"You'll have a drink?" Vathok suggested.

"Thank you, yes. I suppose I can sleep here. And what is this place called?"

Vathok sighed.

His drink was certain.

He chuckled.

"It's not called anything, anything I ever heard of. We just call it "the houses." I don't think it has a name. I wonder if I ought to give it a name!" The idea amused him. He was liking this stranger.

"You're the local lord then?" said the stranger.

"I'm the lord of more territory than has Grood," Vathok remarked affably, and drank.

"You're probably Vathok."

Vathok snorted in his drink and held it down. The stranger was drinking calmly by then and Vathok, unwontedly, waited.

"I was told about you. My name's Scridol. I'm an artist. I didn't expect to meet you here."

"Did you come to meet me, then?"

"By the Yolk no. But I expected to be robbed. Though a little." He leaned forward and tapped his head. "I keep it all here," he stated pugnaciously, "and there's nothing in these dans but roots—and leaves," he added as one always precise in small things.

He accepted Vathok's rank amazement as his due. He was used to this.

"To make dyes," he explained.

"I understand," said Vathok, who didn't. "And what do you do with the dyes? Sell them?"

"Man, I *paint* with them, and color woods, and—even some metals. I told you, I'm an artist."

Light broke in on Vathok.

"A painter, by the Moon."

"No, man," witheringly, "an artist. Anyone can paint. In a way. But—oh, what does it matter? But I hope you'll warn your cut-throats to leave me in peace."

Vathok, besieged on his own dungheap, stared, tensed, chuckled, relaxed and red humor glinted in his eyes as he scanned the pert sparrow of a man, and placed him in his mind with satisfaction. This man was a leader. That, then, was why they liked each other. Respected would have been an apter word.

"Oh, they'll leave you alone, not worth their while," he laughed.

Scridol didn't take it wrongly. He'd gone out of his way to dress so that he would appear not worth molesting. He would make no effort though to disguise his pugnacity, not dwarfed with his size, nor to hide any merit he knew he possessed.

The woman hovered about them bearing in her arms a small broached barrel.

Vathok handed her his gourd.

She filled it awkwardly.

"It's to your taste?" she asked.

"Perfectly," he said in brief politeness. And he nodded.

"Will the other two respected masters be arriving tonight?" the woman asked.

"They will. I've had word they will be leaving the court of Grood tonight," said Vathok, and drank again, deeply. He shifted his body back about half a foot's length and leaned against the post there. Scridol nodded, to himself. That was as it should be. A man of the forest would know just like that, without looking, how far to move.

"I'd better sweep out their rooms then," the woman said and prepared to leave him, thankfully.

"And for this estimable lord," Vathok told her, "my guest.

"For if you've no gold," Vathok said to him as the woman went, "how else could you stay?"

"I thank you, and accept. I've one gold paring. And that a little one. But it would have done for here. And I should reach Grood in a day. But I was sore of sleeping in trees."

"A gold paring! Even a scraping would be too much," Vathok told him scathingly. He leaned forward. "But don't go to Grood." He shook his head. "I tell you what to do, come with me. You can gather all the roots you want, you can have baskets of them." He grew more generous, gloried in his opulence. "You can have scores of great baskets. The forests are full of roots and leaves. Why do you want to go to Grood? They're a pestilential people. No, I know what you should do. And I'll tell you and when I've told you all I know of Grood, and that's a lot, by the Moon, you'll agree with me, and you'll go back to Nipsirc with my half-brother and my nephew, for why should someone like you want to end his life in the bear pits of Rugul?"

"Well, I'll listen to you," said Scridol, draining his gourd and laying it thankfully down, for its shape and its incurved rim irked him, and he didn't much like the drink either.

Layne came in with a torch and stuck it in its socket.

"Bring some food," ordered Vathok, "and fill the cup of my friend here. You'll need it. Take it now, Carpen'll turn it all sour later."

Scridol lifted the cup and sipped it, his eyes still on Vathok.

"And is your brother a bandit, too?" he asked.

Vathok laughed. He was about to speak when another aspect of the remark struck him and he laughed more.

Scridol smiled in sympathy, and waited patiently for the big man's mirth to subside.

6

There seemed now to be a moaning sound among the trees. It must be just the breeze.

Bulinga quickened her stride.

She glanced behind again. It was an effort and yet it would have been more an effort not to.

She hurried on.

Her bundle was becoming heavy, more of a nuisance to her. It had to have both her hands on it. It wouldn't be cradled under either arm without the help of the other arm and hand. It was awkward on her shoulder. Carried in front it still tired her arms.

Spirits dwelled in the trees, she knew; beings bluish and strange, things which crept at night when the tree bodies themselves slept.

She mustn't think about them.

The thing which made her fearful was definitely a sound, no mere rustling of the leaves.

It was more definite, and seemed to come up out of the night, from the ground. From the ground beneath her feet? She strode more swiftly than ever. There were goblins who lived under the ground. They made things very wonderfully from metals and the roots they naturally found down there, but their characters were twisted and warped. The sound grew louder, and for a moment she was panic-stricken and thought that they were coming up to the surface, even that they were following her beneath the earth, and would come up and confront her at some bend in the road.

Then she realized that the sound was behind her, above the earth and actually coming along the road. She heard a small whinny from some distance behind her. It was a horse she had heard.

She began to run, as swiftly as she could and as noiselessly, but not caring so much for noise as long as she could reach the village before the Thing did.

She had heard many times of the horseman who rode the forest on his ghastly beast.

She would be just another of the legends men told at night, another victim of the Green Horseman, unless she could reach the village before it caught her.

She ran madly, wildly, and the sound was louder and louder from behind her.

The road slid past her feet. Oh, dear mother, there was a light ahead of her.

Then she knew that she was swooning. The sky was obscured by clouds, enormous and more terrifying than mountains. The stars sparked through them intermittently—giddily and dizzily they sparked.

Bulinga slid forward onto the step. With clenched fists she banged and banged again.

"The Green Horseman!" she gasped to the scrovelly woman who looked down at her. "Oh, close the door. Quick!"

The woman gaped, dropped from her hand the fire-sharpened lyewood poker, and slammed shut the door. She leaned against it fumbling for the bar.

"What happens?" demanded a voice from across the room, and another yawned, very audibly, and asked: "Is that my brother Carpen come?"

"Does your brother always enter an inn heralded by the drums of Peralior?"

The sounds of a horseman entered the room through all the cracks and gaps in the time-ravaged wall.

"That'll be Carpen," yawned Vathok.

"He must have nearly battered down the door,"

Scridol grumbled. He felt foul. The bed he should have had upstairs, a badly disguised heap of dry crackling leaves and who knew how much vermin, would have been bad enough. The bed he'd had, the dry warped age-grooved boards of the main room floor, would take him days to recover from. That liquor had been insidious. But how could he have refused to drink with Vathok?

Three peremptory knocks shook the door, and the rattle eddied along the boards of the upper wall.

Vathok opened his eyes.

"Go on, woman," he roared, "open the door."

The woman, after but the smallest pause, obeyed, and Carpen entered pulling off his gloves. More hoofbeats could be heard approaching.

"Drink-sodden," stated Carpen.

Vathok grinned.

"To you the best in a new day," said Vathok ceremoniously, sardonically giving him the full salutation of the time.

Carpen's eyes swept over Bulinga. He looked to Vathok, to Scridol, to the woman, and back to Vathok.

"What's the boy doing here?" he asked mildly, as though it were a little matter but he liked all things explained as he came to them.

"Holy Serpent! How should I know?" Vathok answered equably. "I've just wakened. I think we've drunk every drop in the house. Have we, Layne? Is there anything drinkable?"

"Not another drop," Scridol said, drawing himself up to his full height, stretching his sore muscles. "There's no sense to it."

"No," agreed Carpen.

"But it can be enjoyable, about halfway through," grinned his brother.

They were standing together now, and to Scridol the resemblance was obvious. They were of a like height, well above his own, but where Vathok's nose was bridge-broken and bulbous, Carpen's was high bridged and almost fleshless. One was full bodied, materialistic,

a leader, and dressed in colorless unobtrusive garments of tanned skin, the other thinner, with all the
signs of being a bigot, even an idealistic bigot, and
wearing good town-made clothes—but his long green
cloak hung all round him in sober fashion and not
looped back as was the fashion of the day.

"And who is this?" asked Carpen.

"A friend of mine."

"I thought as much."

This didn't please Scridol. He fixed Carpen with his
eyes.

"My name is Scridol."

Carpen bowed his head, politely, but without interest. Then, as his eyes came up, Scridol saw in them
the spark of awakening remembrance.

Vathok took from him all the drama of his intended
announcement.

"He is an artist, he says. But he's a friend of mine
for all that. And I never thought a man could know so
much of brigandry. He talked last night. Snake, how he
talked. He drowned me in words and words."

Scridol saw that Carpen knew him. He was not now
in the mood for fawning traders.

"I'm going to the stream for a wash," he said, and
walked to the door.

His movement broke the setting. The innwoman bent
to Bulinga. "Get up, boy," she said harshly. "You with
your Green Horseman. Upsetting folks. What do you
come for?"

Bulinga stood, flushed.

"You do not have the right to speak like that to me,"
she began, and stood back to escape the sudden entrance of a man younger than Carpen, whom she had
last seen sitting near Carpen at the long table in the
Great Hall of Grood.

"Best day, Vathok," sang the young man, and
stopped at sight of Bulinga.

Bulinga could not escape his immediate recognition.
There was no escaping his expression either. His eyes
swept downwards and Bulinga drew herself more erect

and met his eyes squarely, daring him to absorb further
the fact of her long legs.

Scridol, too, had stopped.

He moved a little sideways and sat himself on his
worn carry-alls.

"Who is the boy?" Carpen asked Vathok.

"I told you. I do not know. But it looks to me that
Gatil knows. Some snotty page. I'd not have thought
they'd send after you, here. But, hold it. The boy came
first. Holy Serpent, there's not all right, here. Are you
not expecting messages from Groodian lords? Has
some lordling misliked your plans, brother Carpen?
Gatil!" he shouted. "Who is the boy, and why do we
have him here?"

"It is the Princess Bulinga," blurted out Gatil.

Scridol snuggled his seat into the cushion comfort of
his worn leather dan. This was all very interesting. He
screwed his eyes, the left more than the right. "And a
princess, eh?" Why did he never have paper and brush
to hand when he needed them most?

The innwoman was several thoughts behind the company.

"He thought the Green Horseman was after him,"
she offered.

Bulinga blushed.

"Green Horseman. Oh! my cloak!" said Carpen.

"Your cloak!" hooted Vathok. "By all the Snake's
Scales! The Green Horseman! I'm the Green Horseman! If there is one. The Green Horseman, Carpen, is
a spectre. At least we pretended there was such a one.
To keep Groodians in their beds at night."

Carpen's thin lips came down in a disgusted and
contemptuous grimace.

"It is significant that they should believe so easily.
But I suppose the young have little choice when their
elders so easily err. Then some is explained." He
paused and turning squarely to Bulinga, with his feet
properly together made the correct apology, his voice
pious and sharp. "Let it be forbidden that I should

ever willfully frighten any fellow creature. However lowly."

"The last part hardly fits," observed Vathok, drily. He walked over to Bulinga.

"So we have a princess here!" There was no respect in his voice, but it was neither contemptuous nor ribald. "You seem unusually garbed, lady, but there's little space for doubt on the matter. Do you know of me?"

Bulinga did.

She had, she thought, stepped from the pot to the fire. What evil chance had made it all so? Here was where her wits must help her. Even the dagger Emalf had suggested would be no use in meetings like this, unless she used it on herself. And there was no dagger.

She braved him, steeling herself to do so. These men must not see one of her blood afraid.

"I know of you," she admitted coldly.

"Then you know this is *my* kingdom," said Vathok. "Here, Layne, we want a meal, and within the moment, though it'll have to be a cold one. You'll get no time for niceties, Carpen, now."

In three steps he scooped up the barrellet and drained it into a gourd.

Carpen regarded him silently.

Scridol crossed, with dignity in his rags, to Bulinga and made a fashionable bow.

"My name is Scridol, Estimable Lady. I am here—well, because of a long walk I undertook—for reasons it would take eons to explain. If you believe you need a friend—and I think you may—I am here. I'll stay, too."

Her eyes met his, and her lip trembled.

There had not been in his manner, either, all the respect she was accustomed to. But—it was there for her to see that he was, like herself, of this gathering by some queer twist the "little gods" had dealt. He seemed not so small nor, somehow, so useless as she had thought him a little before when Vathok was saying much.

She summoned him a smile.

"Thank you."

Scridol had made no effort to hide his words. His tones had carried.

Gatil moved, a little awkwardly, across to them.

"And I too, Your Tranquilness," he said. "I, too, offer you my help, whenever you need it."

Scridol looked him over in disdain.

Carpen snorted.

7

Bulinga was enjoying herself.

She had never had a meal like this, and she had lost her fear. What the outcome of this meeting would be was something she had wondered, several times, even in the shortness of that meal; but she had lost all her fear.

Carpen she didn't like.

His few glances in her direction made her not so much uneasy as rebellious—though she didn't think of it in such terms.

Vathok?

She couldn't fail to understand Vathok. He had many of the qualities of Rugul—the faults too. Perhaps Vathok was more decisive. But she couldn't tell. She'd never seen her father being a king.

Scridol she liked. She gathered he was rather famous in the world outside Grood. A man who created beautiful things.

Gatil! He was young. He was handsome, slim, dark, gay, and respectfully admiring. She liked Gatil very much.

It was very little of a meal. Gobbets of cold smoked deer ham, spiced with walnuts, and sliced off the bone by Vathok's broad dagger. Gobbets of coarse unsalted seane bread, spread liberally with the jelly of thorn fruits, and a full gourd of goat's milk.

Vathok would spend no time in talking; he knew, he said, what was to happen and it wouldn't happen till he'd eaten.

The others fell silent, too, after a moment. Vathok had said if they didn't eat now they might be sorry later.

Vathok had eaten with the considerable help of both hands and his large knife, and he finished before the others, wiped the knife on his sleeve and cut off from the ham a large hunk which he stored in the right sleeve of his leather jerkin, his arm being no longer there.

This Bulinga had seen done by workmen. There was a queer grace in a garment worn thus; one shoulder and arm clad, the other bare.

Vathok then loosened the long broad leather strip bound round his waist and hips, wiped his knife again, stuck it down the sleeve pocket, licked his lips and all round them, had a last long drink of the goat's milk and leaned back against the great pillar post.

"By the Scales of the Serpent," blasphemed Vathok, "I needed that. Here, you—what's your name?—Tord, come here."

Every head swung round in the boy's direction. He reddened and shambled to his feet.

"Come over here. You know the palm pool? Eh! Well, go there. And run all the way. There are men there with horses. I want—how many do I want? I want three, three horses—better make it four. And we'll meet you along the road."

The boy turned, and at once started off on a long lope, through the door and away.

"You," Vathok told the woman, "get the shutters down, I want some daylight. These torches stifle me."

Bulinga looked round.

All the holes and splits, which an hour earlier had emitted streams of yellow light—when she was outside —now let in daylight, streaks and beams of morning light, cold but with the promise of air and sun.

As she turned her hat fell off. She combed fingers through her hair and wished she had taken it off, earlier. Her head felt unencumbered.

She knew the eyes of all the men were on her.

"If you're going to be a boy, you'd better tie on your hat," Scridol remarked.

"Yes," agreed Bulinga. "I had to leave in such a hurry."

"The rosette on the front unties," said Scridol, kindly.

"Oh!"

She picked up the hat, and tried it.

It was as he said.

She smiled at him.

"I hadn't thought of that. I was in such a hurry."

"I can imagine that. This whole adventure is nothing less than bizarre. I suppose I am correct in surmising —though I admit it is none of my business—but you *are* leaving home?"

Bulinga nodded.

"That is what Emalf told me," said Carpen, soberly. "It is that which caused me to be half a day ahead of my intentions. Emalf was of course correct in advising me so. It would have been dangerous for an outlander to be in Grood on the same morning that a trader and a princess had left, she against her family's wishes and the known laws of her city. I know of many reasons why a maiden should wish to leave her parents, a few of the reasons being adequate. If her parents were bad followers of the faith and hindered her devotions, that would be a good reason. Knowing Rugul's court, that could well be the reason in this case." He stood. "But nothing excuses the indelicacy of a maiden wearing the dress of a man," he added accusingly, harshly.

Bulinga frowned.

"Trader," she said coldly, "I am not beholden to you. You forget your manners."

"I forget nothing." He leaned forward. "You are a princess but in name now. You have relinquished your rank and position and it is well that you realize that. It would be well too that you realize that to sit and eat, to be with men, in that costume, is the act of a wanton, and will always be construed as such."

"What else was the girl to do?" asked Vathok.

"She would have reached here in skirts."

"No doubt, no doubt. But if you were running away would you hinder yourself with skirts to the ground? You make a fuss over little, Carpen. She'll be less bother to me like this. But you'd better wear your hat, girl, and hide your hair. Use the hat as Scridol told you."

"Her hair! Yes."

"Eh?"

"I was noting her hair."

"You'll want it cut off, I suppose?"

"No. Oh no." Carpen drew a deep breath, still staring at her hair.

"It is pure milk white," he observed in awe. "By the Fallen Moon. There is good in you and it will surely come out, despite yourself."

"Despite myself!" Bulinga was infuriated.

Carpen laid his long cold hand on her head.

"White hair is given only to those favored from high," he said. "How any feminine person could desecrate her body with clothing originally intended for, perhaps even previously worn by, someone of the other sex is inconceivable and nauseating to me. However, I am one in whom Faith is strong and I would not harm any, nor judge harshly where there was only foolishness and no evil was intended. And therefore if you at once change your clothing for that of a female I will allow you to reach Nipsirc in the company of myself and my nephew, which is the goal I believe you desire."

"Where she goes will be known later. Maybe not till

she's been there," Vathok stated. "And by your same moon, change she won't." He moved to the door and threw it wide open, looked out, and gestured the others out.

"You can walk with the others, Gatil. I'll ride your mare. I have a lot to say to your uncle. I suppose I'll have to listen too. Come. We're losing time. There'll be a mount for you, Scridol, in very little time."

"I'll walk with the Princess willingly enough," Scridol assured him. "She can tell me of Grood."

"Layne," shouted Vathok, "I'll be sending Tord to Grood." He slammed the door behind him and joined the others in the roadway. "Though if Rugul, your father, lets young Tord out of Grood with his skin not hanging from him like ribbons from a packman's tray, I'll set him up in business in Nipsirc, for there'll be no luckier man alive."

"Oh!" said Bulinga.

"No, don't worry me about that now," laughed Vathok. "Get on. Look you, girl. You're in my hands now and if we dawdle, you'll maybe reach Grood with your skin in ribbons. Rugul has no horses, but his cats can follow a trail and run without a noble's hand on the halter."

"You mean they'd set cats on her trail?" said Gatil.

"It's possible, isn't it?" said Vathok, sardonically.

"It's also doubtful," said Scridol, quietly, but during a quietness which made his words ring like a shout.

Vathok's mouth straightened. Then he laughed.

"Perhaps you're right. They'll want her back in one piece. But we'd still better hurry. They'll do something. And one of their lesser fools can easily be stupid enough to loose some cats on the trail."

Bulinga shuddered.

Scridol shouldered his bags, took her arm and led her off. Gatil followed.

The two on horses came behind.

After a moment she gently removed Scridol's hand.

"Why no horses in Grood?" asked Scridol.

"The cats," explained Bulinga. "Horses are uncontrollable near cats. So Grood gave up horses."

"I've heard so much of those hunting cats of Grood. What are they like?"

"Oh—they're big. We have bred them for ages. No one else can breed them for we never allow males to leave the city."

"Yes. I've heard so of course. And that they are descended from a now extinct kind of tiger. But they are not striped, are they?"

"No. Of an all-over dun color, except that their feet are white. And under their bodies . . ." she paused. "You really do know that already, don't you? You are engaging me in conversation, to put me at my ease!"

He smiled.

"And have I succeeded?"

She nodded.

"I don't think they will send after me. Not yet, for some hours. Isn't this glorious country?"

"Off the road," bellowed Vathok. "Take the path to the right."

"You still expect pursuit?" asked Carpen.

"No. Well, perhaps. But I'm taking this road to save time. It cuts off a curve of the ancient road. Means we descend into a gully and cross the river again but it still saves time." He looked aside. And shut his mouth again on a word. Carpen was so obviously lost in his own thoughts. Vathok's eyes, and the curl on his lips, reflected his displeasure at having his words ignored. And Vathok was angry with Carpen and with his nephew Gatil for another reason. Neither had so much as inquired after the wellbeing of Kcus, Vathok's son. Neither had even mentioned his son.

The path they took soon left the road altogether.

What a beautiful morning, Bulinga was thinking.

She was free. And the world outside Grood was well worth her escape. Never in Grood had she walked through such a lane. The palace garden was never allowed to grow sweetly and naturally; every tree and bush was shaped and every slightly irregularly formed leaf was pruned at once. Eight gardeners were kept to see to this inhibiting of nature, so one could never run in the gardens and lie on the grass beneath the trees because the very tree beneath whose shade one was lying would be continually prowled around by someone who examined each leaf with cruel exactitude.

On each side of this path were golden leaves thick and sweet with rustling fragrance.

"I like this," said Bulinga, breathing deeply.

"We must walk even more quickly," said Gatil, looking anxiously behind at Carpen and Vathok. "Come, Your Tranquilness." He took Bulinga's arm.

She stopped and looked pointedly at his hand.

He, after a moment, reddened and loosened his grip, then took his hand away a moment later.

"But we must hurry," he said. "We must get to the horses and get more quickly away."

Carpen and Vathok stopped beside them.

"Should you not give the Princess your horse?" asked Gatil, of Vathok.

Vathok laughed.

"Get on," he said briefly.

Bulinga paid little attention. She was already ahead again. She had liked the feel of Gatil's hand on her arm. It was different from Scridol's protective hold.

Gatil went on after Bulinga.

"I had no idea the forest was so beautiful," said Bulinga, turning to him as he reached her side. "It is not—beautiful like this in Grood."

"You were unhappy in Grood?" asked Gatil.

"Obviously, boy, since she ran away. I, myself, ran away to see all this."

"And who are you?" asked Gatil disdainfully. "The Prince of Dejanira?"

Scridol was unruffled.

"No. The Prince of Artists."

Bulinga laughed.

"What do you propose to do with this princess?" Carpen suddenly asked Vathok.

"Nothing. She can go where she will. After I have had my ransom. And that is something else, brother jeweler. No plans go ahead for a day or so. Until I have that ransom. Then when my men are in Grood, to do as you require, no one will worry much of their Princess. You do not want me in Grood, and I quite see that. You need the strength of my men but you want them to appear as your High One's men. Well, you can have the men. It all fits in, d'y'see? They'll be *your* men, for a while. And when all is settled and your new priests and your churches are pleasing you, I will be still in the forest, taking my toll of travelers. And there'll be more in the future, won't there be, Carpen, my brother, when Grood is no longer itself but part of your High One's little empire?"

Carpen blew out breath in disgust.

"You will not prosper. You cannot. Did I not believe that all is from the One and that use can be made of all to the begetting of the Ultimate Purpose, I would despair. Knowing what I know I can only despair for you. But you chose your own path, and your everlasting negation would be no loss." He shrugged shortly.

Vathok smiled, unamusedly.

"I live for the moment. I have found it to be a good plan. And I hear many things, Carpen. I hear for instance that there are those, in the Good Islands, for instance, who think your High One misguided. Those in the Islands have power. But it doesn't affect me." He looked shrewdly at his brother.

"What do *you* propose to do with the girl?"

Carpen ignored this.

"Your men are ready?"

"Oh, all ready, and more. When your priests arrive at the meeting tree they'll have force to take onward with them. You need have no fear. I'm being paid enough. But what do you intend for the girl?"

"I intend her for the Temple in Nipsirc," said Carpen shortly.

Vathok whistled.

"You think she'll like that?"

"She'll learn to."

"You'll force her there, I suppose?"

"Why not? She is young. And the young take years to learn unless they are helped. She may not be other than somewhat shameless. It is her life she has been given in Grood," said Carpen magnanimously. "One with such hair and coloring should be in the Temple. Why else was she permitted—no! I put it wrongly. Why else was she *made* to leave her father's court and her steps turned in my direction?" He paused. He said, more to himself than to Vathok, "She will be a fine gift to the High One."

Vathok's lip curled in amused tolerance.

"By the Great Snake's Belly," he thought, "you'll have no easy conquest of that girl, even if you get her in the Temple. I might take a hand myself, there. Great Yolk! Now there's an idea! I wonder! She'd raise a fair price in the market at Nipsirc! After I've had her ransom. Carpen, my poor one, this can be thought about. And I'll not be needed here awhile . . ." His eyes dreamed after Bulinga striding ahead like a boy in her long violet-dyed stockings.

The path wound on, and downwards between root-bound banks, over pools of pink and creamy flower-lets—tiny three-petaled blooms whose accompanying leaves, narrow and streaked with olive and black, quivered incessantly. A footfall on the mass of colors caused every single pointed leaf to stretch, almost to strain, upward.

Bulinga was enchanted, and bent to touch.

"No. Leave them," warned Scridol quickly, "they will make your fingers taste for days to come."

"Truly?"

He nodded.

"They are rank."

Bulinga lifted her hand, regretfully, and looked beyond and her voice rose in ecstasy.

"Oh. How lovely!"

They had reached the stream.

She hurried forward, Gatil beside her, Scridol following more leisurely, and stopped at the watery brink.

"Isn't the forest lovely?" she breathed to Gatil.

Gatil let her enjoy the scene. He had no eye for it, and his mind was becoming turbid, unable to think but upon one theme. He wanted this girl.

Last night, as he had caught his first glimpses of her, his desire had been poisoned with the envy of the unattainable.

Today, this morning, she was walking with him, in the forest, away from Grood. She was practically in his grasp.

Gatil's hand moved, and he stopped it.

Not yet.

He must woo her a little. But he would have her.

Bulinga's eyes glowed and she swayed almost to him as she turned again.

"Isn't it truly beautiful?" she breathed.

Gatil's hands lay still by his sides. By the Yolk, but he would have her. He had the recipe now.

"There is hardly a loveliness to equal such a dell," he agreed self-consciously. "Look how over there the shadows shimmer into the water."

"Yes."

Bulinga's eyes rested where he pointed. Unthinkingly—or was it truly so?—her fingers leaned on his arm.

"There are other valleys, and other beauties," said Scridol, from behind.

"But this," Bulinga cried, "this has the beauty of my first such scene. Is the world then full of such valleys?"

"There are millions, Princess. All different and all alike; all enhancing the other beauties of other scenes, of deserts, rocks, and of man-made artistry. There are the heavens too," he added, as an afterthought.

"The heavens," blurted Gatil. Was this artist fool to follow them always, or was he going to stay with Vathok? He foresaw trouble between Scridol and himself. The little beggar might even *be* an artist of note but he was being an intolerable nuisance.

Gatil turned round. "Do we go much farther?" he shouted. "The Princess is tiring."

"But indeed I am not," said Bulinga.

"If Gatil tires that is enough to distress us," said Vathok. "A few steps farther, little Gatil, a few steps beyond the stream and we reach where Tord should wait us with the horses—that is, if my man Shelig has brought them," he finished in a growl.

"Do we cross the stream?" asked Gatil.

"Cross to the twisted tree," shouted Vathok. "It's only ankle deep."

Gatil saw his opportunity.

Swiftly he lifted her, took the two steps which was all the width of the stream, put her down, relinquished her.

That, he thought, should help.

He felt, rather than saw, Bulinga's eyes follow him up the other side of the tiny valley. He was quite satisfied.

8

They entered the clearing by the pool as the knife was drawn from the body.

Shelig looked up, and there was Vathok.

Shelig wiped the long broad knife clean on the bundle of rags and limbs at his feet, his eyes never breaking the link with Vathok's.

Vathok swung across and steadied the horses tethered to a tree. The boy Tord was there but doing nothing to relieve the fear of the animals.

"Hell welcome you," Vathok said, restraining anger. "Why, in the name of all the Snake's Children, did you have to kill him?"

Shelig balanced himself more easily on straddled legs.

"We quarreled."

"I can see that," roared Vathok. He shrugged, regaining control of himself, half turned and addressed the others.

"Get over there and choose what you're riding. Mine is the tall chestnut. Shelig, tumble that into the bushes." His voice rose again. "Though why you have to pick a time like this to quarrel is beyond me. You know we want every man. Holy Snake, you misbegotten guttering, must I always be everywhere to keep you all at peace? What was the fight over?"

Shelig had lifted the body by one wrist and one ankle.

It hung from his hands, heavy and dead.

Scridol, without a word, stepped in front of Vathok and unfastened the belt buckle; taking belt, sheath and knife.

Shelig spoke over Scridol's head.

"We were never friendly."

"Never friendly!" exploded Vathok. "You were always threatening each other. Oh, I suppose it was bound to happen. Perhaps better now. But keep your knife cleaner among us. That's three men in a week, and two by you! If I could keep you all in traces I could sack Nipsirc and conquer the Good Islands. Oh, rest you, brother," at Carpen's restive annoyance, "I'll never do it. Not with these knifemen of mine. Why can't they practice on trees instead of on each other?"

Scridol, mounted, had led the chestnut over.

Vathok took the rein, and said: "Is all quiet at the camp? Had you any message for me? Is all as I said it should be?"

"Kcus said all was as meant to be."

"Is that all the message I get?" bawled Vathok, but there was a different quality in his roar. He was pleased.

Scridol shook his head, amused, contemptuous of these sudden changes of mood.

Vathok laughed.

"Kcus is my son, Scridol. He'll have all as I want it."

Scridol urged his mount over to where Gatil held the mane of a horse and a deep shovel-shaped stirrup for Bulinga to put her foot in.

"Atlan's Lights, but I am surrounded by weaklings and fools," growled Vathok ferociously, in good humor. "Tord, come here, boy. What happens over there, Gatil? By bellies and breasts, Princess, aren't you going to mount? What's the matter now, Carpen? I'm not blaming your boy! It's our prisoner holds things up."

"I find your oaths distasteful, Vathok. Can you not cease swearing and blaspheming for an hour even?"

"Oh, hold off me, I live as myself. What's the matter here? Sna . . . Oh! Great Yolk! Are you up, then, Bulinga girl? Tord, why did you not meet me with the horses? Eh?"

The boy looked up sullenly.

"I . . . they would not come with me, one said, so they fought . . . he . . ." he nodded to the trees, "that one . . ."

"Well, he's dead now."

"But, Vathok, there was said . . ."

"Forget what was said, boy, and do not forget what I say. You will run from here to Grood. Can you?"

The boy nodded uncomprehendingly.

"Can you go to the palace and ask for Rugul?"

The boy nodded, but his eyes darted at Shelig.

"Pay me attention, Tord," emphasized Vathok, "never mind anything else that troubles you. Go to Rugul. Say, 'The Princess Bulinga is in Vathok's hands. You can have her back for two thousand gold parings.' And, listen, tell them if you return harmed their Princess returns harmed. You mustn't forget to tell them that, boy. Because if you don't . . . But you will remember, won't you? Now repeat it to me, boy."

"The Princess Bulinga is in your hands. They can have her back for two thousand gold parings."

"And you must be unharmed, too," warned Vathok. The boy nodded.

"Well hurry!" roared Vathok, and the brat loped off.

Vathok wheeled his horse, and, followed by Carpen and Shelig the bandit, cantered after the others.

Bulinga, clinging to her saddle, Scridol one side of her, Gatil the other, set her mouth hard as her horse lengthened its stride into a canter, and was agreeably surprised to find this gait easier. There was less bumping. She could sit almost unperturbed. She began actually to enjoy the rush through the air, the feel of the slight breeze on her face and hair.

Perhaps it was by this very road that her mother had reached Grood. Surely she had come along the ancient road?

Bulinga recalled her mother's teaching.

No one now knew of those who had made the road. It had been made by people of a long long ago, long before the cataclysm, before the moon had fallen. "Before the moon had fallen," she repeated to herself, almost with her lips. What had earth been like then?

The moon, she knew, had been larger than the sun and it had lit the night. Life must have been queer in such a time when there was always light, light of two different kinds, warm yellow light by day and cold white, blue-white light by night. So little though had been remembered by people and handed on as knowledge from before the cataclysm.

Now there was only darkness at night. No moon.

This road must have been worn for ages to be so smooth.

It was not worn by any constant use of this time.

The older civilization, whose chariots had been broad, whose brains and workmen were capable of carrying out the making of a road which was smooth and straight and wide enough for their traffic—they had used it themselves for ages. After the fall of these people their roads were still straight and hard. Savages had come who founded the little town-kingdom of Grood and they had used the roads triumphantly. "These great civilized long-dead people are our servants; they have made roads with great labor, taking years over the planning and the laying out and the wearing down; when they had perfected them they died and left the legacy to us." So said the Groodians. The Groodians who could not see that they hedged themselves in and made little if any use of the roads.

Bulinga wondered if it led on and on and on to the coast. She must find out. Perhaps it met another road, as street met lane in Grood, another road which led to the sea from where one could take ship and float on water to Rutas-Mu, to the Good Islands, to Dejanira —and perhaps to Atlan. Atlan of her mother's nation. Would they know her there, if she ever reached Atlan? Would her mother's name mean anything to them, and would she be welcome?

Gatil's mount must have slackened speed.

He was beside her now.

Gatil's hand rested on hers on the horn of her saddle. He bent sideways to her.

Bulinga could not catch his words. They floated away behind her on the wind which she realized was stronger now. She knew he was comforting her though, inquiring if she were all right. She nodded and forbore to move her hand from under his. She found comfort in his hand. She realized she had been lonely.

The horses cantered on.

Bulinga looked behind.

Behind was Scridol, and behind him the outlaw who had killed.

Gatil finished speaking, withdrew his hand and hastened his horse to catch up those in front. Her own horse quickened to stay with his.

Bulinga smiled, turned her face, and let Gatil, riding beside her still, see her smile.

The horses went on and on.

Twice the party, at Vathok's command, slowed to a walk and stopped, each time by a little stream where the horses drank, and where the humans drank. Only Vathok had food. He offered none to the others.

Abruptly they left the forest behind.

The road now ran flatly and in better condition for the most part. Every so often they reached a wide split not only in the road but stretching sideways brokenly, like the jaggedness of lightning, far into the countryside, from twenty to a hundred yards in width. The horses picked their way down a little into the broken piled earth, trod delicately, climbed out, and with Vathok in the lead always again took up that distance-subduing canter.

Bulinga almost drowsed. The clatter of the horses, the skinkle of the metal in the harness. She was tired, she was tired, tired, tired. The clatter was louder! Why? Bulinga pulled herself back into full consciousness, became aware that the murderer at the pool, the bandit who had been riding last of the cavalcade, had spurred on, past Scridol, past her, past Gatil, past Carpen and with an extra turn of speed past Vathok whose stentorian bellow, hurled by the wind about Bulinga's ears, never reached the man and horse who were now drawing far ahead.

She could see Vathok unsuccessfully endeavoring to gallop to catch up with him. She guessed that the smaller build of the murderer—for that was how she thought of him—gave him the advantage. Vathok was a big heavy man.

They caught up with Vathok again. The pace slackened a little. Vathok's horse was in some difficulty.

Bulinga, like the others, made no attempt at speech, at questioning him. It could readily be seen this was no time to question Vathok. He was an angry man.

There was something amiss. Why she felt it was so serious she could not know.

She pulled on the reins, nearly reined in. A sense of the futility of doing so stayed her. Well, she would ride on. They must be stopping soon now, for all the animals showed signs of exhaustion and distress. There would be some explanation to her where they eventually stopped. And if it did not please her, she would be off again, somehow, on her own.

No princess descended of the line of Atlan was to be coerced into a flight not of her own choosing.

This morning she had readily fallen in with any plans involving putting much distance between Grood and herself. This afternoon that distance was achieved. But where were they bound? In what direction?

All this day circumstances had given her no opportunity of ordering her own existence. That state must not last.

Bulinga looked up from the waving mane of her horse and saw ahead in the light which was now that of late afternoon, a dark bulk, not only trees but buildings which each moment became clearer. The horses settled into a walk. The buildings were old—old as old was—ruined, massive but ruins, and girt and knit by trees whose roots and trunks bent and twisted where they so preferred, cracking the masonry.

The horses clockered across the stones and stopped in a paved dark unroofed yard.

Bulinga, tired and hungry, slid her feet from the stirrups and stretched her toes to the ground, till the tendons of her knees seemed to crack and wither. Now, even off the horse, she felt the ghost of its presence between her legs.

She mustered her courage and resolution.

Here she must face Vathok and win her way.

Vathok had entered a black lopsided doorway. A tall thin villainous-looking man with a limp in both legs was leading Vathok's horse to the same entrance.

Scridol paused. His hand collected the bridle of Bulinga's horse, pushed it to Gatil.

"See to the Princess's mount," he said, and went on.

Bulinga, repudiating a growing stiffness, crossed

the great paving stones to the doorway. As she reached
it a light sprang up within. Momentarily surprised, she
quickly realized that the light was not newly born, but
was merely invisible beyond the doorway. She had
approached the doorway at an angle.

She went in.

A mere step inside the doorway was a stone screen
which explained why the light had not emerged.

Bulinga found herself at the top of a short ramp,
its floor grooved across to help foothold. Vathok's
voice could be heard, but not loudly, and she could
not see him. He must be round the corner lower down,
for the room below her was wider than the ramp.
Bulinga went down, steadying herself with a hand on
each wall, for her feet and legs felt unreliable. She
knew she should be interested in the light, which was
clearer and colder than that of the torches of her
experience, but other matters took preference. She
must have food and a knowledge of what was going to
happen to her. Food she would presumably be given;
the others must be hungry. Knowledge she must get
from Vathok. And never again would she appear to
acquiesce in others' plans for her. She must immediately question Vathok. Vathok was the prince of this
area, a brutal prince whose sheer beneficence she must
doubt.

At the far end of the long room were the horses,
their wants being attended to.

Near her, on one of several rough wood stools
which surrounded a tomb-like block of black stone,
sat Vathok and another man. This man was smaller,
wiry, much older and grizzled, and by his thin beard
and the yellowness of his skin Bulinga knew him to
come from a land far away. Her mother had told her
of this yellow-skinned people.

Bulinga paused, to collect her strength, and the
pause gave freedom to her anger, anger against all of
them that they should so treat her, as if she were of
no moment, a nothing, an unlovely nothing! Her anger
swelled and burgeoned into a passion.

Her hand went down, in a forgetful moment, to gather the folds of her skirt. That it was not there disconcerted her—added exasperation to her anger.

Disregarding bruises, she knocked aside with her knee the stool in her way. She placed both hands on the cold slab of stone, ignoring the food, the flat bread, the meats and the pile of fruit, and glared with ill-simulated composure at Vathok who turned from the yellow man beside him and eyed her as if his eyes were focused not on her but beyond her.

"What's the matter with you? Sit down and eat," Vathok told her mildly.

"I don't want food. I want . . ."

"But you must be hungry! Sit down like a good girl and fill you up your belly."

"Have fruit first," said the yellow man.

With her forearm she pushed aside the pile of fruit.

"Surely I have been silenced long enough," she exploded. "Exactly what are your plans and how soon am I to be escorted to Nipsirc?"

The distance left Vathok's eyes and a faint humor entered them.

"Go on, girl, eat," he said. "You'll get to Nipsirc soon enough."

"That is not sufficient answer," she replied. "I desire to know all that concerns me in considerably more detail. I do not expect court etiquette from you but I am in no degree pleased with the manner of your help. I am, naturally, grateful for your help but . . ."

"There's no need to thank me," Vathok assured her jovially. "I have pleased myself. Now will you eat?"

Bulinga's chin jutted. Cold dislike modulated her voice.

"I can easily understand that you are accustomed to be autocratic. I have already emphasized I am not one of your band of brigands. I assume that . . ."

Vathok stood.

"Oh, Snake's Scales, assume what you like. You're

in my hands, you'll go to Nipsirc all right, as and when I want. Make the most of Scridol, and young Gatil, if you must pretend importance. But eat."

One large hand gathered three of the flat circular loaves, the other a small leg of goat, and he clumped away.

Bulinga's fingers clasped the red roundness of a fruit she knew to be soft and juicy. The temptation to throw it at the vast retreating back asailed her. She sat. There was fear more than anger in the ascendancy. More than lack of manners was behind his treatment of her. As she ripped the skin from the fruit misgivings crowded on her as never before.

The yellow man watched her.

Bulinga badly felt a need of support. But there could not be trouble before her. Gatil or Scridol would have warned her. No. She was without support. However . . . This Vathok was not to be relied on. Clearly she must now make her own plans. And if they differed from his? Well. He was under no compulsion to take her anywhere. A horse, and she now had one, would take her to Nipsirc. She let her brows relent, cease their tensed meeting.

Her teeth hit the stone in the fruit.

Vathok returned to the table.

There was fire, authority, absolute disregard for the company in the tone he used and Bulinga rebelled.

"Get on with eating, as you move, and stuff what you need in your sleeves," he said. "The horses are fit for more yet, and we go at once."

It brought them all to their feet.

"I do not see why that is necessary," Carpen stated.

"Then stay here. By the Fallen Moon, you can do as you like, but I am not being caught here. Dris, Yelna, bring that girl to a horse, and fast, we're moving out."

"I do not go," said Bulinga.

Vathok glared.

"You go. You can sit the saddle or be tied across it like a sack. You go."

As the two men grasped her she screamed. In the same moment, before her scream had reached its crescendo, Scridol was standing before Vathok and in Scridol's hands was the long broad-bladed knife he'd taken from the murdered brigand. His elbows were bent and the knife held in a peculiar way with the edge of the blade uppermost. It might have seemed an ineffectual threat but Vathok knew better. He cursed.

"Hold!" he shouted.

The struggling stopped.

Bulinga, still held, stood.

"They must let her go," Scridol said.

Vathok, eyes never leaving the blade which could disembowel him with a twist, gave the required command, and Bulinga clenched her fists. She would not rub her released wrist, not in front of these men.

Scridol moved a step back, and slipped.

With a grunt and a movement so fast as to be only a blur to those watching, Vathok's foot shot out, caught accurately the side of the blade and sent it from Scridol's hand and in a slither across the stone table. It swung to rest before Carpen.

Scridol looked down at the knife in Vathok's hands, held just as his had been held. He laughed.

"You're a fool, Vathok."

Vathok put away his knife.

"Yes, little man. But not the only one. Get your Princess on a horse."

Scridol shook his head.

"By the Twelve Temptations and the Twelve Virtues, of which last I desire none, why I suffer you, I know not. I said get your Princess on a horse." His voice roared, "Get to the horses," and his arm shot out to grasp the smaller man and thrust him where he was to go but Scridol shifted his feet, half turned, grasped the wrist with clever thumbs and as the sweat broke out on Vathok's brows and the groan left his chest Scridol pulled the giant's arm down and forward.

Vathok fell heavily and Scridol, swinging clear of the mass of his body, chopped hard with the side of his hand.

Vathok's body slumped inertly.

Scridol turned, and was met by the points of two blades—held one in each hand by the yellow man. In the yellow man's eyes there was no expression at all.

Shuffling was heard from where Vathok lay.

No one moved, certainly not Scridol, but as Vathok, breathing like a dragon, got to his feet, the tension of the yellow man eased.

Vathok clumped across. A moment, then the yellow man was grasped from behind and hurled aside.

Vathok regarded Scridol.

"By the Belly of the First Mother, tell me why I don't kill you?"

Scridol smiled and spread his fingers, relaxing.

"Perhaps," he suggested, "you're afraid of me."

Vathok's laugh was uncertain.

"Look, Scridol, we're wasting time. Get to those horses."

"Is haste then so necessary?"

"Holy Serpent! You will madden me! Bellies and breasts, man, do you think I give orders for the fun I get from it?"

"It could be so," said Scridol coolly.

"It isn't so, you misbegotten calamity. May Hell welcome you, Atlan's Father forgive me for ever befriending you. If we do not soon go from here we may be trapped. Already we've wasted time."

"Trapped! By whom?"

"Damnation of all, and the Five First Curses of the First Mother!" roared Vathok. "Must you have the case in its points? Since reaching here I have learned my men are against me. If they have any sense at all they'll . . ."

Carpen's voice, cold and precise, won over Vathok's.

"So your men are in revolt! You promised much, to what end? I would indeed be justly annoyed did

I believe you to have learned this earlier than you would have me understand. Am I, then, here to no purpose? Is the High One's use for your men in Grood all spoiled?"

Vathok whirled in anger.

"It is you who have spoiled things. Because you would insist on more men than I had I scoured the forests for masterless men. I got them, to the number you needed. But they think apparently that I am no use to them. Me! Me! Long ago would they be all with the Moon were it not for me. All right, you can have it all! Then perhaps you will move as *I* say. If we're caught in here we can make no defense. In the open we can. I go as quickly as I can *to* them. Can you see the value of that? *To* them. All this has arisen in my absence! By the Yolk of the Egg! I know how to rule. And more than that hangs to it." His voice lowered, became vibrant. "My son is there. And his life therefore is in danger. There is no time to lose," he enunciated slowly and very clearly. "Now Curses be on you all, will you move, or stay to be slaughtered?"

"Why take the girl then?" asked Scridol.

"Because, Breastcursed, she is my prisoner. How can I get ransom if she is not in my hands?"

"Then you will return her to her father?"

Vathok smiled.

"I never said so."

"Then what . . . ?"

"The next days will know," leered Vathok. "She'll buy for a price in Nipsirc maybe." Then, "What does it matter?" he roared. "Get on horse. No. Stay your distance, get on horse or you walk."

Scridol paused.

Vathok's last phrase settled matters.

"We go," he said, and went to the horses.

Bulinga, feeling deserted, looked at Gatil; he looked to Carpen.

"You, Carpen?" growled Vathok.

"We too will ride with you, Vathok," said Carpen.

"If you no longer command I must speak with those who do. Mine is no dangerous position. I am the representative of the High One. It is I who am paying them, and paying them more than might be considered necessary for what they have to do. The High One has accepted their unworthy help, and I hold the money-bags."

"Not the only money-bag, when I hold that girl."

Bulinga again looked to Gatil who, hesitant, opened his mouth to speak.

"Silence, Gatil," adjured Carpen. "All else can be settled later. If haste is necessary we have used up too much time."

"Soul of the Yolk," bawled Vathok in extreme blasphemy. "Didn't I say so hours ago?" He took the reins of the horse led to him by the long thin ruffian and, in grim satisfaction, watched the others scurry. Then he led his horse to the doorway.

Bulinga stood by the table, fingering the hilt of Scridol's knife.

There was chance here for escape, she thought.

She felt sure it would be easy to outwit them in the dark—though, she thought wryly, her whole body shrank from the idea of mounting again—but she had only to do so and surely she could get away so easily in the dark.

With this knife in her hands . . .

But the knife was being taken from her hands.

Scridol sheathed it.

"Climb on the table, lady," he said, "and slip to your saddle from there. He'll stand, while I busy myself with this."

Then, the light was extinguished.

Bulinga clamped her lips together. This blackness was like no darkness she had ever experienced. It frightened her. She scrambled to the table top.

"Where?" she whispered.

His hand caught hers and guided her. The horse moved, and she gasped.

"Just hold still and sit," came Scridol's voice. "I'll lead you doorwards."

Bulinga marveled that he could see, then decided that it was not so. Not sight, but sense of direction governed his movements.

Obediently, she depended on him.

Moments later she wondered if perhaps she could have Scridol go with her. He didn't intrigue her. What such bundle of decrepit rags could? But he had shown himself the friend he had said he would be.

Gatil was the ideal companion. He, too, was her friend. More so, she thought, than Scridol. Scridol had been so near to Vathok that his actions had taken her attention. She had not seen what Gatil was doing and had no doubt he'd been doing something. But Scridol had been so much closer.

She must separate Gatil from his uncle.

She felt the horse stumble up the ramp, and sensed the twist at the passage end, and it was lighter outside and the air felt cleaner. They were all there. Seven she counted. They were all there, Carpen coming last, behind her. She couldn't distinguish Gatil in the gloom. He must be well out in front, near Vathok with his two men. She must try and work forward and ride near him again. She had no hankering for being near to Carpen who seemed a just enough man, according to his conception of a just man, but his philosophy was so different from hers; he was no friend, nor did she desire him as such.

There was a tenseness, even in the evening air. The fighting inside as well as Vathok's insistence on hurry would cause that.

Someone yelled, horribly.

Bulinga's horse pawed up, fighting the bit.

Something—thrown stones?—clattered among the hooves, setting them in panic.

"Off," shouted Vathok.

Hooves scraping and sliding and stamping, the slither of steel from sheaths, unnameable thumps,

curses, shouts queerly inarticulate, hoarse breathing—
that horrible yell again.

Bulinga clung to the saddle, to the neck of the unmanageable animal. Another horse squealed. One escaped—she heard its hooves thodding into the distance
—and her thanks to the little gods that one was away
mingled with her wish it had been she.

There was less sound now. The horses were to one
side against the wall of the court; a scramble of figures
surged nearer her and away again. Bulinga could see
clubs rise and fall with sickening sound.

Vathok, center of the *mêlée,* thrust savagely,
dropped his knives and grappled—he staggered sideways almost falling into the way of Scridol's wickedly
upstabbing knife. More figures ran to the scramble.

Gatil edged his way along the face of the ancient
building, clinging with shaking fingers to rotted stone
lintels.

Bulinga, still struggling with her horse, felt the stirrups leave her feet, felt the slam of another hysterical
horse against her own. Hers lost all chance of balance.

In the same instant the crowd was about her. She
fell among a thrash of whirling legs. Irresponsible
hooves hissed past her, the blade meant for her stuck
instead in some other body.

Gatil, above, trembled.

The surge in the courtyard moved from beneath him
with sudden speed.

He could see why. One, someone, had run—had attempted to run to get clear and was inexorably engulfed.

Gatil tried to look upwards, to ignore what occurred
below. He dare not climb higher, even if he could.
He didn't know what to do. Perhaps it would be best
to stay here, still, escaping notice.

He shifted one foot, then his hands, wriggled his
torn fingers along the ledge to a more secure hold, he
hoped.

Bulinga wrenched her shoulder painfully, trying to
move the weight of the lifeless thing which held her

down. She wriggled, crawled clear and raised herself up on one elbow, holding her racked shoulder. Two running figures made towards her.

"A weapon! If I only had a weapon," moaned Bulinga to herself.

She found and grasped the weapon of the man who had been slain. The hilt was sticky and her fingers slid.

The thin trickle of graveled age-powdered mortar which fell near her attracted no attention. She leaned backwards to free the knife. The two men paused and peered.

"This'll be her. Look at the hair," one said with a guttural grunt of satisfaction.

Above them, Gatil, frantic, panicked. He could feel his weight moving the stone he stood on.

The two men lunged forward, Bulinga cowered back, and as the assailants floundered in the bloody mess at their feet, with no warning there crashed down on them a long narrow but deadly stone—and Gatil, all limbs and sobbing sound.

Bulinga, some intuitive instinct forearming her, had pushed herself still farther back.

The intervention seemed miraculous. In the brief moment which was all the occasion allowed for thought, her mind had woefully decided that the rescue was again from Scridol. As he rose rubbing one leg, wondering fearfully what would next befall him, she saw that it was Gatil.

She was able only to give him the faintest of welcoming smiles before she fainted.

9

Gatil was in a position of some danger.

The thought made him stop rubbing his thigh and glance round at the conglomeration of fighting bodies.

He glanced at the horses. There was one, there, not his but did that matter, which stood still cropping at some grass growing from the wall. It would be the best thing he could do. He would be killed if he remained here. When he had the horse at his command he could have a look at Bulinga. If she were not too badly hurt it might be a good idea to take her with him.

There was a cracking sound from the wall.

Gatil hurried over to the horse, keeping well away from its hindquarters.

Curse the thing.

He'd got it, this time!

Grasping the bridle he dragged it from the deep blackness close to the wall, and looked up in terror as gravel and small stones dropped on him.

Gatil almost slavered as he hurried to get his foot in the stirrup. But the horse kept passaging away from him.

The wall was going to collapse!

Ah! He had it!

He gripped bridle, mane and saddle and swung up, urging the horse forward before he was seated. The horse started forward as the stones began to fall. He prayed feverishly that the others would not see him, would be unable to stop him, but at once a hand gripped him, the fingers lithe and capable to hold in spite of his twistings and the forward pull of the horse.

"Get off that horse," said a contemptuous voice, and before he had time to obey he was dragged off.

Gatil received a ringing clout across one ear and the side of his face.

"Get the horses against the other wall! Quick," he was told, and was shoved into a run.

"The Princess! Where is the Princess?" yelled Scridol after him, and swooped forward to where the bodies lay.

Three great stones fell, breaking into fragments, scattering the fighters. There was a shudder along the whole length of wall.

Gatil crouched, shrouding his head in his hands.

As the wall fell Scridol found Bulinga, roughly lifted her, and got clear. Four of the forest men turned and ran to the entrance. Vathok stood, leaning on his hips, his head back, his voice jeering. The fight was broken off, but its consequences not yet over with. Vathok's last victim lay decapitated at his feet.

Stones tumbled and slid; crashed, racketed down, cannoned from one another, split, disintegrated and thundered all about the all but deafened humans.

Vathok's two ruffians sprang to where the horses huddled fearfully.

Vathok stood, mouthing incredible oaths, for the first time in years adding new permutations to his prideful vocabulary. He stepped to the little height of some of the great stones so very recently piled beside him and, with some anxiousness, eyed the walls.

The noise subsided.

There were still crackings sounding, but fewer falls. The dusty air still whirled.

The way out was filled; moreover before it the yard floor had given way and over the jagged uncertain edge of the great hole he could see no bottom.

But in another part, where had formerly been solid impenetrable wall for all the years he had known these ruins, there was now a way out, a path which probably would lead his party clear away.

Vathok tested with one foot the balance of the

stone on which he stood, then jumping down from it strode purposefully in the direction of the new-found passageway.

It seemed good.

He turned back to the others.

The yellow man, who had been watching him, asked: "It is a way out?"

"By Atlan's Cold Lights. Yes!"

"For horses?"

"Yes, man. It winds, but by the Serpent who Laid us, we'll get the horses through. Breasts and bellies, Wheld, you knew who to glue yourself to. And I tell you this, Wheld, if you'd been on the side of those cursed gutterings of mutineers it mightn't have been us resting here now. You'd have been a sore trial to us and instead it was a surprise for them. By Atlan! That misbegotten rat Yelna I killed with my first cut as he turned on me. Holy Egg, Scridol, but you fight well. I'd never heard it was an artist's craft. Is that girl hurt?"

He watched Bulinga, whitefaced, bring herself back to consciousness.

"I saw your arm raise a weapon," he observed. "Did you kill your man, Princess? Your father Rugul would have been pleased to be here, not like my brother, Carpen, who scrabbled off in a hurry. He's too calculating. By the Egg! I fully believe the first thing he did was to count the legs of our enemy, divide it by two, to find their exact number, and decide from such a fact we were certain to be all killed." Vathok shook his head in mock humility. "He didn't know us, did he? Had a long ride back, too, if he's bound for the meeting tree, and I'll bet my share of the warmth in Hell that's where he's off to, to strike a bargain with the new chief. It'll be a shock to them all when we come to them. Dris told me Shelig must have galloped in haste from us to help in the planning of this thing. They were after you, my girl. Two thousand gold parings is an argument of weight to most. Not to Carpen. He planned to give you as an offering to his Temple."

The dust was settling now. Although it was now night, by the age of several hours, there was light enough for them to see. Their eyes were well accustomed—and there were the stars, combined in millions, undwarfed by any moon.

Vathok surveyed the changes in the shape of the ruins and his voice shook with laughter.

"And to think it was your work, Gatil! Oh I saw. Wheld! Are those beasts quiet enough yet? Great Yolk's Guts, it's time we were, ourselves, back at the meeting tree. All my plans are overlaid and nothinged by this. Wheld! man! Who leads these craven cutthroat murderers?" Vathok's loquacity had burnt itself out. His brows drew together and his eyes glinted. His voice now grated. "Who leads this rising against my leadership? Is it that fool Banrod? Eh?"

Dris, the yellow man beside him, tilted his still red knife point upward, fingering it, seeming careless—ready to defend himself if necessary.

"Vathok," he said softly, but in clear unslurred tones so there should be no mistake. "Vathok," he repeated, "who leads is your son, Kcus." He paused, his eyes not leaving the face of his chief. More quietly he said, "I tried to hint as much to you, before, in the room, below there."

Vathok's hands came up, clenched, but the yellow man hadn't moved.

"Wheld!" he said.

From among the horses the other bandit came.

Scridol, Bulinga and Gatil watched.

"Kcus," said the bandit.

After the briefest silence:

"Kcus." The voice was not Vathok's though it came from his lips.

"Your son," Wheld assured him to leave him in no doubt. Dris elbowed him to silence.

Vathok's hands dropped.

He turned, walked away and sat, his back to them, on the fallen plinth.

Bulinga, feeling very giddy, struggled to her feet, took

a step in his direction. Dris put out a hand and stayed her.

Gatil opened his mouth to laugh, saw the faces of the others, and kept silence.

10

Anut sat in his chair by the gate and watched the ants and two brilliantly green mella beetles. What the guards, standing about leaning on their spears and on each other's shoulders, said and thought didn't concern him and it wouldn't have mattered to him if it did.

He had his own life, in a world which was part of Tellur and yet not of it. He saw things differently from others. He was mad.

There were six people sitting on tired horses coming down the long slow road to the ford. At that distance they were no larger than beetles. Anut liked humans no bigger than beetles. They fitted in, better, that size.

But as they came nearer they would grow larger, with a simply extraordinary rapidity. It was queer that they should. It was queer that men were only this size in Dnalgne, queer that they had to grow to come here. Perhaps these people now coming could tell him why. He'd like to know.

There were other things he'd like to know. But no one was ever likely to tell him the answers he wanted. It was all a great conspiracy of silence. They knew, he'd asked them all years and years ago and they must remember because they'd written it down. He'd seen them do it, but he couldn't read writing and everyone knew he couldn't. He could only read the messages in stars and what beetles wrote.

The horses were so tired. A pity. For they'd only get one night's rest in Dnalgne. Nobody but a fool would stay more than a night in Dnalgne. He wasn't going to. He was going away with these people even though he knew there was going to be one of them he couldn't like.

The new people were quite close now. All men, except the horses and the girl who was dressed as a very girlish-seeming young man.

The guard lolled about. There were sufficient of a guard to deal with any disturbance. They weren't even interested. The guard leader, quite an ordinary man whose sole accomplishment was sycophancy, stepped forward and spoke.

"Down to the earth, travelers. This is Dnalgne and in this town now one has to explain oneself, and one's business."

Scridol rode forward, pushing his mount between the others.

"What's all this about, friend?" he demanded. "Since when in the whole width and length of the continent of Handria has it been necessary to answer questions on first entering a town?"

The guard leader smiled. This was almost in the Book of Rules.

"Since the Might of the High One, and his Religious Police, took control of such a town."

Scridol reached up for his reins.

"Oh well, you know all about me, or your superiors do. I am Scridol."

He mounted.

"Where is the inn here?" he asked.

"Scridol!" said the guard.

"Yes, Scridol. Scridol."

"Oh, Scridol." The guard leader's brows met and the effort of memory succeeded.

"You are the artist!"

"I am the artist."

"I am sorry, Estimable Scridol. I have never seen you. How could I then recognize you? But I know well how you are placed in the regard of the High One. Would you be so good as to tell me of all your party?"

"Eh. Oh, there's nothing here for your attentions, leader. This lad is a Groodian noble, with attendants. You know of Grood! And this lad is from Nipsirc." Scridol made as though to move off, but stopped. "You'll perhaps know of his uncle if you know not of him. His uncle is named Carpen. And, I almost forgot it myself, this estimable person is Vathok, brother to Carpen."

"Brother to Carpen!" said the awed leader.

"Perhaps," continued Scridol, "you will now have one of your men guide us to the inn?"

The guard leader was impressed, but troubled. His duty had not been done.

"I will guide you to the inn," said Anut. He looked up at Bulinga.

Vathok's eyes jerked inquiry at the guard.

The leader rolled his eyes up, held one hand flat under his chin and with the other lightly held his forehead.

"Ah," said Vathok.

Anut gripped Bulinga's leaf-tasseled bridle and pulled. The horse followed him.

"I shall report to the Upper Leader who will call on you," shouted the leader.

"So this place has been taken as my men are to take Grood," remarked Vathok.

"Apparently," agreed Scridol, and turned at once to Bulinga, for he realized that Vathok would now remember they were his followers no longer.

"You are quickwitted," applauded Bulinga.

"I think we'd be wise to move on from here without pause," Scridol advised.

"But there can be no danger."

"Danger enough," Scridol insisted. "Danger in plenty. I can deal with any provincial headmen. 'They are all thieves and therefore fools,'" he quoted from the holy books. " 'But fools can be dangerous.' Like the fool who holds your bridle."

Anut's long handsome face turned to Bulinga.

"I will not tell them. You need not fear."

"Tell them? Tell who? Tell them what?" asked Bulinga.

Anut's long stride shortened. He walked easily between the horses. They and the leathers of the harness were filthy and coated with dust and the filth of travel. Anut paid no attention. Nor did the filth transfer itself to his elegant garments. He had the animal grace of the subhuman—his easy lope, the swaying of his body with each step, were themselves significant of his condition. There was always a distance between him and what he was near.

Not even the unevenness of the rutted street upset his balance.

His queer eyes fascinated Bulinga. She knew she feared him, feared him as she had feared the great cats, knew that her fear must not show in her face. His eyes shaded peculiarly from light grey downwards to a dark sea blue. They seemed not to be properly seeing one, yet they stayed, focused, without weariness.

"They will never let me speak with ladies. But I knew you would someday exist for me. They will not know you are a lady. If I tell them they will take me away and—I would not like that."

He walked on, his eyes still fixed in their stare.

Bulinga looked over his head to Gatil who had come up on her left.

"We dealt with that evenly," he boasted. "My uncle Carpen's name is occasionally useful."

"I seem fated from deceit to deceit," remarked Bulinga. "Oh, Gatil, aren't the houses poor things, built so of pressed mud? I have not seen one tree. And they dress so richly. My father's men would overrun the gates at their ease. Mud. All mud. Yet they all dress richly, though one can see they are mere sluggards."

She could not make it out. Even the clothes of the

poorest, recognized by being soiled, were more colorful and elaborate than Bulinga ever remembered seeing, even at the court of Grood. They showed signs of imagination, little details such as collars with unusually long points ended in tassels. And poor, worn and dirty as most of the garments were, they had scalloped hems, slitted and lined cuffs, and tasseled bells on the belts.

"Their trade is wool, you forget, and the fashioning of garments. Even the herds we saw of Angor and Balka goats are not their whole wealth. They range far. And are not worth raiding for the goats are driven to Nipsirc for shearing and killing as food. They keep their flocks alive, just alive, until shearing time. There is no money here. All the value is kept by them in the Market Town. And their herds are so distinctive, no raider could sell even one single animal. There is no real wealth here, Princess."

"Oh look! Gatil! Look. In that pool. Those huge birds. What are they? They are graceful! I thought only eagles and vultures grew so!"

"They are cranes," said Gatil, laughing at her. "Have you not known cranes?"

"I have never seen them in Grood. How big that one is!"

The crane spread his wings and edged into the blue sky. Bulinga's eyes followed him on and up.

"Oh, Gatil," she breathed, "I am so glad I left Grood."

Gatil smiled. He wondered how soon he could kiss her. She was becoming a torment to him. He felt that if only in the right circumstances, in the dark, and with no one else near, he could soon have her as he wanted her—ready to allow him anything. And what a conquest that would be. A real princess. If all these people only knew! It would be something to talk about afterwards. And she thought him admirable, he knew. She was even aware she owed her life to him and to him alone.

Gatil had long since forgotten why he was on the

wall. That too would be something to boast of when he reached Nipsirc.

Wheld couldn't bear even the sight of Gatil.

He turned and spoke to Dris whose pale eyes, as they always did, were storing into the mind behind them all that might one day be useful as help from danger.

Dris didn't expect danger in Dnalgne. Herders were people of no heart. But he had lived long because after the fashion of his race he saw all there was to see.

"That whelp will be slit by me," promised Wheld.

Dris smiled thinly.

"Scridol the artist will be before you."

Wheld snorted.

"Scridol is a man for all his skinny dwarfishness. He doesn't want the girl for himself nor for ransom."

"No. He thinks of himself as a father. He has made himself a watchdog. He will slit the whelp. Unless . . . It is difficult to trap the wolverine," he reminded his companion.

Vathok, riding before, half turned his head, at the same time holding in his horse so he came to ride between them.

"Keep your mouths shut. Tight. And leave Gatil alone. He is my nephew."

"Your family are not always your friends," said Wheld.

Vathok paled. His eyes looked into Wheld's, they were blazing—the hurt at the back of them accentuating the anger.

"By the Belly of the First Mother," swore Vathok. He brooded. He had brooded for days. He was becoming his old self again, slowly. "At least they didn't get the Princess," he murmured. "The little gods must have been with us. To guide me past the meeting tree and to the ruins where—where we were waylaid. Had we not taken her so far, because my brother and that sniffling nephew Gatil wanted my safe escort, we would not now be on the road to Nipsirc. Nipsirc will find her value for us. And for us and no one else."

"If you can get rid of Scridol—and Gatil," Wheld reminded him. "Scridol we can kill. Are we not to kill Gatil?"

Vathok swirled to him.

"Gut of the Serpent. No!" he snarled. "Leave it to me to plan."

Scridol well knew he was now superfluous in the company. No one wanted him, he reflected, humorously. But if that lechering whelp Gatil thought he was going to succeed it would only be when he, Scridol, was not about, and he was always going to be about—between here and Nipsirc. That girl was too delightful a child to be left to learn from her own mistakes. True enough she'd had training of a sort—and had known enough to see the provincialism of her own town-kingdom. But she did not know enough to see that provincialism was in her own alloy.

Though she needed experience the girl was steel at the core, and given her chance would find her proper niche which was neither to be seduced by a canting jeweler's nephew nor to be the fortune of the other uncle—a bragging forest knifeman. What a family they must be, Scridol thought. Some true religion was badly needed in this continent. It was daily becoming worse with squads of enlisted petty thieves and cut-throats bolstering the attempted reign of puritans. Perhaps he should pack up and get himself across the world to Atlan. This adventure was enjoyable. But he must find a home for the years that would eventually come. He would not see his youth again. But the safe delivery of this runaway princess to some people of taste in Nipsirc had become a duty.

Bulinga rode like a queen. In spite of the people's soiled finery this was a poor place. At first she had been somewhat troubled—she had previously visualized all towns outside Grood as cities of glamor. But soon there would be Nipsirc—then Gabebal and Dejanira, and ultimately—Atlan? Atlan's cities would be cities of fantastic culture and wealth.

She smiled down at the back of Anut's head.

She smiled at Anut's head because she mustn't smile at Gatil, and she wanted to. Scridol was too close by and although she owed the little man nothing she did not want to endure his disapproval. He had made obvious his disapproval of Gatil. He was a fiery little man, who seemed to consider himself the natural leader of the party. Yet she would not offend him. He meant well. Gatil. Even his name had grace. He was different from every other man, from every man she had ever known or seen. His courtesy to her was enough on its own to place him above all other men. Groodian men treated their womenfolk as they treated one another. And how excitingly slender he was compared to the squat men of Grood. He was young, with the straight nose and mouth of a courageous man, though she admitted that only in his type were such full lips to be associated with courage. And he wore his neat well-made clothes with an air.

And she would never let herself forget that it was because of his action that she was still alive.

Bulinga was looking forward to a night of comfortable sleep. For two nights now she had slept on the ground, under her a ragged horse blanket, her marten over her. Such sleep was not to be compared with sleep in a bed, with real rugs, long and broad enough for their purpose, and sheets of fine wool.

"How far to the inn now?" she asked Gatil. "Do you know?"

"Very close," he replied. "We are now in the street of taverns. Always in such towns the inns are surrounded by taverns. See, each one carries its own sign."

It made him seem so very traveled.

They must be drinking dens of a very low type, Bulinga thought. In the whole street of crumbling mud walls there were only two doorways, and an occasional small grilled window hole. Bulinga deduced the windows must be on the other walls of the rooms. Till now doors had borne colored numbers, the only relief on the red and yellowy-red walls. Above the doors now near her were rough lettered phrases. "To drink in good company? Here are both!" and "Several good drinks are better than many bad drinks." Somewhat childish Bulinga thought it.

Then, though the street carried on to another gate, seen to be quite near, Anut led them abruptly round a corner and they halted in a roughly rectangular space.

Bulinga looked about with distaste.

Several huddles of colored rags were, she considered, the sleeping forms of men. In one corner horses tethered on too long a rope plundered some bales of grass. A low, broken well-head was near. Round the wall, high up, reached by broken, grass-grown steps, were caves, holes into darkness.

Bulinga was bewildered.

Was this—this!—the inn?

She turned an amazed face to Gatil—to the others —and found Anut regarding her, worry, anxiety in his queerly colored eyes.

"You do not like this," he stated rather than asked.

Gatil came close.

"Of all the holes," he said. "It is worse than I remembered it."

"Bellies and breasts! What's wrong with it?" queried Vathok. "It's a place to sleep!"

"But not to be paid for," offered Scridol.

"But—but inns are *not* like this! They, they *can't* be!" said Bulinga.

"Wait till you see the inns in Nipsirc," enthused Gatil. "They are marvelous. Dining-rooms with tables and even chairs instead of stools, and the bedrooms are . . ."

"This is not Nipsirc," Scridol said shortly.

"I'd—rather sleep in the woods again," Bulinga said. "I can't sleep here." She appealed to Gatil. "You can't expect me to!"

"You can sleep in my house," offered Anut.

No one spoke.

"Here is the innman," said Wheld.

An elderly, broad, protuberant-bellied man with white hair frizzed round a bald head approached, supported by a woman of similar build. They rolled forward rather than walked. Both wore long-skirted fine woolen coats over their other clothing. The effect was ludicrous. Their feet could not be seen.

"The best of the day to you," said the man.

"—sday," saluted Scridol.

"For how many nights?" asked the innman, his eyes roving over them as if counting them again and again. "There is water; there are as many chambers as you wish and," he pointed to the remains of the baled grass, "bedding for those who desire it. And food! You may cook your own, or, if you desire to stroll about and enjoy the town in your time here, you may safely leave your cooking to my wife. She is a good cook. We do not charge much. Just enough to cover expenses."

Wheld and Dris had unsaddled and were rubbing down their animals with handfuls of straw.

Vathok unhitched his girths.

Bulinga looked from one to the other in dismay.

"The horses," Scridol explained gently, "must be rested. There is nowhere else to stay the night." He shrugged. "Unless your beetle-haunted friend can be taken seriously. I suppose he must live somewhere. Here, Gatil! deal with—with the noble's horse. Get off, my dear. The horses must have a decent rest and good hard food if it is obtainable."

He helped Bulinga down.

Gatil was moved to object but Scridol's demeanor suggested that he had better not. Gatil sullenly took Bulinga's horse over with the others to be watered, rubbed down and fed. Acting as groom to a girl was never part of his plan. He breathed sulphurous curses at Scridol to the quiet amusement of the two ruffians.

Dris made no demur when Scridol approached him. Without a word he took the little man's horse. And Scridol went to Vathok.

"Vathok," he said bluntly. "What do you advise?"

Vathok eyed him, commiseratingly.

"You are thrice born a fool, little man," he said.

"Let the girl stay here. Snake's Scales! It won't harm her. She's lived too soft. Better for her to forget this princessness of hers. By the Seven Curses she is no princess here. Let her learn so."

Scridol shook his head.

"It is against all custom to accept the hospitality of a madman," Vathok reminded him, low-voiced for once. "You know it is so. We cannot and we need not. And with those swads of Religious Police in the town! If they were my men it would all be easy. But I know, and you know, that the slightest excuse for plundering us will do."

"You are Carpen's brother."

"Oh yes and I'm also an outlaw. Their group leader will perhaps have heard of me. By Atlan's Lights, I tell you, Scridol, I have no mind to attract too much of their attention."

Bulinga walked over to them, with Anut following.

"I am going with this man, if two of you will accompany me," she stated flatly. Her chin rose as she faced them.

"I have no least intention of staying even half of one hour more in this noisome inn. Our cats are better stabled."

Vathok straightened up from the inspection of his horse's hooves.

"He is a madman."

Gatil, breathless, hurried over. He nudged Scridol.

"At the gate," he blurted.

Scridol turned.

"Ah! the group leader," he said, and walked away two paces.

"Bulinga," he called. "Come with me."

Mutinously, why she moved at all she could not tell, Bulinga moved leisurely after him.

"Princess," Scridol said, "this may not be your idea of a welcome for one of your rank. But more than your comfort and your dignity hang in the balance. These Religious Police are the cut-throats and criminals of the cities, officered partly by puritans. They must not

know you are a girl. Can you appreciate the serious-
ness of it to them? Remember Carpen's attitude to you.
I go to meet this officer. You were best to come with
me, and remember you are a young noble. But leave
me to talk. Don't underrate their power." He smiled
grimly. "They have all the power a princess, in Grood,
would have. Come!"

He took her arm in his thin long-fingered hand and
Bulinga walked with him.

Bulinga, confused, meeting a situation she never, in
all her day dreams, could have imagined, reluctantly
accompanied him.

Her mind had no measure by which to work. This
was all wrong. Yet, though Scridol had said so little,
his quiet forceful words had thrust themselves, each
one, into her mind.

Halfway, she thought of Gatil. He would be of more
use. But Scridol urged her on and at that moment the
group leader spurred towards them, leaving his men to
follow.

Scridol walked steadily forward and when three or
four yards separated him from the approaching horseman, he raised his hand in a peculiar salute. A salute
which was repeated by the surprised horseman.

He pulled his mount to a stop, looked down.

"No one can rise so High," he said, attempting a
casual tone.

"Except One," replied Scridol gravely, replying cor-
rectly.

The horseman dismounted.

"I see you are one of us. I am one Telbir. I command here."

"My name is Scridol."

"The gate leader told me of you. It is not a name I
know. But you have the 'words of grace.' "

"It may not be known to you, Telbir. It is known,
however, to many others. Is it superfluous for me to
point out I had never heard of you?"

The other glowered.

Bulinga didn't like the look of him. He was much

too much like Carpen, not in appearance but in *feel*. His own appearance was nondescript. Afterwards she could not even recall his features or height.

Scridol's upturned hand indicated her.

"This lad is Buling. He is a young noble from Grood whom I am escorting to Nipsirc.

The man bowed, shortly, to her. Turned again to Scridol.

"So I have been informed. You have a somewhat tatter-demalion company. Has that any significance?" He gave a toothy but unlovely smile. "My guards at the gate were far from impressed. Even if there is a reason for—oh, well, anything, you must know that I am entitled to demand explanations from those who enter the town I command!"

Scridol laughed.

"You mean my rags! Save you, man, there are many things to do, and ways of doing them, in the service of the High One. You can consider, for instance," he turned and pointed. "See that tall, big man? He is Vathok. He is an outlaw. He is also, if it interests you, the brother of a man named Carpen, whom, until I met him, *I* had not heard of. I met him as a jewel trader, but discovered soon he was more than that. That other youth is not of the party, yet. He was with his uncle, Carpen, as a jewel trader, in Grood. It is by his uncle's desire that he travels out from this area where things are due to happen. Carpen was with us till two days since. He is now engaged in organizing the followers of his brother Vathok, organizing them towards a new venture. The town-kingdom of Grood is their objective. I expect I can leave it to you to make the necessary inferences, to understand why I travel to Nipsirc, with an outlaw, brother of a full and valued member, his two followers, and a young noble of Grood."

The other's face had set into portentous lines. He nodded.

"Well!" he said. "You stay tonight? here?"

"That," observed Scridol, "is what concerns us at

the moment. Our horses must be rested. Unless," he said brightly, the thought having just struck him, "unless we can trade in those we have for some of yours. Ours are almost forespent," he added ingenuously.

Telbir was not to be drawn on this. He remained impassive to the suggestion.

"This inn, which," went on Scridol, "will doubtless be so very much improved when more important matters have ceased to demand all your attention, this inn is all right—for outlaws. Vathok, his men, the other youth, even myself, we could and would all accept its imperfections. Buling is another matter. He is not bred to such rough living." Scridol bent forward and almost whispered. "The High One," he stated, without even a blush, "is desirous of this noble receiving the best of treatment on his journey. You see," he said, straightening up, "it is difficult. Now we have been offered the hospitality of that madman there. You, a man in your position, must surely know whether we can accept what, in ordinary circumstances, it would be against all convention to accept. For, by the High Steps to the Sun, somehow to accept the invitation of the madman is the only solution I see."

Telbir was softening. He nursed his chin.

"Have you considered approaching me?"

Scridol smiled.

"Naturally. And as naturally put aside the idea. I know the strict rules."

"Yes," the other agreed, his brow clearing. "Yes, although I do not really believe that Rule Fifty-Four means that in such circumstances as this a Leader must not be hospitable. I was taught that by it I must not in my official position play host to friends. I can see, though, that you are one of those who are strict in their rulings."

"I try to be," Scridol lied easily. "Until I saw the state of this inn I knew no necessity to look for other lodging. Nor had I intended to approach you, burdened as you must be with large responsibilities. To approach you was, I thought, to irk you with trivialities. But as you are here perhaps you will advise me. What can I do? You are doubtless overburdened already with junior officers in your headquarters. This Anut appears to have wealth enough to entertain this noble. Should I accept the offer? Remembering that 'conventions must be ruthlessly torn aside when the cause demands?' "

"That is a paragraph of Rule Ten," observed Telbir. "Yes. I believe you should."

The two looked at each other and Bulinga looked from one to the other. She realized that for her sake Scridol was pretending to be what he was not, and that of the rules which bound Telbir's actions Scridol knew at least enough to create a fine impression. It was ridiculous that men such as Telbir should have power and should have to be placated. She was beginning to understand that her desires were apt to inconvenience her companions. That this should be so did not seem to her to matter. They would of course accept that as something which must be.

Telbir was impressed.

Scridol knew contemptuous satisfaction.

The pretentiousness of this prig, as he had expected, was the weapon to use against him.

"As well as keeping as strictly as I can to the rules we have been given, I like to abet the ordinary decencies," Scridol observed, mendaciously, and with such a flood of smugness he himself almost believed it. "Has this Anut parents or a guardian who might reasonably expect to have invited us before enjoying our presence?"

"My authorization is sufficient. He is under the care of the town headmen. His father was a headman. As it happens there is no other house here in which I could quarter your young noble, were I approached for help in finding one. No. There can be no objection by any."

Bulinga was becoming restive.

The boy's clothing she wore kept her silent, though her foot was tapping the firm clay of the path.

She sensed someone beside her.

It was Anut.

After a little silence he said:

"Man Telbir, this estimable lord is my guest."

Telbir inclined his head.

"So he has informed me."

Scridol took back to himself all his contempt. This Telbir, then, had compassion for the afflicted.

Scridol said to Bulinga:

"You will require attendants?"

Bulinga's mind absorbed all the implications of this. Yes. She could not go alone. But she was somewhat tired of Scridol.

"I should prefer Gatil and Dris."

Scridol smiled, and Bulinga found fault with herself.

"You have done much for me," she said to him.

Scridol did not contradict her or attempt to deprecate his efforts, which annoyed her again.

Well, she would have Gatil with her, whom she wanted most of all. She was pleased she had been able to say so, so easily. Scridol she could not have endured. Something in her was resentful of all he did, more so since the day before when he had made really plain to her his disapproval of Gatil. Dris was a miracle of self-effacement. She would not notice he was there.

Telbir and Scridol had been saying other things she had not listened to. Now Telbir mounted and rode away.

Scridol bowed to her with a dry nod. She felt the nod was grim. She clenched the fingers of her right hand round the green bundle she held and her chin rose, ready for anger.

"I will tell the others," was all Scridol said.

11

Dnalgne was behind them, behind the seven of them. Anut had joined them.

Telbir had seen no reason to object, having faith in Scridol who had had to endure a whole evening of his company. Scridol had now to deliver Anut safely to the Official Guardian of Nipsirc. Scridol cursed, as competently as Vathok had ever done, but to himself alone, and accepted the responsibility. The day before his mind might have been alert to find obstructions to such an idea. But he had been drained of vitality by a night spent mouthing prim platitudes and religious puerilities he could not himself accept, and which made him feel unworthy and sacrilegious. He rode with Vathok and Dris and Wheld, so tired of the adventure as to be almost oblivious of the wide, fantastically red, extravagantly flat beauty of the tableland across which they journeyed.

There were four days' travel before them and Vathok and Scridol had decreed no hurry. Bulinga had tried, unsuccessfully, to decide otherwise for the company, and although they were fully two hours forward on their journey she rode in frigid uncompromising silence.

Gatil and Anut, the width of two horses between them, were slightly behind her, just near enough to escape the dust her horse's hooves raised from the dry path. They were not on the ancient road now. Vathok had decreed that they travel on this path, cutting two days off their journey. Vathok, Bulinga fumed, made too many decrees.

Since the night in the ruins he had been quieter, feeling the grief of his son's insurgence. His forceful personality sleeping, his habit of command hushed, Bulinga had almost been able to rule until they reached Dnalgne. Now Vathok was again becoming unbearable and Bulinga wished the son had been successful. These men, Vathok and Scridol, they knew she was a princess! Now that Vathok was merely one of the party escorting her there was no excuse for their conduct. Scridol was unnecessary. He spoiled everything. She never had a moment with Gatil! Now there was Anut with them, always treading on her shadow.

Angrily she tightened her pull on the reins and the animal responded by breaking into a trot and had to be restrained.

She was now almost a horsewoman, except for some soreness in her legs and thighs. That also made her angry. Everything made her angry. Everything. This was no triumphant jubilant course. This flight from the rude ignoble inelegance of Grood had somehow proved to be—and that too from its very beginnings—a mere running away to what was ignobly and rudely similar. No. This was worse. She now had no vestige of comfort, there was continued thwarting of her desires, except those so small as to be of no importance; and her inmost pride was hurt; now she seemed to be engulfed by deceit, lies and insincerity.

This was not as she had seen the escapade. This was a running away, an escape! What she had planned for herself was the soaring flight of a bird of precious plumage released from a mundane cage. Not an exodus but an arrival; it was to have been an arrival, with acclamation, to surroundings which were her rightful environment, to the company of princes and personages of note, of regality of mind, to the company of people to whom the elegancies, the refinements, the graces of life were the very being of life itself. And she was to have come among them welcomed as a sun among stars.

It had been in her mind this morning to discard these

boy's clothes and to be, outwardly, Bulinga, Princess of Grood. She would have done so but for the awkward questioning this action must have evoked from these pestilential Religious Police. She had then resolved to change her habit by the road, in the shelter of the trees she had naturally expected. She should have remembered from her view of Dnalgne the previous day that to the herders' town a tree was something mythical. There were none on the plain, only stunted bushes beside the narrow winding sluggish river.

And last night had been a fiasco.

True, she had known the comfort of a bed, and food eaten from a table and not gnawed squatting by the roadside as if she were no more than a female animal. But Gatil had not been with her. Yesterday she must have been naïve. Was it anything to do with Scridol, she wondered, that Gatil, together with Dris the yellow man, had been relegated to the servants' quarters the night before? She had seen nothing of him until the horses were brought round for her leavetaking this morning! Had Scridol done that? It was easily possible. He guarded her as though he were a near blood relative; it was irksome, to say the least. If he considered she should be grateful he was expecting what could not be. She would rather have Vathok's brutal disregard.

Four days of this! Four long, interminable days before Nipsirc was reached.

There, at least, she could meet her peers, and surely there would be those there who would help one of her rank. She almost wished she had gone with Emalf. She knew now that he had been right when he demurred at carrying her for what she had been prepared to give. She had been much surprised this morning when the men were paying their bill at the inn, to see how much money one was expected to pay for the little one received.

The very small amount of her own money rather worried her. It was with a small pang of shame she realized how unfair she had been to the trader in refusing to let him ask what had, after all, been a reasonable price for a journey with him to Dejanira. The price of jewels and cloths bought in Grood from the traders had given her no clue to the price of services on a journey. She had thought she was paying princely prices for her things in Grood. Now she suspected their quality.

She saw that she had been a fool in the ways of the world. But she knew now. This journey had taught her wisdom.

Bulinga glanced back at Anut and Gatil.

Both were looking not at her but to the side, and interested in their own side only. Each saw her turn but failed to catch her eye before she looked ahead again.

Bulinga felt pleased.

They were both self-constituted followers, and each in obvious annoyance at the other's proximity. To Anut, of course—well, what did he matter? Poor thing. It would be impossible ever to gauge his affection. Was she as a woman to him, or did he class her as some sort of transcendant beetle? She knew she was the sole reason for this excursion of his. It was like having a dog. And he was as much nuisance as a dog one really didn't want.

The only good that could come out of his devotion was that it made Gatil more devoted to her. Bulinga knew she could see so easily into Gatil's mind. He worshipped her. He could not know that all her thoughts were bent towards planning a future for them, a future which would raise him step by step in the world so that all would acclaim her choice and forget his lowly birth.

In obedience to a long-drawn whistle from Vathok the horses changed gait to the steady canter which was their talent, and which, so carefully were they bred, they could maintain without rest for mile after weary mile.

Gatil glowered at the back of Bulinga's head and thought of himself running his fingers through and through and through the masses of inflammatory fairness which flared and seethed about her now she had removed her cap. There must be a way. Princess or not, he knew more about her limitations now after three days of traveling in her company, and he would wager his uncle Carpen's chance of high office in the Temple Circle that he would eventually have his desire of her.

The horses cantered on. Bulinga plotted, Vathok plotted, Gatil plotted and seethed, Anut seethed.

12

Wheld and Dris were already scooping a shallow hole in the ground, for a fireplace. Their horses were hobbled and turned loose, their saddles heaped where they intended to sleep.

Bulinga, watching them dismount, had envied their slovenly grace. All their movements had the aptness, the practiced ease, of those who had spent long years in the wilderness. Doing something, they were unflurried. Like animals.

Anut was beside her, holding her bridle.

Bulinga slid thankfully to the ground and watched him as without a word he did all that was necessary for her horse.

It was nearly dark.

Vathok had spread himself comfortably over his men's saddles and extricated from one of Scridol's leather cases a bone still lavishly covered with meat.

"Why in the Name of the Serpent's Glorious Belly didn't you fill both your accursed dans?" Vathok demanded. "For a man who has a head and can use it, Scridol, you show at times a woeful lack of sense. Atlan's Lights, man, there was food by the crate on that table in the ruins. Holy blasted Yolk, there were whole goats' hams you left behind."

"You were hurrying us out of the room," Scridol reminded him.

"Serpent's Guts, man, of course I was but I didn't know what you were doing."

"Would that have made any difference?".

"Perhaps not," Vathok had to agree. "But even if it didn't, couldn't you have taken more of the food there? The fruit would not be all poisonous even yet! That meal in the ruins was spoiled by your fighting me and, curse it all, man, if you guessed we might need food you might have guessed more and taken more." He bit into a loaf. "Gaugh," he spat, "this bread from Dnalgne is poor stuff." He waggled his bone at Scridol, tassels of meat waving fitfully from it. "There was bread on that table, Scridol," he admonished.

"There was no light," Scridol answered. "You should congratulate yourself that I found so much."

"Who extinguished the light?" Bulinga asked.

"Dris, I suppose," Vathok said. "He knows how to do it. When I was younger I searched those ruins from end to end. There were other rooms intact. But only one with the light. I found out how to use it, by an accident. By Atlan's Lights!" He stopped. "By Atlan's Lights," he said more slowly. "I wonder! Cold Lights! By all the bloodshot eggs that ever were, was that one of Atlan's Cold Lights? Was that ruin one of Atlan's cities when all this land was under her rule as the priests say it was? Great Yolk! Great Serpent's Yolk! To think I had *that* in my hands."

"Well, it stopped me getting more food," Scridol said.

"But you had two dans!" Bulinga said. "I was with you. Had you told me I could have filled the other!"

"The other is filled," Scridol said equably, "with what I wish it to contain. As it is I have lost much I had carefully collected."

"It was such good food," Bulinga remembered.

Scridol said no more. He was prepared to offer his share of the conversation, but he now saw his share as being very little. The warm earthy color of the great table-land had swallowed him. He was immersed in inspiration. Never had he seen naked raw color express so much. He should have known, of course. The sky should have warned him. The sky, especially at night—in spite of the complexity of pattern in the arrangement of the stars—could not be more simply designed —yet consider its unearthly beauty! But somehow he had never expected to find in the earth such a glory in all the shades of one color—he had often seen it in the sky but never until now in the earth. This had opened to him vistas down which he could walk for ever. There were other colors, other tones which could be so isolated.

What had once been in the dan he would not mourn. Had the contents of the other, too, been replaced with food he would not now have cared.

This, these pageants of nature, of the Deep God, were what he had wandered to find, this rhapsody on a theme, this wealth of oneness in color.

Should he take earth back with him?

Vathok sat and gnawed and swore, goodhumoredly. Three days, and a little bit, to Nipsirc.

In four days he would be rich.

The girl's form was of a quality—oh, he hadn't the words, but he knew money when he saw it, in whatever form. This was so easy. The idiot was of no moment. Scridol? He could be dealt with. He might even leave the party of his own desire, once Nipsirc was reached. Gatil? Vathok snorted.

Gatil was too afraid of his own nail-parings to be even considered as a hindrance. He would do as he was told.

She'd strip well. By the Great Snake's Belly she was a find. And all so easy! He could laugh at the simplicity of it all.

Complacently he eyed her, she standing talking to his weakling nephew. Those trousers now. They showed off her body as no skirts would have done. Yes, life was good. All this demonstrated what a fool brother Carpen was. To put a girl like that into the Great Temple of Nipsirc was sheer waste. Religion took you nowhere, Vathok told himself. This was the life to live. What was it Carpen had called it? Ah. He had the word. Materialism. Well, why not? It paid! Take these Religious Police. Who were they? To say that Religion paid them was to laugh in the Serpent's face. Vathok chuckled at the thought. They were all ruffians like his. And the good they got themselves out of Religion was good solid gold extorted from people who paid well or were reported to the High One's officers as needing remedial treatment. It was cheaper to pay the Police than to pay the Church.

Vathok had seen rich plundering in Grood, and all coming his way, and snatched away by Kcus, the murdering young scoundrel.

Vathok had not been at all surprised to find his own idea already in operation in Dnalgne. It would be like that in Nipsirc, and elsewhere. There were more cities than one, richer towns than Grood. And Carpen was his beloved brother. It would seem that in addition to the riches Bulinga would bring him, he was going to earn himself a position where ease and plenty were the reward.

Gatil could keep her amused and interested till his uncle Vathok was ready to take her over. They could come to no harm out here on the plain. They could talk all they wanted, till they sickened each other.

"The idiot is asleep," Gatil said with satisfaction, "and at last I have the chance for which I have schemed for days—always to see it pushed from my grasp by circumstances no one could have foreseen. Princess, it is vital that you give me all your attention, for what I have to tell you is very terrible."

He paused at that. That much he had phrased over and over during the ride till he had it perfect. He had meant to emphasize still more the dangers from which he was about to deliver her. But the desirability of her body had always usurped his thoughts and his first sentence was all he had ready.

It was sufficient, he found.

Bulinga's great purple eyes were staring at him. He had all her attention. She was very ready to listen to the least remark he might make.

"I must get you away, alone, with me from this camp and these people tonight," he said urgently.

Bulinga nodded.

All her nod meant was he had permission to talk on. He took it to mean much more and his confidence in himself multiplied and gave his words the semblance of sincerity and truth.

"It can be done, if sufficient stealth is used. You have little to carry. We need only take food, and our few things. Our two horses are the best because we are the lightest weights in the party and therefore our horses are the least tired. You may not have noticed, but I hobbled ours together, attached by thongs so that we could find them easily. You will be sleeping a little way apart. I too have placed my bed some way away." He looked guiltily at those about the fire. No one was even looking at Bulinga and himself. "You must be ready when I crawl to you, when all is quiet," he whispered. "For if you are asleep and make any sound the others will waken."

Bulinga nodded.

"You are the only person I have met whom I have been able to call a friend of my own. I am so very much aware of all you have done for me. I feel again that I have not perhaps shown you, sufficiently, that I know I owe life itself to your daring in loosening the wall base there in those ruins where your uncle took us. It was taking your own life in your hands, as you must have known, and also when you attacked the two men who were about to kill me. Though they may, I think, have been trying to capture me and bear me away, for what they said betrayed they were looking especially for me. You dealt with them in the only way possible to you. I did not know you were above me

I had thought you to be fighting with the others." Bulinga laid a hand on his arm, her face flushed with gratitude.

Gatil placed his fingers over hers and held them there.

"Princess," he said earnestly, "your thanks are much to me. Your continued happiness even more so. You are very probably pleased at our nearness to the city of Nipsirc, but unless I can get you safely from the power of both my uncles you are likely never to leave the city."

Bulinga's inert fingers now tightened so about his forearm he almost squealed in surprise.

"Say more," she said. "Why?"

Gatil recovered quickly. Carpen was not here; he would never discover the betrayal.

"My uncle Carpen," he told her, "intended to present you to the High One as a servant in the Great Temple. My uncle has much power. Even if we enter Nipsirc not in his company he may have made arrangements which we could not—not upset. He—he may be there now. Nipsirc can be reached by a determined man more quickly than by us, traveling as we do. And my uncle Carpen is determined. The resurgence of our religion in his whole desire, and nothing else is of any importance to him. Only by venturing in by a way I know shall we be safe and only if there are two of us can that be done. We must not travel farther with these people—and"—he grew more earnest as a fresh thought struck him—"Vathok, too, is not to be trusted!"

He was very pleased with himself.

The Princess's other hand was now on his arm beside the first.

She was closer to him, very close.

It was darker. The two of them must be only a darkish blur to those about the fire. He had courage for this sort of work.

He savored the strands of her hair which because of the light breeze now floated loose about him, gently touching his cheeks and one ear. She was close to him, so close that although he knew they were inches apart still he felt the caress of her against him.

Gatil breathed hard and kept control of himself.

He would be a fool if he spoiled his carefully worked out plan. She would be all his, soon. He could woo her to his way of thinking quite easily when they were alone together.

But, first he must get her there, into the night alone with him.

What was it he had told her?

Oh yes.

About Vathok.

What his uncle's plans were he had no idea, but— he had a good mind, he could invent.

"You know that, for certainty?" asked Bulinga.

"Yes," he lied, simply. "He proposes to sell you in the slave market. He still considers you as his prisoner."

"But—he has not . . . ! There has been no suggestion of that!"

"Why need there have been? You are traveling willingly with him! He need do nothing to upset your willingness until the very last moment."

Bulinga drew back.

The perfidy! And it was true. He would be like that.

For the briefest moment there flitted inside her mind the thought that none of the family were trustworthy. The thought barely received acknowledgement, so unnoticeable was it.

"The only safe way is for you to come with me, tonight. We can travel all night. If we ride hard we can be in Nipsirc at least a day before anyone would expect us."

Bulinga thought.

It would seem the best way.

Although, strangely enough, what attracted her most to the flight was getting to Nipsirc a whole day earlier than she had expected. It was becoming increasingly evident to her that she had not a vestige of an idea of what to do once she reached there. But Gatil would help, she comforted herself.

She looked at his shape, near, in the darkness.

"Very well, Gatil. I shall never forget this, this

service you do me is—I was about to say more than your last service to me. I know that couldn't be so."

She smiled at him. She knew he could not see the smile, and permitted herself to put into it all the tenderness she felt.

And this was no easy assignment he had set himself for her sake. Both uncles would be antagonized.

Another thought occurred to her, but she thrust away anything unwanted. That both these villainous uncles would become closer to her, being so closely related to Gatil. That was a thought she must not harbor at this time. It might affect her relations with Gatil.

"Dear Gatil," she breathed. "You, at least, are good. I will be waiting for you. I will not allow myself to sleep."

She rested her hand on his arm, just a momentary touch to seal the bargain, and moved off towards the faint glowing of the fire.

Gatil, well satisfied, circled round to where he knew the horses were.

Dris rose carefully from the damp ground and shook the dirt from his clothes.

They'd have to be watched. Women were all the same, princess or not it didn't seem to matter.

Anut waited a little longer before he moved, and he moved, quieter still, after Bulinga.

13

Gatil saw no reason to put off the enjoyable moments he had promised himself.

A two days' journey to Nipsirc with only the beautiful Princess would be delightful.

Gatil went over to the fire. The food was easily picked up, the bag was light. He carried it towards his own bedding. The two horses were there. The large stone he had thonged to the hobbles had kept them comparatively immobile.

The stillness, the fact that those cut-throats of his uncle Vathok were encamped near, that he was about to embark on the most thrilling love adventure of his life, everything combined to make his heart thump erratically, to shorten his breathing and to dry up all the saliva in his mouth.

When he stumbled over Anut and the strong fingers clasped murderously round his throat his own hands were useless to him. He was too untrained for his hands to attack, they clawed at the ground. There was a stone. It was grasping the stone which gave his brain the suggestion and it was pure accident that his arm was able to swing so accurately.

Gatil didn't wait to investigate the results of that wild thrash of his arm, he repeated it, and as that freed his own throat, he got up, staggered a few steps, found Bulinga.

They led the horses, softly, for minute after minute, pausing every now and then. There was no outcry. Obviously the figures by the fire had accepted that the horses, being hobbled, might wander but not far.

It was when they were quite far away that Gatil remembered that he hadn't cut through all the hobbles. The others would be able to catch their mounts with little trouble.

But, he was away, away with his Princess, and everything, except for those hobbles, was as he had planned.

In a little while they could break into a canter and add distance, miles and miles of it, between themselves and the others. Then! Well, there just was no chance of anything going wrong.

He wondered if he had killed Anut.

He hadn't.

Anut's fáce was cut and broken, one cheekbone and part of his scalp laid bare.

He rolled over and snarling like a hunting cat got to his hands and knees. He found moving forward like that very awkward because of the blood which would get into his eyes. There was pain, pain, intense pain, in his face and head. The snarling noise from his throat awoke Wheld and Vathok. It was the noise they made which awoke Scridol.

Anut had achieved for himself a crouching apelike gait, his head rolling from side to side in pain. Sight was almost impossible to him, there was the dark to be added to his pain, but he knew exactly where Bulinga should be. And she wasn't there.

Wheld and Dris had more sense than to approach him.

Anut found the nearest horse. One long slanting slash freed the hobbles from its legs and, caring nothing for saddlery, Anut, sobbing, crouching low on its back, galloped into the darkness.

"The fool is going in the wrong direction," Wheld shouted excitedly to Dris, as, swiftly as they were able, they saddled up.

"Not him," Dris yelled back. "Young Gatil asked me early on what was the direction of Nipsirc, and I told him. And naturally I told him wrong."

"Get my horse saddled," shouted Vathok, lumbering out of the dark.

"Saddle it yourself," Dris told him. He swung up and waited a moment to shout at his dumbfounded chief: "You're too heavy. If the madman isn't caught before he gets to Gatil, Gatil will be dead meat, and the girl too maybe, you know what madmen are."

Dris was away, his last phrase floating back to Vathok over the air. The hoofbeats of Wheld's horse were already faint sounds.

Vathok stood and cursed.

He appreciated the wisdom of the yellow man's remarks.

"Holy Serpent's Blood, Scales and Entrails," he

roared into the night. "See the girl is safe." But even his bull voice was insufficient for that purpose, and at a half-run he made off to the right where his horse should be. He slipped on a tussock of hard polished fern and fell backwards, calling on all the devils in Hell for support.

Scridol, methodically feeling over the ground for his missing bag, also swore.

Vathok found his horse and, spread over its back, urged it towards the flames which Scridol had produced from the fire's faint embers.

"What are you going to do with Gatil?" asked Scridol, and decided to disbelieve Vathok's lucid and picturesque description of that youth's fate. There was nothing to be got from conversation at this moment, apparently. The best thing, the only thing, to do was to trudge about till he found his horse and try to catch up with the rest of them.

"And," thought Scridol, listening to Vathok tearing his way into the darkness, "I don't much care. Riding shepherd to that girl has added to my age. Why should I mother her? I get no thanks. I get little merit for it begins to be apparent to me that beautiful girls have a special providence of their own. They're so interesting to humanity in general that things are certain to happen to them. Perhaps it's an armor of their kind but I've noticed before that they don't really come to much harm. Not if they've really got guts, and this blasted Princess has.

"Now *where's* that horse?"

"At least I've got something out of it all," he told himself humorously. "I now own a horse. If I can find it.

"And, by all the Scales and Entrails of the World's First Serpent, I've a new taste in art to stun the world with."

Vathok lolloped along.

The horses of the others would tire. They were on the wrong road but it wasn't so very wrong. He would catch them up, for horses must be rested. Dris and

Wheld could do as they liked with the boy. What could he, Vathok, do? Even if he galloped all the way, and no horse carrying him could do that, he'd never arrive in time. All would be done, whatever it was that Heaven had mapped out.

Dris and Wheld raced on.

Neither attempted speech. None was necessary. Both knew the best termination to this escapade.

The only thing that occupied the mind of Dris, and, not surprisingly, the only thing that occupied the mind of Wheld, was whether he should tell the other the thought which had reached him.

There was wealth for whoever owned the Princess. Why should Vathok share in it?

Far to the east, on a tiring horse, for its mouth was torn cruelly by the madman who ruled it, Anut from a maze of pain strove to keep fresh one bright illuminating light of near reason.

The man would be killed.

And he would be easy to kill.

He, Anut, avenging the abduction of the lovely girl in boy's clothes, would only have to snatch him off his horse and place a foot on him and grind him into the soil. For now they were far and far away from Dnalgne. They would be small. Very small. He would have to put the girl tenderly into the pocketed sleeve of his shirt and carry her carefully back to Dnalgne so she would again grow to his own handy size and be able to grace his dwelling in Dnalgne.

And the man would die, squirming.

And Gatil squirmed sideways in his saddle and caught the rein of Bulinga and pulled both horses to a walk.

"Now," Gatil told himself. "Not a moment longer do I wait. Just a little wooing, but she is mine, now!"

It was not now so dark to them, their eyes could see—could distinguish detail.

Bulinga could see, so close to her was he, could see enough of his face to discern the animal lust she mistook for love.

She, being royal, must give the cue to begin such a conversation as they must now have. Now she must warn him of the future she had arranged, which was their destiny.

"This," she said softly, "is the journey to Nipsirc, and beyond, of which I have always dreamt. With my own friend. I should be so forlorn if this journey had gone on, and developed otherwise than to this. I should be so forlorn if I had to lose you."

Gatil's full lips were very red. Lust, ignorance— lust and stupidity and ignorance were unhooded, unleashed.

It was a dreadful admixture.

"Because you are the most polite, elegant and intelligent man I have ever met, I honor you," Bulinga explained without embarrassment. "But the warmth of my feelings for you stems from something inexplicable to me," she paused; "and from your valor!"

"Now, little girl," he said, "you mustn't think of losing me. What about now, then?" he smiled, and no longer able to resist showing her how very much more attractive he could be than she had ever considered, he stretched across and took her in his arms.

"Oh! No, no!" she whispered. The color had flushed her cheeks. There was something wrong, though the element had not yet isolated itself for her. She yet felt breathlessly glad. "Oh, but no. You must not! I shall feel sorry, after, until I am *quite certain* that I love you!"

"But, I am only going to kiss you," Gatil said peevishly.

"Yes, but that is what I mean!" she insisted, drawing herself away.

Gatil straightened in the saddle. Her horse had drawn her away from him. He had almost fallen. He reined his horse over till he was close again and grasped her arm tightly, twisted his foot under her stirrup leather so they could not easily be parted by action of hers.

"But, little girl, I think you must let me have that kiss," he insisted smoothly.

Bulinga's eyes opened wide.

Then she smiled.

Men were like that, of course. It was a sign of his love for her. But he must wait, yet. She was no serving sluggard. She was Princess of Grood!

She leaned back, her palm on his chest, her arm straightening.

And the thud of hooves on hard earth reached them.

Gatil wrenched himself away so that he nearly unseated her. He swung his horse about. Sat, a moment, listening.

"It is them," he whispered.

He looked about wildly, for somewhere to hide.

He turned back to Bulinga and she could not in her mind disguise her recognition of his fear.

Bulinga's further thoughts were obliterated by the squeal of Gatil's horse as he kicked it viciously with both heels. He was away.

"Come on," he yelled. "Come on. Come."

Bulinga's decision had deserted her. It was utterly impossible for her to move.

She still sat, thus, but it was no more than a moment later when Anut hurled his horse and himself past her.

Only then, when he too was from her sight, did she act. And, sobbing now, she loosed her hold of the reins and pushed her mount to a frantic gallop.

Gatil was struck by the suggestion that by sweeping a wide arc he would escape.

Why the idea appealed to him he did not attempt to discern. It was a scheme for escape.

He pulled on his left rein. But he pulled too hard and too suddenly. His horse stumbled, lost equilibrium and though it tried gallantly to counter the mischief of its rider, it fell, heavily.

Gatil rolled clear, raised himself on one knee, rose unsteadily to his feet and as the avenging centaur blurred towards him out of the night he turned and ran, fell, struggled sideways, rose again and ran, a horrible keening wailing sounding from his slack fear-twisted mouth.

The hooves, the terrible hooves, thundered at him and the thing that was all Anut had become projected itself, a subhuman sling shot, at the fleeing craven victim.

Now they were rolling, thrashing about, a maelstrom of fear and fury.

Fury won.

Gatil lay, his spine wrenched haphazardly over the small disrupted cairn of a long-forgotten lonely grave.

Anut above him crouched lower and awfully lower.

Gatil, moaning, could not let himself face it.

His outflung useless arms were pinned to the ground, a shoeless foot on each upper arm. His forearms could swivel from the elbow, and he flung them in, but only for the hands to cover his face, to hide from his face the awful oncoming of death.

Anut dropped, his knees almost caving in the chest of the figure beneath them.

He grabbed at the wrists of Gatil, wrenched the hands away from the loathed face and breathing close and closer, mounted:

"I don't like you."

The simple understatement was more awful than curses.

"I don't like you," he repeated, though now the words were an animal mumble. His pain-tortured eyes peered at the backs of Gatil's hands. The fine black hairs criss-crossed over them, sweeping from knuckles to wrists. A frenzy of disgust shook the madman. He loathed fine black hairs. In one moment he dropped, thrust aside the loathed wrists and bashed his clenched hands into the face of Gatil.

The figure of Wheld above Anut plunged the knife deep between Anut's shoulders.

14

Bulinga rode into Nipsirc a prisoner, bound for the slave market. Her arms were pinioned to her sides and her picturesque captors, Dris and Wheld, were unduly surprised to be suddenly halted by as picturesque a group, the Religious Police. They should not have forgotten their entrance into Dnalgne.

Nipsirc was so different from what Bulinga expected.

She had hardly realized they were there until the Police accosted them.

Riding on a road fringed by market gardens and occasional houses and odd hovels, Bulinga had felt free to notice only her own thoughts.

She was too angry to bother much about the fate the two ruffians had in mind for her. Gatil had warned her. And when the time came she herself would have a word or two to say. But what had become of Gatil? Would she see him again? Where was Vathok, and Scridol?

That large square building was no more than a box. Why it should have a stream of smoke from its center was a mystery and even if she thought her captors could answer she would not demean herself by asking.

But this place was undoubtedly a factory for making and firing pottery coffins. They stood in racks, or lay about, plain and ornamented, red, yellow and white, some even painted in geometric designs. In Grood they used wood, but the shape and ornamentation was exactly similar.

That Gatil had fled was so bewildering. It was difficult to connect his flight with the valor he had shown previously when he had saved her life at considerable risk to himself. And there was, too, his treatment of her. It had hurt to find he was so plebeian. That was wholly unexpected.

There must be a reason. Perhaps she was just too inexperienced to know of it. Possibly he had attempted to draw pursuit from her.

It must have been Anut for Wheld said Dris had killed him.

Poor Anut.

Perhaps it was better that his body should be lying out on the plain which freed his soul for life with the Moon that was Gone.

Gatil would find his way back. And find her, and they would start again. The magistrate to whom they were now being taken by these ruffianly Police, he would see some justice done.

Now they were moving along crowded streets, and the houses leaned against each other, supporting each other. The gardens and the trees and bushes on their roofs were strangely beautiful and cast a welcome shade. Gatil must know all this so intimately. This magistrate or ward chief or whoever he was would be certain to acknowledge her rank.

She could rest assured of that.

If only Gatil were with her, showing her all this.

The buildings, all homes surely, now, were much taller than anything in Grood, except her father's Great Hall. But these had balconies high up. Several balconies one above the other, and one could sometimes glimpse hangings by the windows.

The people!

This street was so narrow that if the trees lining it had been any nearer each other their branches would have met and no one would have been able to see upwards.

The party had now become one small part of a jostling multicolored scene, more extravagant than her limited experience had ever allowed her to imag-

ine. The street and the many streets leading from it
were filled by noisy crowds. Peoples of many races,
with skins of white, black, yellow, brown, and an almost red, stood, walked, laughed, lay in litters, talked,
joked, rode horses, bought goods from itinerant ped-
dlers, stared at or ignored each other, ate fruit, audibly
admired the ladies who passed, wagered, shared each
other's flasks of wines, and discussed the news of the
moment.

There were beggars, nobles, tradespeople, the indeterminate multitude. There were men of the city and
of every country and town within a distance of mil-
liards of miles, and from beyond that distance too.

Some carried beautifully ugly lap-dogs. She saw
three monkeys of widely differing types, and there was
more than one leashed and muzzled cat, almost as
large though obviously not so fierce as the great hunting cats of Grood.

The clothes, the ornaments, the dress of the women,
even the rags of the fruit sellers and the beggars, were
so diverse in type, so multivarious, that even to her
own mind Bulinga forbore to describe them.

She, Dris and Wheld, and the gaudy uniform of
her escort, were ignored. It was even difficult at times
for the Police to force a way through the crowd.

"If this is Nipsirc," decided Bulinga, "Dejanira, the
city capital of Rutas-Mu, must be beyond the appreciation of human senses."

And abruptly they were in quieter almost empty
streets. Children sat in the central gutter and threw
stones down the grated drains. Sluttish women strag-
gled across the stones, old men shuffled their crouched
way between the groups of playing children. Dogs,
lean and yellow, slunk into cave-like openings in the
plaster walls of what had decades before been a fashionable quarter of the city. Cats sunned themselves
wherever there was lack of shadow, or stalked majes-
tically about, eyeing the dogs with aversion.

Bulinga watched a dog worry at one of the cats,
barking and circling the cat, foolishly, impeding its

progress. The cat stood, twisted, and crushed a huge paw down on the dog's back. There was a slightly nauseating snap, the dog lay squealing, and the cat walked on, dangerous but restrained and suffering one of the gutter brats to call it names and to kick it in the ribs.

Grood had had no such slums. That a city could house two such differing scenes and so close to one another was not within her understanding. Bulinga supposed the people must wish to live like that. What else could make it so?

The party went on till again, almost imperceptibly, the streets were cleaner, wider, lined with trees, the people better dressed.

The Police stopped before a building. Bulinga, Dris and Wheld were ordered to dismount. Clutching her now bedraggled and dusty bundle, Bulinga was ushered inside.

"Is this the magistrate's house?" she asked one of the Police.

"It is an inn which he has made to be his office," was the reply.

She followed the others along a wood-paneled passage and into a large airy room; the hinged shutters of the wall to the house's central garden had all been folded back. The room was bright with light reflected from the wall beyond the little lawn. A vast table was covered by stacks of thin metal and porcelain book-sheets and records. There were a long wooden bench, a few solid stools, and a thin-faced forbidding figure seated to one side. Bulinga, startled, was sure she must be wrong, but the recognition in his eyes was unmistakable. It was Carpen.

The Leader of the Police bustled forward and saluted with the peculiar hand motion Bulinga had seen Scridol use in Dnalgne.

As the man began to speak Carpen waved him to silence.

"I am conversant with all facts relating to these people," he intoned. He looked Dris and Wheld up and down, his distaste and disapproval of them manifest.

"Take these two men away for work in the mines. The other will stay with me. I have been awaiting her arrival."

The Police saluted and left.

Neither Dris nor Wheld uttered a word. Bulinga watched them go, feeling that she was being deserted. At the door Wheld turned, winked broadly, and was gone.

Carpen made her uncomfortable.

"You are destined for high things," he said.

That, from him, surprised her.

"I may find them in Dejanira or in Atlan," she said.

"You will find them in Nipsirc," he said authoritatively.

He lifted a small handbell and rang it.

In a moment a woman came.

"Attend this lady," Carpen told her, and to Bulinga:

"It is my wish that you change your dress to garments more becoming to a female. Under no circumstances will I permit this ridiculous imposture to continue. When you are clad in a decent and womanly manner, whether in clothes you have with you or in others obtained for you by the servant, I wish you to rejoin me here."

He bent to the tablets on the table.

Bulinga was not to be dismissed like that by a mere jewel trader turned by some fate to the controller of a city ward.

She regarded him.

"I suppose I may assume that there will be available a bath and all the comforts a princess is accustomed to," she said.

But Carpen did not look up.

"Yes," he said, flatly.

Bulinga waited, tried to think of some way of annihilating him. She was unsuccessful.

The stairs were unlike those in Grood, the treads being thin and unsupported except at the ends. Accustomed to steps which were baulks of heavy timber, Bulinga felt afraid to trust them with her weight, but the woman, a heavy woman, went before her and it seemed to be safe enough.

There was a plainness which comforted Bulinga about the appointments of the rooms. Though in reality this was no more than an inn meant for traders with incomes of a few milia it approximated to the comforts Bulinga had known in Grood. She was able to bathe and dress in comfort. She made no attempt to discuss matters with her attendant. That would not be the action of a princess descended from the Royal Line of Atlan.

But it was unadulterated bliss to be rid of the clothes of a page of Grood's palace, to strip off those long coarse stockings, to watch them, the now loathed trunks, and the rest of the dust-impregnated things dropped with disgust into a pottery vase of hideous color and ugly shape and to know they were all, clothes and urn, to be dropped into a fire and consumed by flames.

Her own clothing was ready to use. Deft skillful fingers had made it so while she attended to her bath and the grooming of her hair, hands and feet. Unguents there were in abundance. Salves to take away the fire of the sun's rays, creams to help roughened skin recover its softness, and there were blades and flat-pointed pins with which to attend the needs of fingers and feet. Bulinga was pleased to notice that her skin had not suffered for her several days spent in the open, except for one or two tiny, really quite piquant, freckles. It was still fair, almost white.

It was a rejuvenated Bulinga who descended to rejoin Carpen, but also a Bulinga who was hungry, deeply uneasy and puzzled as to many things.

She knew Carpen's plans for her.

Somehow she must escape from him, somehow find help to live her own life.

Bulinga was at the foot of the stairs before she remembered to be surprised that Carpen was here. That he knew a quicker path between Grood and Nipsirc was already obvious.

She was not very taken aback when she found Vathok and Gatil in the room with Carpen. They, too, must have been arrested on their arrival in Nipsirc.

"Atlan's Lights," Vathok's voice boomed at her. "You don't seem the same person."

His critical, measuring gaze made her redden.

"I prefer you as a page," he decided. "What did you do with those rascals of mine?"

"You may meet them," Carpen said drily. "They have gone to the mines."

Vathok's large hands spread out over the desk's edge and he leaned to his half-brother.

Bulinga tried to keep what he did out of her consciousness. She was more interested in Gatil's reactions to her reappearance. But Vathok's voice won.

"Serpent's Blood," he swore, "am I being threatened?"

Gatil's attempt at insouciance was a pale thing.

"My uncle had just told us you were here."

Bulinga nodded.

"You erred when you trusted yourself to him," Vathok said to her. "If I hadn't come across him and caught his horse for him he'd be wandering still. By the Moon that is Gone your madman would have stood you in better stead. What happened to him?"

Bulinga swallowed.

"Wheld slew him," said Gatil. "The madman was just going to kill me."

"Wheld told me it was Dris!" cried Bulinga.

Her eyes widened. It seemed many people lied whenever it suited them. Not that it mattered who had killed the poor madman. But Bulinga felt, at this late mention, more regret for his death than she had before.

"The madman was just going to kill me," Gatil said.

"And Scridol! Is he, too, in Nipsirc?" Bulinga asked.

"Oh, he'll reach here, tomorrow or sometime. He may be walking," chuckled Vathok.

Carpen, still sitting back, eyed him sourly.

The silence stayed.

Carpen rose.

"There has been a meal prepared. You may both accompany the girl and myself and partake of it. I will know better, later, what I should do. You will always be an embarrassment to me, Vathok. You should not have come here."

He left the room and Bulinga followed him.

It had been a stilted, unsatisfactory reunion.

But Bulinga believed she might be able to resolve some matters of importance during the time of the meal.

Gatil was behind her.

"You like Nipsirc?" he asked.

"I find what I have seen most interesting," she agreed.

"Tomorrow I may be able to show you the fashionable quarters, and the market-place. They," he enthused, "are the best part of the city. They'll open your eyes, I can tell you."

A sniff from Carpen's direction quieted Gatil. He subsided, exuding shamefacedness.

Vathok's chuckle did nothing to help him.

Carpen felt it was necessary to point out to all that though he did not approve of eating for pleasure, he yet recognized the necessity to recruit strength and vitality. Still, they should remember it was unwise to fill a stomach with dead flesh and vegetation more than was necessary to quell hunger.

"Well, I am always very hungry," said Bulinga.

"I do not doubt it," said Carpen, ironically, and glanced at her with contempt.

It was hours and hours since Bulinga had eaten, days since she had sat at table in a civilized manner. She bent to her meal and missed the way his contemptuous glance left her face, and dwelt on her hair, and lost the contempt.

Although uninterested she had come to the conclusion that his must be a religion different from her own.

She had thought that the same religion held from Dejanira to Grood, and beyond, but it was quite possible she had been misinformed.

But it would seem he would have to let her go. His idea for her was voided by that difference in religion.

She had, too, other things to think of.

So had Vathok.

He ate heartily and quickly, Bulinga noted, and she was not surprised when he laid down his spoon halfway through a dish of cooked fruits and, with a muttered word which was his contribution to the idea of dining-room courtesy, strode purposefully from the room.

Carpen paid no attention and Bulinga blushed slightly and kept her eyes on her plate.

The minutes passed.

Bulinga heard Gatil clear his throat, and looking up her eyes met Carpen's.

"Why do you stare at me?" she asked bluntly.

"I am staring because I am interested in your face."

There was still a half-glass of wine before Carpen and he sipped it slowly, not draining it until she had fully finished her own meal.

"I have much to say now," Carpen told her.

"And I to you," said Bulinga. "You know who I am, although, throughout our acquaintance, you have been strangely loth to accede to me my proper title, even from courtesy. I am grateful to you for the opportunity of changing into my own clothes again, and for the meal. But as I would not wish to be insulting I shall not offer payment. Nevertheless I must now leave you."

Carpen shook his head.

"No. I could never permit a second departure from here."

Bulinga did not understand, but Gatil did. He stood.

"Is—is Vathok gone?"

Carpen squashed him with a look. Gatil sank back to his seat; and half rose, staying like that under Carpen's superciliously contemptuous stare.

"Must all my guests wish to leave? Sit still, fool boy. Or go, if you so desire. If you stay with me I may succeed in converting you to becoming of some value to the community, perhaps even in the service of the High One. It is for you to choose."

Bulinga marveled at the cold inhumanity in his voice.

It seemed he cared little whether Gatil went or stayed. She would, she thought, prefer that Gatil went. He stayed.

Carpen said:

"Your hair is white."

"That I know. I know also I am not to be constrained here against my will."

"My daughter," he said, ignoring her tone, "what is your religion?"

"Mother," she pleaded silently. Somehow she must outwit this cold religious puritan.

"I find it hard to tell you that," she said with a semblance of frankness. "I have never heard of any other than my own. I believe in a God Whose Name is too terrible to be told, Who created this cosmos and all in it from an egg He laid. I believe there are Eight Roads to Heaven and each must be taken in its proper order. I believe in the Twelve Temptations, and in the Twelve Virtues which I always strive to possess. I believe that the Nameless God has Children who have been entrusted by Him with the governance of fields and crops, love and hate, the elements, and life and death. To these I pray. Is there another religion in this world?"

"You are grossly misled.

"That is the old, the false religion of Dejanira and Gabebal and Edrigir and your own little town-kingdom of Grood. The High One of Nipsirc is causing to be spread across the continents the true Religion which I have held to since I first heard it. It is spreading from town to town, from city to city-state, and soon it will only be Dejanira, our enemy across the seas, which withholds the truth from itself. Ours is a religion which preaches of all that is good and noble."

"Yes?"

"I am informing you," Carpen said. He rebuked her, "Your tone is without reverence."

"I cannot have reverence," she replied, "until I know more, and find it to be something to reverence."

"I am telling you," he insisted, once again. "We believe that God shows Himself to us in the form of the Sun, and that not to worship the Sun is to blaspheme."

"The Sun!" gasped Bulinga, scandalized.

"It is from the Sun that all comes to us. All life-giving qualities are from Him in that way."

Bulinga sprang up, offending him with her sudden and precipitate movement. "Do you actually mean," she cried in horror, "that you believe the *Sun* is He Who is the Nameless One?"

"Yes."

"The Sun, great as it is, is only part of His work. Because it is great and away from us, it is a symbol of the Great One Who is Nameless. It was He Who *made* the Sun."

"You speak like a fool," he said harshly. "He *is* the Sun. You talk of children of the God, children who govern life and death, and so on. What warrant have you? Where are they? Nonsense. You are no more than pagan. There is nothing unseen. There is no supernatural world. God Himself is visible! Oh, I do not state that the Great Being is a disc. That is what we see of Him. He is the Sun shining in the sky to light and warm our way. All Heavenly aid comes down from the Sun Who arranges circumstances, weather, seasons to our advantage. There is no Heaven. Heaven we will make on earth, when all hear the teaching of our Religion. Those who say that God is invisible are attempting to open up a whole new world, imaginary, baseless, invisible and so, of course, non-existent. They believe in that which obviously is not. They are denying a real

God. Cannot you see that? By denying a real God they blaspheme!"

Bulinga brought her fist down on the table.

"Your Religion is crude and raw!" she cried. She rubbed her hand for it hurt. "Do you deny the existence of your emotions? of your thoughts? of scents? Show me that which is life itself, which makes the difference between a body alive and dead! You cannot! These are all invisible."

"Peace and silence, child," rapped Carpen discordantly. "You do not know what you say. You will have time enough to learn answers to all your arguments. But you need not endeavor to quell me with sacrilege, as is the delight of all your kind. I feel no surprise that you wish to go to Dejanira."

"Do you not? Then I will not waste time with you. You have been trying to convert me, I believe. Your logic was not sound enough to convince one who is royal. We must part now."

"You will stay. Listen to me awhile. You have white hair."

"Is it an offense to your code?"

"It denotes an inner purity."

Bulinga began to laugh.

"And you detain me for *that* reason! *You* think *I* have inner purity!"

"Those who are fair and are virgins are demanded for use in the Temple."

"Where I may be, in time, converted!" she sneered.

"I have told you. By your fairness I know what is your destined place. From the obscurity of a small unimportant town-kingdom rarely reached by any but traders, and never left by those who reside there, you have been brought here, on your travels escaping considerable peril. One has only to add to that a description of your person and no one of the true Religion would doubt that holy intervention has brought you here. Your fairness is supreme. In you has been manifested the purest type. Never before have I seen such fairness, nor had I expected to. I should be helping you to evil if I permitted you to escape me. I know where one with your coloring should go. I cannot permit myself to be diverted from the full accomplishment of a plan which will give to the Temple that which belongs to it."

"You will have to use force," Bulinga said, and knew his answer long before he gave it.

"I will use force if necessary," Carpen said.

Bulinga ran to the doorway through which Vathok had gone. For one wild moment of hope and triumph she thought she was away. She gained the passageway. Then Carpen's arm was around her waist and his other hand on the back of her neck forced her body over; forced her to fold. The pressure was cruel. She struggled and fought. Carpen held her easily, impassively.

"Let me go!" she stormed. "How dare you lay your hands on my body! Take your hands from me. I will not be used in the Temple!"

He pulled her back, her heels sliding over the plank floor. She had nothing to grip. She tore at his hands unavailingly. He threw her roughly to a chair.

"You will come to no harm. All your life you will remain virginal. That quality is also necessary. You will serve the true Religion by appearing in Temple dress, faithfully carrying out the duties allotted you, at the Times of Reverence. You will be taught, and you will learn."

"But it is freedom I value!" she raged. "It will be worse than what I escaped from, in Grood, if I am to be incarcerated all my life doing paltry tasks! Let me go! Tell your people of the Temple they can have you for their petty maidservant. I suppose you are pure enough!"

Carpen stood silent in front of her.

She looked past him at Gatil. She had forgotten he was there.

Gatil looked down at the table.

Surely Gatil could not remain inactive. She could not believe there was no help forthcoming from him.

Was he—was he deserting her? Was it a sham—all his love for her? Surely he intended to do something to help her!

Gatil could not bear to meet her eyes. He sat sullenly, digging the point of a knife into a joint of the table, watching the small splinters of wood he displaced, almost more interested in the hole he was making.

If only he could do something. He was sorry for her, too. She was so very beautiful. Must she be beyond his reach?

He hated Carpen.

Vathok was no more than a brute beast. But Carpen was a puritanical contemptuous swine.

Why shouldn't he, Gatil, rescue this princess who thought so much of him? How could he get Carpen out of the way?

Carpen had not forgotten his nephew.

He stood back a few paces from Bulinga where he could see both Bulinga and Gatil.

He spoke without passion, very nearly without inflexion.

"I do not know, Gatil, whether what I have done to further your interests is sufficient to discharge my responsibility. Never would I countenance in myself forgetfulness of my responsibilities, and I promised your mother, my sister, that I would look after you. But your willfulness and insobriety of character are always a hindrance to my plans for you.

"I have no doubt you planned to enroll this girl as your next mistress. Fortunately your plans miscarried. It would have been unforgivable had you cheated the Temple. Your action was irresponsibly irreligious."

Gatil flushed, awkwardly digging the knife into the table and twisting it.

"I . . ." he began, and stopped.

"I am expecting a visit from Stapo. I would prefer you were not here. There is a room upstairs. Go to it."

Bulinga watched in fascinated disbelief as Gatil rose and without a word, without looking at her, left the room, brushing roughly past a small boy who stared after him in annoyance. Then there progressed importantly into the room a man whose fat shook as he walked, he being as blackly flabby as a slug.

15

"So you have her? Good!" said Stapo.

He looked at Bulinga.

"What a prize, eh! Her hair is white! Where did you pick up such a prize as that?"

"I became acquainted with her in the course of my recent journey," said Carpen briefly.

"Good. Very good!" said Stapo. "Now, my dear, shall we be off to the Temple now?"

Bulinga glared at him from under her brows, her under lip out, and did not answer.

"Well, well, not all of them are willing," said Stapo indulgently. "Not at first, anyway. Come along, my dear."

"Can I have my money now?" shrilled the child.

Carpen regarded him sternly.

"I requested you to do me a service," Carpen said. "I did not envisage the necessity to make you a payment."

The child stared, amazed.

"But I always get some money!" he said.

"Would you only help a fellow creature in return for payment?" Carpen scorned him bitterly.

"But, estimable sir . . ." began the urchin, pugnaciously.

"Well, well, my boy, perhaps it is to me you should look for payment for your service," said the Temple official. "You have done us a great service, you know, in helping this gentleman here to bring this young lady to our notice, and you must be paid in full, must you not?"

"Yes, respected sir," muttered the child.

"And what have I here but a quite new link of silver," said Stapo, taking it out of his pocket. "Well, how does that suit you, my friend?"

"Thank you, respected sir," mumbled the boy, and, ignoring Carpen, he bowed his head to Stapo before leaving.

"And now for this young woman," smiled Stapo. "Perhaps we should secure her wrists."

He took a short leather strap from the pouch which hung at his gem-encrusted belt and fastened Bulinga's arms uncomfortably together, behind her.

"Good, good," he said, stepping back to admire his work. "And now we shall have to take her down to my litter. You, Estimable Carpen, will have a fit reward when the High One himself is informed of your help! He is very anxious at the moment to obtain more fair-headed virgins, and this one is, how can I put it, *unusually* fair. I prefer redheads myself, but one can't have them in the Temple, of course. What do you prefer, respected Carpen?"

"My fear is that she may not be virgin," said Carpen. "But I naturally felt it to be my duty to afford the Temple the opportunity of refusing her. I desire to emphasize that it was my duty to act as I have done, and it would be against my principles to accept a reward."

"No doubt, no doubt. Yes. We know of your probity and value to us. But I know, respected Carpen, that some high office is the High One's intention for one of your worth. I will say no more. Well, come along, my dear," he said cheerfully. "It'll do no good not to use your legs, we'll only have to carry you."

Bulinga submitted, to reserve her strength, but she did not intend to resign herself.

The moment she was clear of the outside doorway

she began to scream and scream as loudly as was possible.

Stapo laughed.

He stood, still holding her tied wrists, making no attempt to stop her screams.

There were horses there, a litter, and men wearing the mark of the Religious Police, a double sash of cerise with, on back and front where the sashes crossed, a super-imposed eight-rayed sun in gold.

No one of these, and not one of the passers-by, so much as seemed interested.

"Did you think everyone in the street would rush to your assistance?" chuckled Stapo. "And attack me and my men, when we wear the sign of the Temple! Now, come along. Down the steps."

She preceded him quietly down the steps, realizing the futility of resistance if all Nipsirc was subservient to the power of the New Religion.

Stapo helped her into the litter.

"You'll have to sit, my dear, with your hands behind you like that, and I'll pull the curtains, for you shouldn't really be seen outside the Temple. And you can watch the scene because you'll see through them. I expect all this is new to you."

He entered the litter with her, the eight litter bearers raised the shafts shoulder high, an almost unnerving experience to one unused to litters, and the party moved off.

She felt something uncomfortable beside her and found it was her own bundle of possessions.

Stapo chuckled at her look.

Bulinga considered him through her lashes.

He was a big man, though not so large as Vathok. He was black, black-haired and dark-skinned, surely showing some admixture of race, and the gem-encrusted clothes made him seem fatter than he probably really was. In spite of the joviality of his protuberant mouth his small eyes showed no humor. They were like flat black stones.

On the orange stuff of his gold-edged cloak was a

blue and gold eight-rayed sun, and the design was repeated on a huge gold and enamel circular brooch on one shoulder.

Bulinga judged him to be dishonest.

Had she been his superior she would have distrusted him. Therein might lie her hope! But she had nothing with which to tempt him.

Plans and wild improbabilities chased each other frantically through her mind. When they passed through a crowded thoroughfare she might hope to become lost in the crowd if she swung quickly out. Then, her foot touched the curtains which had descended at Stapo's touch. The fine net was unmistakably metal. That hope was dead.

Bulinga moved her foot from the netting, afraid that her motives might be suspected. She had no wish to do anything but lull Stapo's suspicion at the moment. As she shifted guiltily away her eyes met through the net the eyes of the mounted policeman riding beside them, as one of Stapo's escort. She recoiled a little. Such a brutal, such a leering, face. Bulinga shrank onto the cushions behind her, feeling afraid and trapped, while the sunlight dropped between the metal mesh, hard and brazen in its heat.

There was a commotion at her side of the litter and she turned her head again, and saw with relief that the back of the mounted ruffian was now towards her, and he was shouting at some beggar who had importuned him.

"Away from my stirrup, fellow!" roared the horseman. "My master has not money for such swine! Away or by the Sun's Backside you'll feel the lash-end of my whip!"

Stapo had leaned forward. Bulinga thought he would reprimand the man for blasphemy and for being so brutal, but Stapo, watching intently through the mesh, applauded softly: "Go on, man, beat him! That's right. And now again."

The beggar was slow in leaving, and the ruffian, leaning forward, struck him once across his face and twice across his back which sent him, screaming curses, into the crowd.

Stapo leaned back, well satisfied.

"Impudence!" he said. "They would never dare to touch me in attack, but just because we are officers of the Religion, they think that from us they can beg everything they need!"

"It seems to me that you preach benevolence and practice brutality," mocked Bulinga.

"I am afraid you will have to be given a little lesson in general manners. Pain—er—*never* does any harm, my dear."

Bulinga, her lip quivering, remained silent. Threats made her lonely, afraid, indignantly determined, and angry.

And surely they would not torture their Temple girls for fear of disfiguring or maiming them? Though she would believe that, unknown to the High One, anything might be done by corrupt and dishonest officials such as Stapo who obviously felt no loyalty to the Religion.

Stapo looked at her, silently.

She kept her head erect, her eyes from meeting his.

After a moment he turned away again, and Bulinga hurriedly brushed away a tear, and kept her attention on what could be seen outside the litter.

They moved slowly through the press, even the shouts of their mounted escort doing little to clear them a path. Movement was impeded in every direction by the disorderly traffic of carts and barrows, horses and people, cats and children, beggars singing over and over again a version of their life-histories in which none of them seemed ever to have had a moment's happiness or good luck. Stapo threw one of them a coin, presumably because this man's monotonous intoning pleased him, and the man snatched it up without bothering to thank him or even to stop the continuous autobiographical moaning.

Houses were taller and taller as they neared the center of the city. White stone was used more in their composition.

Each succeeding street was cleaner and nobler than the last one, till at last she saw that they were in a fair avenue, up which the litter's progress was smooth.

Litters in uncountable numbers were passing up and down the broad road-pavings. The gold-flicked curtains shimmered as they swayed; high ladies waved with gentle cordiality at acquaintances in the other litter, which passed them; fat men, dressed in jewels, sat cross-legged on much-jeweled cushions, their curtains drawn well back, but they themselves looking not to the right and not to the left; chattering fops, three to a litter, with bared oiled chests whose muscles shone iridescently because the oil had been rubbed in with gem-dust, and jewels pasted over their nipples; courtesans, austerely dressed and too sought-after to acknowledge the accosts of any but the highest in the land, reclining on cushions and furs which, dripping with gold tassels, fell halfway out of the litter; noble-children, laughing and shouting at each other, being conveyed to their school by their fathers' gold-liveried litter bearers and attendants. There were lesser businessmen and merchants and diplomats, their curtains almost invariably neatly half-drawn, their litter bearers running at a trot, and there were Religious officials who leaned out and gave Stapo a cold salutation of the hand, their eyes glancing curiously through the metal mesh at herself.

Beyond the river, reached by a marble bridge, was a hill, a great mound of palaces. Crystal and marble, chiseled silver and platinum, these were the Great Palaces of the most ancient families of Nipsirc. Their towers and pinnacles and crystal points were treated reverently even by the sunlight.

She hoped they would pass closer to these palaces which made hers in Grood little more than a peasant's hovel—but the litter was carried to the left along the river bank, away from that glorious sight.

Soon they entered a great crowded open paved space which was a pandemonium of noise.

A hubbub of cheering broke out every time a litter passed in which there was a princess or a courtesan popular among the people. Above this rose the yelling of stall-holders; and the startling ululation of the wandering vendors with handcarts of fruit and sweetmeats which had begun to simmer and bubble in the heat.

The litter was forced through the crowds until it was accosted by the owner of one of the many canopied dais upon which slaves stood waiting to be sold.

"Stapo! Hey, Stapo!" said this man through his teeth, very agitated.

Stapo signaled to his litter bearers to stop and looked at the man inquiringly.

The man approached the litter, in a harassed manner, and spread out his hands, appealingly, to Stapo.

"Awful trouble has swallowed me, Estimable Stapo! The visiting Prince Dedn has this morning done me the honor to send a man of his to buy from me a slave girl to share his bed during his visit in Nipsirc. Alas, alas, alas! I had and have no slave girl beautiful enough. He will be very displeased, this great and powerful prince, if the leading slaver of Nipsirc cannot provide him with satisfying bed-pleasure when called on to do so during his goodwill visit here! Yet look at the girls I have at the moment! What can I do, Most Estimable Stapo?"

Bulinga, a laugh momentarily in her thoughts, turned to look at the maligned girls he had indicated among the slaves on his dais.

Indeed they were none of them more than passably pretty; not one of them seemed really fit for a visiting prince. One had very pretty hair; but the same girl had pimples and freckles all over her back and neck. This was not very noticeable, and as her figure was neat she would be worth some money to a struggling businessman; but she was not suitable to be given to a great prince. The others also were passable, but they were lumpy like the women of Grood, and all of them had skins a trifle too brown.

"But, my man, this is a dreadful thing!" he said. "What under the Sun can we do?"

"I don't know, respected sir. I thought you might know," said the slaver worriedly.

"I don't know what can be done!" cried Stapo, striking his forehead in an effort to set his mind cogitating more successfully.

Bulinga laughed.

"I don't suppose you know, Estimable Stapo, but you are just like a fat hen or a proud housewife who has been caught unprepared for a very important guest!"

Stapo turned to look at her.

"Dergors!" he squeaked to the slave-holder. "Give him this slave girl who is probably not virgin now anyway, it doesn't make the slightest difference, they never are! Several nights with His Dignity won't hurt, and when *his* visit is over we can give her to the Temple no more than a couple of weeks late, with no harm done and money in both our purses! Yes, that is the unparagoned solution!"

The brutal policeman who had struck the beggar slid a glance from under his brows at his master.

Bulinga didn't like his smile.

"What if the respected man Carpen tells the High One that she is to be expected?" asked another of the mounted escort.

"Then I will tell the High One I found her out to be a whore all the time," exclaimed Stapo, rubbing his forehead again with a fat bejeweled hand. "Dergors, sell this girl to His Dignity!"

"Very good, respected sir!" said the slave-holder glancing at Bulinga, and obviously appreciative of the plan.

"Well, thank the Heavenly Aid of the Sun for that!" gasped Stapo, in perspiring relief, manipulating the curtains and giving Bulinga a push so that she slid down between them into the arms of the slaver below.

"Thank you, Most Estimable Stapo!" said the slaver as the litter moved away from him again, and Stapo, his fat face twinkling with sweat, replied with affability, "I am glad to have helped you!"

The slaver led Bulinga, not ungently, to the canopied shade of the top platform of the dais on whose ledges stood the girls and other slaves, young and old men and some older women, and told her to sit down on the small heap of cushions by his own place.

Bulinga saw that at the moment escape was impossible.

The slaver stood right before her and would notice her smallest movement. In a moment he came and fastened round one of her wrists a long thin chain whose other end he fastened to his belt. He put her marten cape over her hair, telling her that it might cause a disturbance if its color were noticed in the market.

Bulinga thought, "If I am to be put in the palace of a prince, I may be able to escape more easily than if I were taken to that Temple!"

She could pretend that she was quite willing to be the concubine of a great prince so that they would see no necessity to keep any strong watch on her.

Bulinga sat straight and squared her shoulders. It must now be not very far from noon.

She looked up and saw that the shadow which had startled her had been cast by the slaver, who was bending over her with a cup in his hand.

"You would like something to drink?" he said in an expressionless voice as she looked at him blankly. "It is very hot, and I myself have just had something to drink."

"Thank you very much," she said and took the cup from him, jockeying ruefully, and as unobtrusively as she could, round the rim to find the least grubby place to put her lips. "What is the drink?"

"Wine," the man said briefly, and turned back to his selling after he had told her to set the cup down in the shade when she had finished the drink so that the dogs who were sniffing round the market in many places should not come upon it too much.

Bulinga hurriedly put the cup down in the shade, the wine unfinished, and stealthily, at regular intervals when his back was turned, poured the drink out down the steps of the dais, until it was all gone. She was not going to drink from a cup into which it was possible dogs habitually snuffed and gurgled.

Another burst of cheering attracted her attention and she saw three disdainful-looking young women descending from one of the litters. Dais-holders rushed forward to elbow away their attendants and to assist them to alight: they accepted the ovation without glancing either to left or right, and prepared to move on foot among the stalls of the market.

Bulinga admired their poise; the arches of their chins were high and their gilded eyelids drooped.

This was the sort of person Bulinga had left Grood to find—the poised cultured aristocrat whom she felt to be her rightful associate.

If she could contact these three great ladies surely they would recognize her for what she was, of high and royal blood, and help her.

Bulinga, though reluctant to demean herself by appearing curious, touched the arm of the slaver.

"Could you tell me who those three noblewomen are?" she asked.

"They are higher courtesans of the city," he answered.

"Oh!"

But—they did not walk at all as though they were courtesans. They walked beautifully—all three with their eyes set straight in whichever way they happened to have turned their heads. There was coldness and austerity rather than coquettishness in their gait.

One of them stopped at the dais and fingered the clothes of one of the slaves upon it. Then she looked up at Bulinga.

"How much is that girl?" she asked in a mincing voice.

"I am sorry, she is not for sale," said the slaver. "Now this one here—if you are looking for a housemaid, she would be useful as well as decorative."

The woman reached up and touched Bulinga's hips, thoughtfully. "I would pay much for this one," she said.

"I am afraid she has already been ordered by His Dignity Prince Dedn," said the slaver, not without pride.

The woman raised her brows as though the information were boring to her, stepped down from the dais, and moved onwards through the marketers, who were all clamoring for the distinction of serving her.

Suddenly she and the other two courtesans were knocked aside as the crowd surged forward to acclaim a woman who lay upon the cushions of a litter carried by four huge yellow men. She was blatantly and ostentatiously a great courtesan. Scorning the discreet dress and cold aloofness of her lesser rivals, this woman made it obvious that she was by profession the delight of great men.

Her eyes, green as polished malachite, every now and then glanced languidly over the crowd; her eyelids were heavy with iridescent paint. Each of her lips curved like a shining red petal.

She lay on white fur cushions; against them her skin could be seen to be smooth and faintly orange. The voluptuous pose caused the tight gold dress to gape almost down to the waist. A sea of cerise and rose hair fronded about the face of the woman: one bare arm hung down over the side of the litter. The crystal shapes with which the white curtains of the litter were edged shook and shickered against each other in tinkling disharmony; in their shadow a girl sat fanning her mistress.

This litter passed on through the crowd, and in it yawned the divine courtesan, the courtesan of great lords and higher nobles; her eyes flickering, her mouth scarlet.

Bulinga thought that Nipsirc was too vulgarly crowded

a city. Since very early morning she had seen it crowded. In Nipsirc the religious fanatic and the degenerate noble lived side by side; the High One would find it harder to convert his own city than Grood and Dnalgne and Taryb to his beloved Religion.

Bulinga blinked at the unending flow of bright colors, winced at the din, unceasing, unmerciful, and shuddered at the heavy, nauseating smell of heat and sweat on unwashed bodies. Big shining flies vibrated over the fetid puddles and dogs' messes which lay everywhere on the ground.

Suddenly the market began to thunder enthusiastically. The slaver himself started up and shouted and waved, all the slaves waved and hastily wound themselves into attractive attitudes. Bulinga caught a glimpse of the top of a litter moving slowly past. Was it the High One himself? Or an extremely great lord?

A burnished silver-blue-green sheen of peacock feathers lay over the litter. There were fourteen bearers, and their cloaks were made from drifts of the tail feathers of white peacocks.

In it a man lounged. He glanced over the crowd, as he acknowledged the excited acclamation of the market. His mouth only half-smiled. The faintly satirical eyes met hers. Bulinga felt as if she had been stabbed. The litter passed and the market was delirious with its yelling.

"Was that the High One?" asked Bulinga. "His eyes hurt me."

"No, he was the visiting Prince Dedn," said the slaver.

A fly, shining like a piece of lapis-lazuli, darted round her face. Brushing it away, Bulinga raised her eyes to the face of the slaver.

16

The man's gaze was brief, critical and authoritative.

"Yes, she will do," he said.

He handed money to the slaver, and there seemed to be much of it.

The slaver bowed.

"I am glad to have been of service to His Dignity," he said.

"This is a barbarous city," said the lord Hylun. "In another city at least one concubine would have been offered to us with the palace and attendants."

"The High One is in command in Nipsirc," explained the slaver, briefly.

The lord Hylun nodded commiseratingly and walked down the steps again.

The fan bearer came up the steps to take her bundle and escort her to the litter.

She was helped in after the lord Hylun, and with a bow the fan bearer handed her her bundle. In his hand, against his white peacock uniform and the resplendent interior of the litter, the green bundle looked pathetically small and lumpy.

Bulinga was afraid and her heart was beating oppressively. But, oh, here it was cool, and she leaned back on the cushions, settling herself well in the shade.

Somehow, somehow, somehow, she must escape.

She had no one to turn to for advice or help. No Gatil, he had failed her. She could see easily enough that his environment had been too much for him, the personality of his uncle, Carpen, too strong. Would she ever see him again? And if she did, what would be her feelings?

"What's happened now?" thought Bulinga with a moment of wondering panic. The litter had stopped.

Another litter had drawn up close to them. It was white, tinkling and twinkling with crystal shapes and in it, fanned without stop by her maid, reclined a woman whose pose on her white fur cushions was languorous and voluptuous. Her curtains were drawn back so that all could see her without effort. Her foot servant was speaking to the lord Hylun.

"My lord," he was saying, "the lady Lelahla gives to you her esteem, and offers her services to the visiting Prince, His Dignity Prince Dedn."

The lady Lelahla lay silently in her litter, her eyes dreaming behind their net of lashes.

"I am sure," the lord Hylun said smoothly, "that Prince Dedn will be gratified to meet the lady Lelahla."

The litters moved on, together.

Bulinga's mouth had opened. "Could this mean," she thought, "that the Prince Dedn will be so taken up with this courtesan that he will not look at a slave!"

Her spirits rose. She rummaged in the green bundle and when her fingers found the little silver pangolin she drew it forth and lay there clutching it.

She was quite sure now that escape was hers.

How glad she was that she had escaped from Grood!

These scenes, wonderful as they were, would be as brass to gold when the actuality of Atlan, her mother's country, was reached.

With the little pangolin firmly curled between her fingers and her palm, Bulinga decided she would not lose faith again. The dangers of her journey and the dreads of this morning were all surmounted, surely with her mother's help!

Bulinga looked out through the slits in the curtains.

There could be no doubt.

The Being Whose symbol was the Great Serpent would never permit a daughter of a princess of Atlan to suffer final degradation. She must remember that.

They had left the market behind: the market which had grown to seem a part of her during her long morning on the slaver's dais. And they were so obviously bound for that unbelievable pile of palaces she had seen earlier that morning. The river flowed beside them. The beautiful marble bridge was near. Trees hid the palaces. Now they were almost on the bridge.

But the bridge, the masterpiece of Nipsirc's most famous architects and artists, poem that it was, was the entrance to a conglobation of palaces beautiful not only as an entity but composed of pieces, each of which, no matter which of the thousands it was, was in itself an artist's jewel.

The litters came to rest in a marble, crescent-shaped courtyard.

Men came to assist Lelahla alight. She rested jeweled fingers very lightly on the arm of the lord Hylun, her small feet, thrust again into her gold sandals, touched the ground. Then she waited upon the steps until orders had been given for the disposal of her litter and its contents. There was no such deference shown Bulinga. She was a chattel, the plaything of a prince for those nights when he was visiting a strange city.

At the summit was a long colonnade and here, among the blue shadows, they stopped. More guards stood here, their dress, Bulinga later discovered, the age-old uniform of the Imperial Guard, a remnant of the days of centuries before when Nipsirc had been the center of a flourishing monarchical state.

Bulinga looked below.

A man ran up the steps and joined Lelahla. It was her foot servant. He carried a large silver and enamel box.

"I would go to a woman's room of my own," said Lelahla, her voice artificially husky, "and my man shall accompany me to bring my box."

"Certainly," said the lord Hylun. "I will myself show you the way. Jarrold! See that that young woman is placed in the room adjoining the informal ante-chamber of His Dignity."

"Yes, Estimable Lord," said the man with Bulinga's bundle, and led her away.

Lelahla had been escorted along the colonnade. It was a procession, Lelahla, her maid and servant, the lord Hylun and three guards.

Bulinga was led by one man between the tall wrought-brass pillars and into a hall.

From where Bulinga stood she guessed it to be roughly square, and to measure one hundred and fifty of the paces of a tall man, but it was the decoration which fascinated the eye, and the mind. There were pillars of glass, clear but with leaf designs either ground in or perhaps incorporated in some other fashion she had no knowledge of, and these pillars, surely in no way assisting to support the many-faceted ceiling, curled and curved upwards—and within each pillar soared queerly shaped bubbles, each differing in color from those which preceded and followed, and each carrying its own aura of color complementary to itself. After watching for minutes the pattern of the bubbles became apparent—almost, she said to herself, the musical pattern of their ever rising rhythm.

It was movement near her feet which distracted her attention.

In horror she gazed at a spot two paces away.

The floor too was of glass, faintly rose-tinted glass, again with opaque, chiseled-seeming designs incorporated. And, that not being enough, beneath the floor was a shallow labyrinth, a myriad miniature passages with doors in profusion bewilderingly opening and shutting.

In a passage two paces away from her was a snake, a giant python, the cream, brown and green of its scales writhing ever and ever closer to a rat-like animal which waited with no sign of fear. Then Bulinga realized the little animal was a mongoose.

And as she waited, horrified, for the battle—the door between them closed.

The man, standing patiently beside her, proud of the palace, pleased at its effect on her, chuckled.

"I cannot wait here all day, girl," he said.

Bulinga sidled slowly after him across the floor, trying to see everything at once, the long silver and green ropes which intertwined and all but veiled the glory of the painted panels of the ceiling, the wonderful ice whiteness of the albino peacock tails which swayed so gently in the perfumed breeze blowing from she knew not where, but bringing inexplicably to mind the fabled Isles of the Blest beyond Atlan.

The small room she was left in, empty but for two couches and a gentle fountain sunk deep into the floor, was quiet after so much magnificence. Only later did she realize how rich it was, by more ordinary standards.

Jarrold had left her and joined a group of guards who were playing some game in a corner of the room into which hers looked. The soldiers were pushing money across to each other. The soldiers, Bulinga concluded, were deaf and dumb, for Jarrold made signs to them to which they replied in the same hand and finger language.

Bulinga peeped three times past the side of the curtain but the soldiers continued to play and she concluded that she had the privacy she had longed for. She had clear water which she could drink and in which she could bathe and a couch on which easy sleep was a certain thing.

17

Bulinga awoke.

A drear light of dawn leaked through the hangings. The soldiers were gone!

The servant who entered would have tripped over her had she not seen him coming and slipped hastily aside.

He carried a tray piled with fruit. There was also a large cup of smooth shining black juice.

Bulinga waited till the servant had gone—then she began to eat as quickly as she could. Had she not been so hungry she would, she thought, have escaped at once.

She would not tolerate such an interference with her freedom, such an arbitrary choosing of whose woman she should be. She had a fundamental horror of being taken by anyone she did not love—Bulinga knew that she would fight as hard and as long as she could to prevent that.

She knew enough to look for Carpen—and Gatil would be there.

That Gatil needed her far more than she had ever needed him was so obvious a thing that she should have seen the truth of it before. Except that away from Carpen he showed qualities which melted before the puritanical taskmaster who stood to him as a parent. If she could separate him from Carpen, and she didn't see why that was impossible, she could give him tasks of another sort.

Her own plans, born in the desert, still stood.

Bulinga was certain she could do much with Gatil.

What he needed was someone in place of the mother he had lost. It was to her he would look for that, and he would find it.

With methodical haste, excitement quivering within her, she drank and washed in her fountain room, took up her green bundle and her cape and cautiously stole out. Bulinga crossed to two huge beautifully adzed doors of inlaid woods. One door was half open, and from behind it she heard, faintly, voices.

Of the voices one, unmistakably, was Scridol's.

The other voice was speaking now.

"—Naibara did, and I have always understood that it was your dictum, Estimable Scridol."

Scridol! Scridol, here!

"This," that was Scridol, "is the work of an hour only. But of two days of seeing. As I maintained in our first conversation last night, the soul, the brooding of the spirit of any scene . . ."

"Then you do not accept this New Religion?"

"Illogical unreasoning claptrap," Scridol's voice declaimed.

Bulinga slipped past the door.

For one moment she had considered claiming his help. But through other doors she could see a garden over which dawn trembled.

It was a gracious garden, ordered but with art, and she was pleased to note that the marble wall seemed to have been designed and built to be easily climbed.

That garden wall was tempting.

The other door swung so easily that the strength Bulinga exerted brought it back against the wall with a resonant clank.

"Great Yolk," swore Bulinga, paused in surprise at her own voice saying it, and dashed through and along the colonnaded gallery, down the steps and almost reached the wall before she heard the running footsteps behind her and almost at once two figures passed her, one on each side, and she was brought up short by crossed spears in her path.

"I am sorry, lady," one soldier said. "No one may pass from here."

"But I am a guest here!" Bulinga expostulated, brushing the tousled hair from her face.

"I am afraid you do not understand," the soldier persisted. "The order is that of His Dignity Prince Dedn."

"Oh—did—did he think I would try to run away?"

"I cannot say," the spokesman said impassively.

"But I am the concubine of the Prince!" cried Bulinga. "I—would not wish to run away!"

There was a laugh from behind her and she twisted about. There stood the Prince Dedn.

The soldiers removed their spears from about her and saluted him.

She stood silently.

"So you are the slave girl from the market?" he said. "It is a very early time to walk, is it not, my slave?"

She said nothing.

She saw that his eyes were searching her face and she dropped her own eyelids obstinately.

When next he spoke, his voice sounded amused.

"I think," he said, "you had better learn to accept me. Perhaps you were not even told to whom you were being given. I am Prince Dedn."

"I am Princess Bulinga of Grood!"

He laughed.

"I have heard of the obscure town-kingdom of Grood. Their Princess would never be here as a slave. And the women of Grood are all flabby."

He had satisfied himself that she was slim, of more than medium height, with big beautiful eyes of some dark color, with a pale oval face and with a cloud of very beautiful white hair. Her form was good. Now he looked closer and saw that in her face, with its jaw set firmly, there was fear no less than anger, and that she was far younger than he had at first believed.

"What is your name?" he asked more tenderly.

"My name is Bulinga," Bulinga said.

"I am not sure how you came to be given to me," he

told her, as his eyes considered her, "but I am certainly going to keep you. You are of far rarer worth than I had thought."

"No, I am not," Bulinga insisted.

"Do you find me unattractive?" he asked.

The purple eyes became soft, and the mouth he thought so desirable became soft, too.

"Yes," she said simply. "There is only one man I have ever found attractive. I had thought he might come and rescue me from the market-place, yesterday, but I now see of course he couldn't. But he did save my life, twice."

"And what is his name?".

"Gatil."

"And what sort of man is he?"

"He is young, of course. Not very tall. He is dark, and slim. But he has two uncles. One is a bandit, who tried to kidnap me. The other, most unfortunately, is a puritan, quite highly placed in the Circle of this New Religion. It is with him Gatil lives. He—he browbeats Gatil. Gatil needs a mother."

"I see. You propose to supply that place."

"He does need looking after. Only thus will his good qualities be given free rein."

The Prince earnestly gazed at the wall, some few feet away.

"Tell me, my Bulinga, what is your age?" he asked. "In actual years."

"I am seventeen. I am sorry," Bulinga added, "but I do find you unattractive and I can only belong to the man I love, and who loves me, as his wife."

"Yes," he said, distantly, "yes, I see that."

"He does not believe me," Bulinga thought indignantly. "He doesn't take me seriously. He thinks I am trying to make myself more desirable by being harder to win. Every woman he has ever met has wanted to be his concubine because he is a prince, and rich, and handsome."

"You are not keeping to the traditions of your city," he pointed out. "In Nipsirc, marriage doesn't matter

and to be the mistress, successively, of many rich men,
the more the better, is a great honor for any young
woman of Nipsirc. Why, my own official mistress during my visit here, the lady Lelahla, is the most respected
female in the city, and each time she lives with someone of importance, the esteem in which she is held
rises proportionately. That is Nipsirc!"

"Yes, it may be," Bulinga retorted. "But I am not
Lelahla, nor am I an inhabitant of this city. I am the
Princess of Grood."

They had been strolling about the garden. He
stopped. He said in a lazy voice: "Yes, you said that
before. Are you really?"

She nodded.

"Why are you here?" he asked, and they began to
walk again.

"I ran away," she told him. "I am making my way
towards Dejanira, in Rutas-Mu, because it seems the
best place for my purpose."

"I think I should like to take you back with me,
when my visit is over. What, incidentally, is your purpose?"

"I wish to get to Atlan. My mother was a princess
of Atlan."

"Ye-es, that would explain much."

"Atlan of course is the head of the world," Bulinga
explained.

"And Rutas-Mu, the feet of the world!" suggested the
Prince. "Being south-east of Atlan—which is northwest of here."

"Yes," smiled Bulinga.

"That would make Nipsirc the pelvis of the world,
which accords well with its reputation," observed the
Prince.

They had reached the steps again and mounted them
in silence.

Bulinga wondered what he intended to do with her.
She was afraid to ask.

Abruptly, carelessly, he said: "I shall most certainly
take you back with me, my child. The lady Lelahla will

probably not consider leaving Nipsirc, and I find you most amusing."

Bulinga, in a silent fury, mounted the steps and, beside him, crossed the colonnade and entered by the adzed door.

Inside stood Scridol.

"Princess Bulinga!" he said in extreme astonishment.

He looked so different in a long brocaded gown, with a jeweled ceremonial dagger through his tasseled sash, and boots stiff with enamel to ensure an awkward, stiff-legged gait.

He bowed.

"You know this—lady?" Prince Dedn asked.

"I met the Princess while on my so recent journey," Scridol said, smiling.

"I never expected to see you again!" Bulinga remarked cordially.

"Nor I you, lady." He turned to the Prince. "I am more than ever glad I met Your Dignity last night, and accepted your invitation to discuss art here with you."

Prince Dedn beckoned a guard.

"You will conduct this lady to her room," he commanded.

Bulinga saw there was nothing else she could do. To stay, to say even one word after dismissal, was to lose all dignity before Scridol and the guard.

Still, Scridol was there, he was her friend. This Prince was very obviously now disposed to credit her royalty. She could leave it to Scridol to get her free.

She turned away and went with the guard.

The two men watched her mount the stairs.

The Prince took Scridol's arm and they re-entered the room they had left.

"Tell me," said the Prince, "about this journey of yours."

He walked to the window.

Scridol smiled.

So the Princess had found a home, had she? It would seem his presence had been opportune.

He told of his adventures, choosing his words carefully.

The Prince walked about; listened to most of the story standing before the artist's painting.

"Then that settles it," he said, when Scridol finished. "I take her to Dejanira. I believe I discern in your voice a measure of regard for this princess!"

"Yes, Your Dignity."

"I presume I may understand that she wishes never to see Grood again?"

"It would not be wise, Your Dignity, for her to do so. And she, of all people, would understand that, knowing their barbarous customs."

"If I tell you that there is, now, no necessity for anxiety as to her future, and that if she pleases me I may even install her as my favorite, will that satisfy you?"

"Most definitely."

"Then," said the Prince gravely, "I do tell you so."

"Thank you," bowed Scridol. "I have felt some responsibility in the matter. But what to do, I didn't quite know. She couldn't be left alone."

"It is now my responsibility," the Prince assured him.

18

As the Prince who was her owner had commanded, breakfast was brought to her by a servant.

With the breakfast was a written message which stated that he would do himself the honor of visiting her this coming night, that she would be accompanying him when his visit to Nipsirc was over, and that her friend Scridol was entirely satisfied that in his protection she would find her safest future.

Bulinga, suddenly overcome by the futility of her escape, bowed her head and wept unrestrainedly.

Life had ended now for her, in spite of her bid for freedom, her escape from Grood. Here her deep real self would die.

Pitifully, she saw she had only traveled by a round-about road to exactly the same thing.

How, how, how could she escape? She did not want to go with this Prince to his home, no matter where it was. She wanted to get to Dejanira—to Atlan.

Was that just another of the dreams which were never to be fulfilled?

She buried her head in the pillows.

Voices attracted her attention. They came to her quite clearly through the fabric-covered grille of the door—the great curtains had not been drawn over it.

There were two men coming up the stairs. They were talking, in an apparent amiability which resolved itself into less than that when they came closer and she could distinguish words.

Bulinga went to the door and listened; her ear was caught by a familiar note.

"Of course," said a light, oily voice, which somehow had beneath it a current of nervousness and uncertainty, "I would not willingly invade your privacy except that it—er—is—er—rather important that I should discover whether . . . That is, the High One had commanded me. I have only to see the lady—er—quite quickly. It is not that I wish to disturb you."

"But you do disturb me," said the second voice, lazily and with a good-natured scarce-hidden contempt. "You have followed me almost to my bedroom. Must I tell you yet again that as I bought this slave in the market-place I must be permitted to consider her entirely mine? I do not wish her to appear in the Temple."

"But it is only for one service. Your Dignity . . ."

"What is that to me? I am not a follower of your Religion, which you must well know. I would not interfere with whatever you consider necessary in the observance of your Religion—except where it inconveniences me. And this would."

The voices went past her door.

"Your Dignity," pleaded the oily voice. "Just for one special observance this afternoon."

It *was* Stapo!

The footsteps stopped, some distance away.

"I have not the least intention of permitting you to see my slave," said Prince Dedn, finality in his voice. "I am taking my slave with me when I leave. You should have, if you required her, bought the slave. You cannot buy her from me. Now will you go?"

He leaned over the balustrade.

"Guard. Give this official free passage."

"Yes, Your Dignity," called the guard.

Bulinga heard the click of a shutting door.

She leaned against the wall.

She would be offered no other, better, opportunity.

If it were only for one afternoon . . . ! There was no time to waste. All in one movement Bulinga had her bundle in her hand and was out of the room and running swiftly along the thick carpeting to the stout figure at the top of the stairs.

"Stapo!" she called softly, still running.

He stopped, and turned.

As she caught up with him she saw the guard waiting at the bottom step.

"Oh!" she gasped, pulling back.

Stapo chuckled.

"They will not stop us," he assured her and took her arm.

At another time that would have been fiercely resented by Bulinga. Now her mind was all escape. One faint remaining shred of suspicion advised caution.

"Only for this afternoon," she whispered. "That was what you told Prince Dedn."

Bulinga looked for the guard, but he was no longer there. Of course, they would not obstruct a high official of the Temple.

Stapo got her through the heavy curtains into the great hall, and paused, and blew out his great purple cheeks.

"You see," he went on, when his breathing had returned to normal, "the High One discovered you were destined for the Temple and there will be trouble if—er—you are not instantly taken from the care of this heathen Prince who, because we have been very successful in the number of towns we have taken over just lately, is no longer an object to be—er—considered. Yes. Not to be considered now. That will surprise him. You see, my dear lady," he said, starting off again across the hall with his hand still grasping Bulinga, "this Prince was invited here in the hope that he would be interested, but the High One found him to be oh, much more interested in—er—well, slaves, for instance. He is not now in favor with the High One, on account of his paganism you must understand, and the High One has now lost his fear of offending that powerful country. We may take it—er—under our wing, very soon."

"I think I will escape from this silly old man before we reach the Temple, even," thought Bulinga. "If it's at all possible, I will."

"Oh! Hurry!" she urged Stapo.

He negotiated the steps with unimpaired pomposity, folded himself into the litter with her, the shafts were raised high by the bearers. There was a guard of three at the gate, and all Bulinga's fears surged back. She need not have entertained them. The guard bowed discreetly at sight of the eight-rayed sun and the litter joined the *cortège* which waited on the marble-paved roadway outside the crescent courtyard.

Bulinga noticed with barely repressed excitement that Stapo had not brought down the curtains of metal mesh. And to distract his attention and safeguard the avenue of escape she asked:

"Weren't you going to tell the High One, if he found out that I should be in the Temple, that you had given

me to the Prince because you had discovered I was—
a—a whore?"

"My dear," he replied without rancor, "you may
think me very incompetent if you wish, but I found
it impossible so to—er—deceive the High One." As
he continued Bulinga turned for a last look at the
magnificence of the palaces, then hurriedly gave him
her attention again. "You see, he has a great respect
for me," Stapo was saying. "I am Second in Command of the Temple and direct all the business of
slave and Temple attendant procuration. However—
er—a certain other official, you saw him the other
day in his litter, is trying hard to have me deposed
and to gain the favor of the High One and my place
in the Temple. This—er—pestiferous person surrounds
me with spies. I really cannot trust anyone but my
own litter bearers—who would be faithful to me were
they to die for it. And," he continued with compla-
cency, "they would die were they not faithful. Well,
this man obviously has a spy who heard me lending
you to the slaveholder for him to sell you to Prince
Dedn of—what under the Sun is all that noise ahead?
Oh well, I suppose it will die down soon. And this spy
must have heard me make that—er—decision to try
to convince the High One as you have just said. So
you see, as I also have my spies—what man in my
position can dispense with them?—I discovered that
I should be in disgrace did I not at once take you from
His Heathen Dignity, whose reputation as a lover, I
may add, is somewhat to be—er—envied.

"Ah, a merchants' train passing, eh! That makes the
sixth today. Too many. There is far too much inde-
pendence in that quarter," he said, and to Bulinga:
"Traders' trains are always a nuisance, and smelly.
Especially if they have camels. You!" he shouted. "Put
down the litter. Only tires them out," he told Bulinga,
"standing holding us up. Then they loll and drop one.
One would think bearers easy to get if one didn't know.
They have quite a short life."

Bulinga lay back, nodding agreement to him. He

eyes were closed to slits so he could see no telltale emotion in them. In one moment she would slide out and be off. Their litter was surrounded by others. They'd never catch her.

Stapo turned and looked out over his shoulder.

At once Bulinga's feet were over the side and he caught her shoulder, and held her.

He grinned mockingly. She saw he had expected that bid for escape from him.

"No, my dear. I think not. Back to your place."

Stapo watched her leniently.

"I believe I understand how you feel, but consider *my* feelings were I to return empty-handed to the Temple! I should be greatly blamed."

The litter had been lifted and was being jockeyed to a position nearer the front of the crowd.

"But . . ." began Bulinga, and stopped.

The thought which her optimism had so rigidly repressed flowed, strengthened, to the foreground.

"You will tell me now," she said bitterly, "that you lied when you spoke of this afternoon only."

He nodded.

"I do tell you so."

Bulinga looked out. She was in despair.

The last of the traders' caravans was passing. Seated on a black, shaggy, dusty caparisoned horse was a figure she knew. He was competently directing the many animals and their burdens, pleased at the ending of his journey. He was so close she could see clearly the firm curve of the smile on his lips.

"Emalf! Emalf!" Bulinga shrieked wildly.

Swiftly Stapo's podgy hand was over her mouth. Emalf had heard her shout, for his face seemed to search over the crowd, but Bulinga, firmly held, firmly gagged, had to watch the interest die out of his eyes, to watch him shrug, turn back to something one of his men had said, and to ride on out of her sight.

He would have helped her, Bulinga sobbed within herself. Emalf would have helped her.

19

Stapo leaned out of his litter with a good humored wave of farewell. The little gold stones which were set into his broad nails glittered affably.

The green-gowned servant who was with her, knowing just what should be done and where he was to take her, did not speak, but she knew that when he preceded her she was to follow.

There was no absolute silence, no cold stillness as though they were in a great sacred stone vault, but the atmosphere of the place, though punctuated by familiar small noises such as the buzzing of flies, or a voice in the distance, was not a welcoming one.

Bulinga went with him without rebellion or resistance of any kind. The great size of this place, which she could feel but not see, seemed to be pressing about her all the time they walked, as if to tell her that escape would be impossible. She felt numb.

They walked without swiftness or urgency by much thick, plain white stone which exuded a very slight mustiness.

After some time the passages began to widen out a little, and soon she noticed that the musty smell had appreciably lessened. Soon even the character of the walls had changed; there were little narrow friezes cut along the tops of them, and pink round stones had been set into the bases of the columns.

"Where are you taking me?" asked Bulinga presently.

"To the Room of Abondil," said the man briefly. "And I would know your name, that I may enroll it."

"My name is Bulinga," said Bulinga.

He nodded curtly, committing the information to memory.

They had come, within a few minutes, to a door of stone which was opened for Bulinga to enter the room behind it.

Before she could even cry out he had swung the big stone door behind him and she was alone. She could not see to distinguish the door though she knew where it was. She could not open it.

Somewhere a bell rang.

The floor was uneven, so that she had stumbled a little, and she looked fearfully around, hoping that there were no pits in it. No torch or brazier or lantern of any kind was left in the chamber with her, but a greenish pallor seemed to emanate from the floor. This unhealthy green glimmering everywhere in the black chamber reminded her of the phosphorescence which she had been told flickered from rotting corpses.

Bulinga held her bundle to her as though it could comfort her, and sat down on that discomfortable seat.

"When I have counted to twenty," she thought, "I will get up and begin banging on the door for help."

Shivering slightly, she squared her shoulders and forced herself to sit waiting there.

A door opened in another part of the wall.

"Who is it?" breathed Bulinga.

A golden glow from a lantern had fallen across the floor, and someone came forward as she shrank away against the wall.

"Only me," announced the cheerful voice of a large woman with a paint-raddled face.

"Come along, my child. I was busy when the bell rang. It's not a nice room, is it? It's part of the oldest Temple, ages and ages old, but till we get a new entrance built it's the only connection between the Temple corridors and the attendants' rooms. The woman attendants, that is."

The diaphanous draperies with which her rotund

form was hung were so light that she literally whirled Bulinga across a pleasant corridor—to a room which was gently cool. In the center of the floor a fountain splashed and sparkled.

By the preparations going forward Bulinga judged she was to be given a bath.

She laid down her bundle and submitted to being stripped. One could think of this woman as a maid, quite easily.

The woman was deft and competent in her craft.

Bulinga had never been so rapidly bathed and dried before, although it was rather too much like being groomed like a cat for judging at the Great Birth Celebrations.

"Now, I shall deal with your face, my dearie. You're much too pale. Color is what you need. And quite a lot of too.

"Now let me start on your mouth. A—a vivid scarlet, I think? With your skin and white hair a vivid scarlet it *must* be!"

With expert exuberance she applied the vivid scarlet to Bulinga's lips.

"Oh, please leave me alone!" Bulinga said. "I don't want to be kept in the Temple all my whole life!"

"Now," said the woman with vexation, "do keep still, my dear. Do you think I haven't enough to do without silly girls ruining my handiwork? If it's a life-long celibacy you don't want, don't let such a thing trouble you, my dear. It's quite easy to manage to take lovers after a little, which helps us all, and you'll have lots with your unusual coloring, and body."

Still talking she wrapped round Bulinga's slim figure masses of white-edged blue, which, when the flowing panels were folded into place and smoothed down, seemed to have no thickness whatsoever.

"Just think," she chattered on with kind intent, "you will have to do so little work, keeping the candles going, sprinkling perfumes, and polishing the holy altars which can only be touched by the hand of pure young girls, and all the rest of the time you'll just

loll around in the Attendants' Courtyard—lovely food
—and all these jewels . . ."

She paused in her soothing to unhook from a tray
an elaborate headdress of thin gold hung with blobs
of lapis-lazuli, which she proceeded to arrange in her
charge's hair.

"White hair. This is the gem you need," she said.
"I give to girls with pale yellow hair—ebony. And
diamonds to those with bright golden hair." She sighed.
"I often wish we could be allowed girls with dark hair
in the Temple. They would be so lovely in pearls."

"I didn't think the High One would permit jewels,"
said Bulinga.

"He does as he pleases. He is the High One," was
the woman's shocked answer.

"Serpent's Blood," she swore, the old religious oaths
coming easily to her tongue. "I've forgotten your feet!"
and she bent to attend to them, rubbing fine scented
powder over them and clothing them in soft slippers
of doeskin, the fastenings being high up over the
ankles, protecting Bulinga's flesh from possible rubbing of the jeweled anklets clasped over them.

"Can I . . . can I see myself in a mirror?" asked
Bulinga as the woman fastened round Bulinga's neck
a heavy gold necklet and slid several wide gold bracelets on each arm.

"I haven't one, dearie. We're not allowed mirrors,
but you do look nice," smiled the woman.

"I've one in my bundle," Bulinga said, and stopped
to where she'd tucked it below the stool.

"Ah," said the woman, and scooped up Bulinga's
pangolin.

"Oh!" cried Bulinga, thinking it was being taken.

"How lovely!" said the woman. "It just needs that
below the gold necklet. Here, give it to me. I've a
chain here will fit it perfectly and hold it taut where
it should be." Her fingers twisted over the fastenings.
"There. Let me put it on you."

She stepped back.

"Such a pity you'll have to be in the back row of

girls today, being new. But you'll soon be in the front row, with your beauty. And then you'll have all the men chasing Stapo for nights of you. I can see you'll be a favorite. Of course, you shouldn't really be painted. But the High One doesn't realize that if we didn't the beauty of the girls would be lost in that great dim Temple."

Bulinga tried hard to ignore all this and inspected herself in the little polished bronze mirror.

She turned her face, in critical wonder, from side to side. She seemed to have an infinitely rarer, a more exotic kind of beauty than ever before. Her eyes seemed even larger than they were in actuality, their soft purple brought up and accentuated by the smooth long gilding of the eyelids above them and the black applied to her already naturally black lashes and arching black eyebrows. Her mouth was painted in such a glowing scarlet that it was vibrant to the sight. Jewels shickered and sparked against her skin, shimmering from her ears, casting a light on the young flesh of her throat. And there the pangolin nestled, in the hollow, beautifully apt there, and reminding her of her mother who would, she knew, have loved to see her like this.

A great regret entered her mind that Gatil had not seen her like this.

20

There were no seats.

Some of the people had brought surreptitious folding stools but these were confiscated if seen by the Religious Police. There were Police stationed in galleries at ceiling height around the Temple, though not everyone knew that.

Only reflected light, and very little of it, reached the packed crowd. The few windows were mere slits and cleverly placed in deep niches high in the walls.

So in the dim light conducive to worship the motley thousands swayed and perspired, separated into two groups by a vast pile of masonry, a pillar which rose up and up till at the height of eighty feet from its base it spread into a capital in the shape of a five-petaled flower.

There was a line marked by a double line of circles which interrupted the uninspired geometrical design of the tessellated floor. The crowd was not allowed to surge beyond this.

Opposite the crowd was the simple altar, high up on the wall and reached by two long flights of steps. Immediately below the altar, on a draped platform, stood the throne of the High One, a massive chair of caldon wood. Below that, on the floor of the Temple, facing the crowd, stood three rows of Temple attendants.

Seen from where the Temple attendants stood, the faint white of the thousands of faces rose in a gentle ascent towards the masonry of the back walls of the Temple's interior. The crowd stood on a series of four-foot-wide but very shallow steps.

From the doors at each side of the Temple entered long processions of dignitaries, all in flowing gowns, all bearing prominently on their cloaks the eight-rayed sun in gold. They arranged themselves about and before the female attendants.

There was much shuffling, throat clearing, rattling of small metal links, for today there was to be a collection of voluntary gifts to the Temple.

The woman who had dressed Bulinga entered the small room in which she had left her. She burst into the room like a bud bursting into flower, the light draperies flowing up and out were utterly unmanageable.

"Oh quickly, dearie," she gasped. "You'll be late!
I forgot all about you!" and firmly grasping Bulinga's
wrist she pulled her out.

Bulinga followed helplessly, still holding to herself
her green bundle which she'd been hugging for comfort.

"I must get you there before the High One," the
woman threw over her shoulder.

Bulinga's earrings were smacking against her neck,
her head was sore, she was hungry, the anklets felt
like lead weights, her skirt draperies were flying all
over the place and two panels had become knotted.

She was led, still at the same speed, through a
long wide low-ceilinged hall and as they reached the
three arched doorways at the end the woman noticed
Bulinga's arm-cradled bundle.

"Oh! You silly girl!" she cried. "Put that down."

She tore the bundle from Bulinga's arms, dropped
it on a small stone seat beside the doorway, and started
off again, not, as Bulinga had expected, through the
arches, but towards the right wall, where again they
paused so that the woman could lean heavily on a
stone peg which emerged a bare inch from the level
of the wall.

All the doors were like that, thought Bulinga, watching this one swing out, and all blocks of stone. It was
going to make escape somewhat difficult.

She was hustled through, along a short passage,
through another door, into the Temple, whisked along
behind the last line of girl attendants and plunged into
place at the extreme end.

One of her earrings dropped and she bent to pick it
up.

On the instant all the girls began to chant.

Bulinga found herself endeavoring to copy the lip
movements of the girl beside her. She stopped herself.
Why should she chant? She wasn't here of her own will.
She wouldn't chant. And the words, being broken up
into unusual syllables, were hard to follow and understand anyway.

There were faces everywhere.

Bulinga became conscious of the expanse of shoulder which was bared and tried to right it, but the dress wouldn't stay up where she wanted it to.

From the great door away to her left a figure was entering the Temple.

It was impossible to judge his height. Perhaps it was the size of the Temple which made him seem small. As he came nearer, walking slowly but not in a stately manner, Bulinga saw he was neither gross nor slender, and, but for the abnormal tininess of his mouth, might have been handsome.

His gown was of a nondescript green and fawn. His large, fleshy, ugly square hands were innocent of any ring. He wore no ornament whatsoever, not even an eight-rayed sun.

One could tell from the way he walked that it had never occurred to him to doubt his own divinity of purpose and character, and his dress was as plain as that of the poorest in the congregation—in fact, though he very possibly did not realize it, his clothes were as distinguished for their bad cut as for their lack of ornament.

He was the High One, of course.

To the accompaniment of the intoned voices of the entire congregation, who had joined in the chanting of the girls, awkwardly, his feet moving nearly in time, he crossed to the steps farthest from Bulinga and slowly mounted to his throne. As he reached it the chanting stopped—for an instant only—then burst out again, and continued.

After Bulinga had several times thought, "This chanting is endless, will it never stop?" she reached the conclusion that it was the main item of the worship. By now she had heard enough of the words to know that it was extolling, in great detail and humility, the Sun's many virtues and also the life-history of he who, on attaining the ancient office of High One, had reinstated the worship of the Sun. There was interspersed, too, much about the overthrow of their enemies, the enemies of the Religion, and vilification of those individuals or nations who adhered to the old wicked faith.

Bulinga had begun to feel giddy and apathetic with the weight of the chanting continuously in her ears. She looked about for relief. She looked at the congregation, at the building and at the dignitaries near her.

The monotony of the chanting was reflected in all.

Then she noticed that the little door she had entered by was still open. In her haste the woman had forgotten to close it!

Holding her draperies to her Bulinga calmly left her place, walked briskly towards it, entered the doorway and, finding and pressing the knob, closed the door behind her.

Now she was alone and could think in peace.

That awful chanting was only a faint murmur from behind the wall.

But what was she to do next?

Presumably everyone was in the Temple. With such a puritanical creed no one would be allowed exemption. No one would have the audacity to follow her.

If she could find the right doors she would soon be out of this.

Exhilarated by success Bulinga searched the wall for little stone knobs.

She found one.

She leaned on it and the door opened. She stepped through and found herself in the Temple again.

And she couldn't return for a Temple policeman closed the door behind her and eyed her with interest.

Alarmed, Bulinga looked around quickly. Near her were the long lines of dignitaries and attendants—not far away the thousands of ordinary worshippers.

The policeman's hand went out towards her, Bulinga sensed it coming, stepped forward, and walked towards the crowd. Her determined walk broke into a run as she became aware that her behavior had been noted. Two of the Temple officials nearest to her were walking as determinedly as she in a direction which would cut her off from the safety of the crowd. So she ran. It would

be safer among the crowd, she told herself. She reached
it and pushed a frantic way among them.

The chanting had broken out on a new theme, chanting faces melted before her, bodies moved aside. The
fringes of the crowd knew her for a Temple attendant
and made way for her, but as she penetrated deeper
she came up suddenly against a figure which didn't
move. The stolid unblinking face stayed there in front
of hers, the mouth continued to open and shut and the
eyes stared into hers. Bulinga turned about and became
struck with desperation when she found her passage
had left a winding lane through the crowd and along
this lane proceeded a Temple official and, now, two of
the Religious Police, while the other official stayed
farther back.

She looked about wildly and scrambled off sideways,
upsetting people, caring nothing so long as she could
be lost, desperately trying to hide herself and each
moment growing more certain of her ultimate capture.

Although the chanting continued it was now well in
the background. All about her it had stopped. People
pushed and shoved, some to see and some to let her by.
The second of the two policemen was trapped and engulfed in a moment as the crowd swarmed over him.
He yelled a threat and his head was banged against the
floor.

The leading policeman swung about, knocking over
a woman, and started using his fists to clear a space
about himself.

Within seconds a score of arms flailed back at him
and he too went down.

The Temple official, an old man, found himself alone
and shrieked in alarm, and his shriek became the fore-
runner of many as a squad of Religious Police charged
into the swaying milling jumble of bodies.

Bulinga had reached a wall, and had come against a
group of people who were staunch adherents of the
Religion; unlike the bulk of the population who were
merely acquiescent and subservient.

Bulinga flattened herself back against the wall and

tried to edge sideways past the disapproving cold stares.

One of the puritans raised an arm and shouted that "the girl was here."

Bulinga was grasped and lifted, legs and feet threshing, and placed on the wide ledge running round above the base of the great central pillar. Now she was in full view of all and the Police and officials pushed their brutal way towards her.

She must get quickly round this corner and let herself down among the other crowd! . . .

Bulinga tried that.

Some of the more rough-looking men tried, laughing, to pull her down.

She could see three more groups converging on her.

And still the chanting went on and on.

But there was a more than distrait note in it.

Close to her one or two people, one or two small groups, still tried to continue as though nothing unusual were happening. But, though most of the people were silent, even fearfully silent, some were shouting angrily against the Temple officials, or wrangling among themselves. And these were growing in number moment by moment.

Bulinga was becoming distraught. In one lucid minute she realized that if she were caught now, she would never again have the slightest chance; no opportunity for escape would be left her.

She leaned back against the stones of the pillar, covering her eyes with her hands, trying to prolong the moment of coherent thought, searching for reason, for the power to reason, for knowledge of what she should do.

And where the first Police party had reached there was now a *mêlée*. Men with grudges, and tempers inflamed by being treated in the only manner known to the Police, permitted themselves the pleasure of kicks and jabs. Their action brought harsh, brutal retaliation on whoever was within reach. The same thing was happening in other directions.

Now the chanting tailed off and as Bulinga felt the steps behind her and backed up the first three, horror-stricken at what her action had started, she saw fighting break out farther in the crowd.

There were shrieks now, shouts, the squeals of those hurt and loudly bawled commands. And there were catcalls and curses which should never have been heard within the Temple.

A policeman, a giant of a man, yet with his clothing torn and his face bruised, reached the pillar near her. Bulinga, white-faced, her eyes staring, watched him try to climb up to the ledge and saw him torn from it and his shrieks became a horrible gurgling as people trampled.

Bulinga moaned, turned to escape from what she knew was happening there, and saw that she was on the foot of a flight of narrow steep steps which led upwards.

She climbed upwards.

The steps spiraled up the pillar. She did not look down now. To look down was to see a surging struggling scramble, a battle she thought begotten of her.

At the throne of the High One three men stood beside the seated figure looking down in consternation.

Both doors were open. More Police had been brought in and some sober citizens were endeavoring to escort their women from the scene. The doors became jammed—and more fighting broke out.

Bulinga clung to the many handholds provided, rested and climbed on.

"Oh! mother!" she cried, "Oh! mother, please help me! Oh! mother!"

She decided to stop and stopped and looked down, and saw on the steps below her, circling the pillar as she did, the figures of men.

She tucked the flying draperies into twists, knotted them about her and continued upwards. To her panic was added the fear that her feet would slip. She shuddered, and had to wait, clinging desperately till she mastered that. She was, she felt, ready for death. She could see no other ending.

"I can stay here no longer than this," the High One said to the tallest of the three men with him.

The official nodded. For some long time he had been urging a withdrawal.

At the beginning the High One had been imbued with the earnest hope that a realization of his presence there, even a tardy realization, would spread through the congregation and shame them into peace.

He did not appreciate for how long he had been savoring this scene, just as, he guessed, the men did who watched staged battles between animals. But now that he knew how his thoughts had become contaminated he no longer had the temerity to stay by his throne.

Worn, chastened and worried, he was escorted by several officials through a door behind the throne.

He descended the steps within the wall.

In the Hall of Reception there would be peace.

In the Hall of Reception he was met by a minor official who pointed, timorously, to His Imperial Dignity Prince Dedn, Visitor Extraordinary from the Court of The Supreme Calanza of Dejanira, Capital City and Place of Government of the Good Islands, Rutas-Mu.

Towards the center of the low-ceilinged hall, in small resplendent groups, stood the Seven Fathers of the Circle of the City of Nipsirc and the Officers of His Imperial Dignity Prince Dedn.

But although it was in the circumstances incumbent on the Princes and Merchant Princes of the City, and on His Imperial Dignity's followers, to dress in full ceremonial, Prince Dedn had not apparently considered that the occasion warranted such compliments from himself.

And he wore the two swords of a Thank of Rutas.

When the gossiping ceased, and the stares of his followers caught his attention, the Prince ceased pacing and strode purposefully to where the High One stood.

The Prince made a complete if curt obeisance but he made none of the signs of reverence, he neither spread his hands nor bent his knee. He stood.

The High One had made nothing intelligible of the hurried whispering of his subordinate. He armed the man aside, and straightened his shoulders. There was, the Prince noted, a fire in his eyes which had not been there at his previous audience, though this time there was an anxious tiredness, shown by all his slow, even awkward, movements.

"I offer you the greetings of the day," stated the Prince perfunctorily.

"They are received and returned," replied the High One.

"Yesterday I bought a slave, in your market-place."

The eyes of the High One lit. This morning he had had poured into his unwilling ears a rambling spate of what he had considered to be unworthy gossip. He was not accustomed to flying from statement to conclusion but he knew, now, that the Sun had ensured that he should already be conversant with whatever was about to be said. He looked about for Stapo. That official was not here.

No. Of course not. He would be, naturally, superintending whatever was being done to calm the hysteria of that unfortunate girl. He found time to deplore the hysteria which religious observance so often induced in women. Then he turned his attention to the matter before him.

"The buying or selling of slaves does not in any way concern me. If you consider yourself cheated there is a purely Merchants' Circle which has, I understand, been formed to deal with such complaints."

He knew at once that it was a paltry speech.

Prince Dedn bowed.

"The Merchants' Circle has, I believe, that reputation," he agreed.

The High One bit his lip. That *had* been a paltry speech. This man was actually laughing at him. Not

disgracefully so, but he was. And there was no attempt
to hide the contempt which lay behind the amusement.

He thought to regain the lost ground.

"I presume that the affair is of sufficient importance
to warrant an audience. I cannot see that it is so until I
have been more fully informed."

The High One saw from the eyes of the Prince that
this too was not successful, and the irritability, which
he had been containing within himself for nearly an
hour, all but burst forth into anger.

The Prince helped him by speaking.

"This slave early today was removed from my palace
by force and by stealth. The person who so took from
me my legitimate possession was an official of your
Temple and Religion, a person named Stapo. There
can be no doubt of this. Moreover, I had expressly told
this official that I could not permit this slave to be
taken, even for the time of one day or less.

"I have, naturally, come here for redress. To receive
in person the return of my slave and to see some reprimand, at least, administered to one who has put in
danger the relations between yourself and the Kingdom I have the great honor to represent."

"Well," thought the High One. "So it is, then, true."
For the second time within minutes a conclusion
jumped to his mind. He turned to an official.

"Bring before me, at once, Stapo and the attendant
who—who . . ."

"I understand, High One. The girl in the Temple."

"Who climbed the central pillar."

"Yes, High One. I knew it was she you meant."

"She should be by now in his hands?"

"Yes, High One. There would be officials waiting for
her in the Observance Room at the Pillar Top."

"Have her brought here."

The man bowed and stepped backwards.

Another suspicion struck the High One.

"Unharmed!" he said.

The man walked away two, three steps, then—an unheard-of action—he ran to do the errand.

The High One watched him go. He then bowed to the Prince, and walked, with all the dignity he could muster, to the chair which had been placed for him.

21

When Bulinga reached the top of the pillar and entered the little room, there she was easily caught and conducted to the Room of Audience by the official who had been dispatched by the High One.

Her entrance caused no commotion.

To the High One she was an object of distaste and Prince Dedn did not recognize her, at first. When he did, he eyed her appreciatively. He would never have agreed to quite so much jewelry nor so much face-paint. He reflected that the High One's officials demonstrated a significant lack of taste. And yet she had some regality now. He was glad to have her back. She would grace his entourage. Femininity of this quality was not encountered every day.

The High One, after waiting patiently for some lead, saw that he would have to speak first. It was, in any case, right that in his own hall he should speak first. He cast about for something to say, something which would not commit him.

"Come here, girl," he said.

Bulinga was pushed towards him.

As she passed the Prince his fingers closed about her arm and he halted her.

"Stay there," he commanded—and to the others: "This girl is my slave."

The High One looked at him sourly. He considered the Prince's action to be foolish. He was being too hurried. But he was playing into the hands of his opponent, and the High One always distrusted the obvious; his was a tortuous mind.

"That girl," said the High One in an even voice, "is an attendant of this Temple. You will at once permit her to come here, to my side."

He was not at all surprised that the Prince refused to comply with this sternly worded request.

"The girl stays with me," flatly stated Prince Dedn.

The High One could have laughed.

"Prince Dedn," he said, and he stood. "You were invited to Nipsirc by the Fathers of the Circle at my request.

"Let me refer again to matters upon which I touched at our initial meeting of yesterday.

"Each fresh day thousands more of the people of the mainland arrive at the Temple and make their contribution and declare themselves in favor of the reconstitution of the Great Sun's observance.

"City after city, state upon state, is acknowledging that we here in Nipsirc have been blessed in seeing a truth too long hidden, a truth which must not again be hidden nor swamped by a resurgence of misguided thought.

"Because the peoples of the mainland are now united in this their Religion, all subservience to the island of Rutas-Mu is at an end."

He stopped abruptly.

That was more than he had intended to say. He was becoming as naïve a diplomat as this young heathen from Dejanira. But the pause was accepted. He would prolong it a little, collect his thoughts.

But they weren't waiting for him to speak.

They were all listening.

Now he, too, could hear.

It was faint, but it was unmistakable for what it was; the sound of rioting.

The riot must have spread beyond the confines of

this, tired of fighting, tired of Prince Dedn, tired of men.

Of the seven officers who had left the Temple with Prince Dedn, five were still with him when he carried Bulinga into the hall of a looted and empty house.

Bulinga leaned against the wall and regarded them with repugnance.

The Prince was wiping clean his sword on the torn door curtain.

The room was ravaged and fouled, doubtless more being broken than stolen. Bulinga's tired thoughts were able to travel no further than to sympathy for the plight of the owners when they returned—when it was safe to do so. She felt pressed to leave for them what she could of wealth. Besides, her jewels oppressed her. She removed her earrings, the caul of network in gold and smaller gems and the heavy anklets and slid them into the broken remains of a small desk.

Some she must keep.

While the Prince and his officers were talking, and paying no attention to her, she untied her bundle and tucked into it her necklet and arm ornaments. That gave her the warmth of security. She wasn't so poor now. She still had her forty-eight gold parings, too.

This house had long since been passed by the rioting crowds, there were no sounds from outside.

Three of her escorts had gone. While she was repacking her bundle some talk had percolated to her mind. The three had gone to the palace to obtain horses and the few items which, for various reasons, could not be left there. They were all to meet again outside the city limits.

She heard the two who were left being stationed as guards in the passage from the main door.

The Prince returned, seated himself on an upturned emptied chest and gave all his attention to his slave.

There was no courtesy in his attention.

Lazily he stood, stretching his long lithe limbs. He was a splendid figure, but it was not that which Bulinga saw. She was suddenly afraid. She was alone with him; he considered her to be, and thought of her only as, his slave. She had been bought for a purpose. Now he had some time to spare. And she was alone with him.

Bulinga first flattened herself against the wall, and slid herself along the wall, slightly.

She had no weapon—none but her fingers—but she would fight—until she was exhausted.

She straightened herself and looked levelly across at him. Her eyes were narrowed.

Prince Dedn was amused.

He had not moved a step.

He stretched his arms out as if to loosen the muscles, and laughed as he saw her tense herself.

"You yourself have shaped your destiny by leaving the shelter of your father's palace and the guardianship of his arm and rank," he remarked. "What end did you expect to your adventure?"

Bulinga's arm slowly picked up her bundle from the desk beside her and clasped it to her as if it were a shield.

Her eyes watched, without blink.

From the trace of irritability in his voice at the end of his last sentence she judged he was losing his patience.

The suspense was draining her of resolution, but she was still resolved.

A little awkwardly, but swiftly like the scurry of a wounded bird, she jumped to the door and was out through it.

He whirled about, lost his footing in turning, shouted, sprang doorwards shouting to the men to hold her, but his two officers were resting while they could. They too had not expected her action, they were only prepared for the arrival of a noisy crowd of which they would have had ample warning.

Bulinga made no mistake such as turning in the wrong direction. The officer at the outside doorway heard his Prince's shout in the moment she passed him. He paused, waited too long before starting off in pursuit. It was becoming darker each succeeding moment. Bulinga was light, and though her bundle was heavier than once, the men behind her were encumbered by heavy greaves on their legs, by the weight of metal breastplates and by scabbarded long-swords which banged at their legs and had to be held, awkwardly.

Bulinga sped along.

She had won. She was away. She was free. Her heart sang and her mind exulted.

What of his vaunted masculine strength! In what had it helped him? With no weapons except the power to grasp the opportunity his weaknesses offered her, she had beaten him.

Bulinga could hear them, far behind her, but the sound came faintly.

Were it not for the few braziers hanging above they would neither see her nor hear her. She could not run much more, though, there must soon be a cross street, or a square, or a small courtyard she could cross.

The streets were empty.

In these meaner streets there was no rioting.

As she walked her shadow lengthened and shortened, disappeared behind her and swung round before her again as she turned a corner. Sometimes it seemed top-heavy, sometimes its legs were alarmingly wide. She walked in deep thought but her shadow played around her as though it were an irresponsible imp, its unreasoning movements depending on the position of the braziers which, from above, followed the lines of the streets.

Bulinga was certain she was headed in the right direction and that soon she must be clear of the city. She had taken care to counteract the way the streets ran; if one were not careful walking in circles would be easy. But she believed she had mastered that. She must have walked miles, clear across the city. It was night now. She was hungry. She must, she thought, be in the direction opposite to that from which she had entered Nipsirc, for she had seen no sign of palaces.

There was light in the sky, away over there. It was much too strong to be from the light braziers, and anyway they had not been lit because of the rioting.

A man came out of one of the houses, the carved shutters of which had been added to a bonfire still burning in the street.

Bulinga was across the street from him. She felt no fear. He was alone and what he carried, she knew, he wouldn't wish to lose.

He was a large man.

Bulinga crossed the street.

"Have you anything to eat there, Vathok?" she asked. "I'm starving! I've had not a bite since early this morning."

23

Heralded by the squealing antics of the horde of naked small children, Slila and Sluk staggered into the camp. Each carried the corpse of a bear larger than himself. Behind them, very proud of his share in the expedition, head erect, and bow legs twinkling with the short steps all the Arvela affected, walked Slon. He had wound his pink cloth about himself in the manner of a hunter of the tribe, and he carried the bolas of Slila and Sluk as well as his own.

The women were on the bear carcasses before they hit the ground in their drop from the tired shoulders of the hunters.

Vathok, squatting between the two graying patriarchs, grimaced and grunted.

Vathok had made no effort to learn even a word of their language. The lack of a speech in common with them proved no hindrance to any of his activities.

Bulinga said the right things to Mila. It was halting speech and her accent was bad, so that had Mila not known what to expect her small understanding would never have suggested to her what was intended. But Naitok repeated the remarks for her, as a lesson in pronunciation more than for any other reason.

Bulinga liked Naitok just as much as the Arvela did.

Twelve days had come and gone again to the Moon since she had stood on the ridge and watched the blaze that was what Nipsirc had become.

It was the day after that that they had met the Arvela.

Bulinga drew her marten cloak about her, for the wind was snell.

She felt almost happy with these people, though she knew she must leave them within a few more days, when they had reached what for her was easy walking distance from Gabebal.

Vathok had said he would stay—but Naitok had told her he was mistaken in thinking they would permit that. Bulinga had good hopes that he would stay with them long enough after she had gone to give her time to get clear away from him. She did not want the attendance of a ruffian and outlaw such as he when she reached a civilized city.

But this stay with the Arvela was refreshing pleasure.

So too would be her share of the bear now roasting above the fire beside which she sat. She had slipped her feet from the awkward fur boots she'd been given. She knew that of the two sticks Mila was sharpening with a stone, one would be given to her to eat with. Her fingers would have to help, and she would make an even more sorry mess of her marten cape for bear fat was insidious stuff. It got everywhere. It trickled down your chin and all over your hands and forearms and somehow pools of it dried in your lap, and there was no way of obviating all this.

She wriggled backwards a little from the fire.

"Too hot?" asked Naitok.

Bulinga nodded, happily. Such unnecessary remarks could only be said and accepted amid happiness. In other circumstances they would have been tedious.

Portions, sizzling, dripping fat over everyone, their warm appetizing smell sending the children dizzy with delight, were already being handed on pointed sticks to the elders, to Naitok, to Vathok. Hers would come in a moment or two. Bulinga didn't object in the least to the first serving of the tribe's menfolk. The women were well treated, always generously helped with the few tasks left to them. It was a small thing that the men should be first served with meat. Besides, if it had not been so, she might from her ignorance have inadvertently eaten on the occasion of her first night with them, when the feast was supplied by the person of some traveler who had encountered the tribe when they were in a less cordial mood.

It was nearly dusk.

There would be silence soon, silence while the thirty-four of them ate and after that much talking which she would be unable to understand. And she wouldn't get much speech with Naitok for he was an integral part of the tribal conversation.

That was the pattern of her evenings, now.

Then in the morning with the dawn she would awaken; and gnaw, just as would the Arvela, at the piece she had saved from the evening meal. She would get her drink, in her two cupped hands, of the milk of the two ungainly ground sloths which were the tribe's only animals, and she would wander with them all onwards over the scrub-covered desert, towards Gabebal.

Bulinga wondered for how long Naitok would stay with them. For how long he would escape being the feast of these quite lovable nomads. There was still a chance that she would end that way. For some reason it didn't seem to matter much, though it would again tomorrow when she was not sleepy and not so full of delicious greasy bear meat.

She was becoming fatter on the diet. Naitok each day handed her her share of the long slim almost dry leaves which, chewed and relentlessly swallowed, would counteract that tendency to become too toothsome. Although he assured her she was safe, and she believed he thought so, still she would hurry when she said good-bye to the Arvela, because there might, she guessed, be two of the more skilled hunters of the tribe hurrying after her.

Bulinga wanted to reach Gabebal, unchewed.

Vathok of course relied on his knife. He must have, as she had, witnessed a killing. The short length of strong rope twisted and plaited from many bear sinews, with a polished hard stone ball at its end, was a formidable weapon. Vathok would be skilled indeed with his knife if it were sufficient to counter the attack of, say, three Arvelas.

Bulinga shuddered, and pulled her cloak closer about her.

She should not have rushed so quickly from Nipsirc. And she considered the matter. She should have tried to find Gatil. Though that might have presented difficulties, and danger to her. With Nipsirc full of rioting people Carpen would be hard to find, to find Gatil might be still more difficult. And had she met Carpen . . . Well. She didn't want to.

There was much meat on those two bears. Mila offered her guest another tidbit, Bulinga smiled sweetly and tucked the lump into a knotted sleeve of the gown she had filched from Vathok's bundle of loot. She could not have continued in the Temple dress, it was too exiguous, and much too conspicuous.

The air was heavy with the smell of burnt and cooked bear. The small children gorged happily. A small girl child near her patted her little full stomach and shrilly echoed an age-old jest of her elders.

Tomorrow they would travel again—cover what number of miles Bulinga could not even guess, there was nothing in this wilderness to guide her. Naitok might know. She thought he didn't. No. He must. Otherwise he wouldn't know when to tell her to leave.

Two more days of sweltering heat, two more nights of desert cold, after a feast of—bear meat, she hoped. Naitok would tell her if it weren't so. Or she herself would recognize what it was, now she knew what hung over the fires on occasion.

She should have guessed they were cannibals.

Bulinga licked all her fingers, and her wrists, greasy from wiping her chin down which fat would drip. She tucked her green bundle under her head, carefully prodding the metal within it to one side. She curled up inside her cape.

They could talk all night if they wished to. She would think of Gatil, and then sleep. She would meet Gatil again. That she knew would happen. If only Gatil were here with her. She was lonely without him. She didn't trust the Arvela.

She should have known they were cannibals, from her first sight of them. Those awful protruding tusks at the mouth corners.

They were barely related to her, Naitok said. A separate genus of mankind—an earlier joke of the Great Serpent's—Naitok had laughed, and she had laughed and asked him if that were a double joke in view of the fact that he was a missionary from the High One. He was, but he had retreated to the old religion finding impossible all attempts to convert the Arvela.

Those awful tusks.

Yet they had treated her well.

Bulinga curled a greasy hand into a knot under her chin and rested her head on the green bundle.

She hoped Vathok would manage it too. Perhaps they would let him get away, because they'd so enjoyed having him with them. She must have a good rubdown with earth tomorrow; get some of this grease off her skin. Mila would help her.

Mila was a good friend, despite her awful tusks.

Mila might help her to get away.

Bulinga ran her fastest to the trees.

Running was easy in the light sandals Vathok's loot had supplied.

When she had seen the trees she had decided on this action. The bolas would not be so dangerous to her if she were surrounded by tree trunks.

Each moment she expected to hear behind her the whirr of one of those sinew-hung black stones.

From the shelter of the trees she looked back.

The Arvela were quite a way distant. They seemed to be all there, no hunters missing, though she must still be careful.

She could pick out Vathok, huge amidst the smaller, copper-colored Arvela. The pink clothes they wore, hardly two of them in the same way, the two huge lumbering ground sloths, the string of naked children— Bulinga found it difficult to believe that that was another episode which was over and finished with in her life, that not tonight would she, after a feast of bear meat, curl up in her marten cloak and wonder if she were really to escape being roasted and gnawed by all these tusk-mouthed savages.

She waited till they were all specks in the distance before she stripped and scoured from herself the layer of bear fat.

Once, as a pheasant whirred past, her heart almost stopped with fright.

But she was safe now. The Arvela were too distant. No hunter could catch up with her.

It was a delightful copse, especially after days and days in the scrub-covered desert. She still had a large lump of bear meat. And real water, clear clean gurgling dimpling water from a little spring. She could really wash. She could clean her robe, perhaps even get the congealed fat out of the mess of marten cloak.

24

Rain came.

It swiftly became so dark that it seemed nature had decided on a second night instead of one night and one day in this thirty hours.

Naitok had said that if in the morning one climbed the southern slope of the hill between Gabebal and the desert, one would reach Gabebal in the afternoon.

"There will be nothing for you to fear in Gabebal," he had told her. "It is less than a city, it is in fact no more than a huge palace-court surrounded by the houses of servants, but it is true to your own, old, religion. They will welcome you there and, if you still so desire it, set you on the shortest road to Dejanira."

In spite of her determination to reach Gabebal, Bulinga had a lesser certainty of her immediate welcome there.

If spies and missionaries of the new Religion were as prevalent in the land as they must surely be, for Naitok had been sent to convert even such a small and wandering tribe as the Arvela, a town such as Gabebal would be wary of the admittance of strangers. But, after all, when they saw her and heard her speak surely they would realize that she was one whose blood was true.

The sky was purple and drenched by the rain. Tall slender poplar and fir and cypress received the rain in their foliage and turned it to a liquid perfume. The slope of the hill down which she had come was steep above her, it lowered dankly down at her, the height of it black with the great trees.

Bulinga's flesh was stinging from the rain. Her bundle and cape were very heavy. Once she dropped the bundle and had to search for it among the damp earth-slimy roots of the bracken, while the rain fell above her from leaf to leaf and from frond to frond, and finally piercing the barricade of undergrowth dripped about her ears and down her back between the dress and her skin.

She came to a place where the grass and slope were gentle, and she walked over this gingerly till she saw, materializing from the rain before her, a high black line of feathery-topped trees between whose blackness there seemed to be no way.

The rain fell.

She looked back up the slope down which she had come.

The forest was menacing, but it could not reach her here for it looked exactly as if it had been petrified just when it had run halfway down the hill.

Bulinga dashed through the low black drenching branches before her, and found herself in the courtyard of the palace of Gabebal.

There was a melancholy silence to it.

The rain fell puddling and trickling into the gravel of the great empty yard.

When one listened one heard a definite silence unbroken by anything except the little crepitation of the rain in the gravel.

Bulinga went towards the door, swinging careless and open into the courtyard, and passed the stables. There was a horse, lying half inside, half outside, of one of the stall doors. It was quite dead.

Now Bulinga feared to enter the palace.

But her feet took her into the great silent hall behind the door, and she saw men lying here whose sleep was not to be ended. She walked between them slowly, so many men who leaned upon tables and sprawled in chairs and had fallen against pillars and rich curtains, and when she had realized with a gradual cold horror that they were not ordinary sleepers, she had passed too many to go back, and so she continued and found that in the next hall the men wore better clothes and still all of them were dead. And this was the same in the next hall and in the next, and in the next hall too.

Everywhere there was silence, ultimate silence, and everywhere men and women and small pet animals lay and sat and leaned and were dead. There were no children.

No hangings had been torn down; no weapons were visible; none of the dead had wounds upon their bodies. There was no sign by which to tell how death had come upon Gabebal, and Bulinga moved quickly and breathed fearfully for terror of some potent, terrible disease.

The last chamber which she came to was obviously a room of audience. The dead figures here were so numerous that there was frequently no obvious way between them. Food and wine stood about but Bulinga dared not take any. In the chair in the middle of the room sat a woman whose beauty of figure and dress were so great that Bulinga believed her to have been Queen.

The open eyes of this woman were yellow, and her long hair was green-blue; or perhaps the other way around: in after life Bulinga could never certainly remember which.

And this woman too was dead.

High up against the rafters mists of vapor still hung and little eddies occasionally stirred ominously in them.

The ending of these people must have been recent for nowhere was there any sign of decay, but in this chamber there was a smell which was not good.

Bulinga reached an open terrace and fled from Gabebal to the wet of the woods. The sharp staccato of her sandals as she dashed across the marble startled her.

When she reached the wet shelter of the trees her eyes were wide and terror was in her mind.

Only there did she dare to form the words:

"Gabebal is dead."

25

Bulinga stood, shivering, at the curve of the gray road.

Gabebal was behind her.

She wouldn't look at it again.

Before her the road arched over a steep bridge and was level again till, again becoming a bridge, it passed a tiny group of high unbeautiful houses in whose windows were lights, red and unfriendly.

And still the rain dripped neverendingly.

All about her, behind Gabebal too, pale black hill slopes went almost precipitously up, then down a little, then up again at a lesser angle—all in the distance behind the tree trunks. She was in a cup.

But the river swept through, and, unhurried, a dark misty mass came forward. It was a wide, long cargo barge, low in the water and piled with baled goods.

As it paused at the bridge, someone on board shouted.

It was an old, gravely friendly voice, and Bulinga met it gladly.

She raced to the river bank, and waved, and the boat nosed in to her and the small bent kindly-faced waterman beckoned her on board.

Now the river bore her on and the land unwontedly flowed past her, grass, gravel, bushes, trees, earth and gorse, and gorse and hill were all unreal and had so little to do with her that their brief existence was of no moment; except once when, for the time of an exciting count of twenty, there stood, suspiciously, back from the water, three long-necked heavy moropus.

Bulinga held from her lips the heavy clay-lined wicker bowl of soup and watched them in wonder and surprise, her head slowly swinging round to catch the whole glimpse of them before the boat bore her away.

"When I was a small boy," said the old waterman at her elbow, "those moropus were everywhere. In those days half of those bales behind you'd be tied up in moropus skin, and it'd sell for as much as the baling it held. There's the first I've seen for years. For very many years. Did you see'm, boys?"

The two grandsons, one on top of the load, one at the steering oar aft, cried a long low-carrying assent in what Bulinga had learnt to know as the voice always used by watermen speaking against the forward movement of their boat.

She bent her head to her soup.

The boys kept from her as though she were poisonous. She knew it made the old man chuckle, but he made no attempt to lessen the distance between them. He was satisfied.

He took the bowl from her, swilled it in the watercask, rubbed it with earth and swilled it again.

Bulinga protested.

"I could have done that!"

He smiled and made no reply.

Yesterday she had offered to mend, and in the cabin had picked up a jacket, and seen the stitches. She had put it down again. Her sewing could not compete with theirs.

She had tried to sound him, to discover whether some gift from her would be acceptable when the time came for her to go ashore. Directly, and with no embarrassment, he cut short her skirmishing and negatived the idea. It was unnecessary, he said. And Bulinga knew, without the need of further speech between them, that cautious living, the habit of years, had put him above need.

So she was a guest.

He would put her ashore at Tayrb, he said. There were people there.

It was such a quaint way of summing up her needs. And as though he and the two shy grandsons were a race apart. Which almost they were.

She had asked him of Gabebal—expecting no answer, for before her lips had ejected the words it had occurred to her that he could not know.

"They were killed by a smell," he stated, authoritatively. "They held to the old religion, and there were those to whom that was an objectionable thing to do. So now they are all with the Moon, and perhaps they prefer it to be so." He sensed her surprise. "An upriver barge brought me the news," he explained.

"Know you anything of Nipsirc?"

He nodded. Slowly, and, for a small man, ponderously.

"There was grave rioting, and half the town in flames. It was a fine town for trade, but trade attracted women." He paused, and looked at her, and Bulinga blushed, and then, afraid that that blush might be taken as telltale evidence, she opened her lips to speak, but he went on: "You've heard of what sort of women Nipsirc boasts. I never go there. The boys, you see. And myself too, for that matter. But the men who command the Temple have righted all, and now there is peace there."

And ever afterwards Bulinga wondered how he placed her, for his words had still left his decision a matter of doubt to her. But he treated her always as man should treat womankind, and his courtesy reminded her of Gatil and hurt her, for where he was, and whether she would ever again meet him, were as far from her knowledge as were the sky and what was held in it beyond the mists of men's seeing.

These were quite, restful, uneventful days.

Tayrb was on a plain and she first saw it in the

evening. But far away. A sky like a mountain stream
whitish-green, with white flecks in it, was in existence
at the end of that day. There were many many boats
even up from the great seas. There were hours to
wait before she could be put ashore.

When she was helped up the stone ladder, and over
the balustrade, she turned to wave—but the old man
and his two grandsons were working. She waited. And
then went.

26

Bulinga clasped her hands behind her head, and lay
and looked at the darkness of the room and then at the
windowed wall.

Not only was it long since she had slept in a real
room, so that she felt now rather suffocated in the
small space, but other anxieties and worries had come
to her so that it seemed to her that, all this night,
sleep would be difficult.

The days spent in the desert and on the river had
unarmed her, and she had been overawed by the city.

She had intended to be very particular in her choice
of an inn.

Bulinga sighed.

There had been practically no choice by her. This
was far too expensive and far below what she had desired.

This one it had had to be because she was becoming
tired of wandering through the streets and she knew
that her stock of money was as small as or less than
the trader, in Grood, had told her.

In the streets there had been bands of men wearing

the insignia of the Religious Police. That had alarmed her. She had avoided them, slipping into the crowd whenever she saw them and, remembering the importance attached to fair hair, she had kept the hood of her cloak over her head and tucked her hair from sight.

She was annoyed, impatient and angry with herself. She had at first forgotten that she would encounter danger in any town subservient to the Religious Police.

The tardy realization of her danger, as well as the coming of night, had forced her hand and shortened her search for shelter. The room hired, she had at once locked herself within it and endeavored to relax, to rest. And to plan. She was tired and all her problems seemed suddenly to have piled themselves for her recognition.

She had passed through much hardship, much danger, much agony of mind, she had covered many miles, and still she seemed no nearer to Dejanira. And the farther she traveled the more she appreciated the size of the world, and that Atlan, her ultimate hope, was no nearer to her than it had been when she was in Grood.

Life was a bad thing, outside Grood as much as within it. She had left Grood in which she might have been happy had she known that to leave it was not to step at once into a high paradise.

It seemed that in this life one was allowed to attain nothing without hard endeavor, depression long and deep, and heartbreak.

And even one's small triumphs and gains were tempered by difficulty which accompanied their possession as well as their acquiring.

Her necklet and bracelets, which she had filched from the Temple, were valuable, but she might never be able to utilize that value; would not anyone to whom she showed them immediately recognize them as of Temple design and as Temple property, and accuse her to the authorities—to those brutal Police?

The street outside, over which her window looked, was a back street, little more than an alley between houses. In this vicinity dwelt no rich or solid citizens. For some time there had been no sounds from it. Now there were shouts, the sound of running feet. The shouting was mainly obscene curses.

Bulinga turned over restlessly in the bed, again hoping it was not verminous. She must shut out the noise with sleep. It was, she supposed, a brawl, or the merrymaking of rough, drunken men.

She must sleep.

She needed rest, she needed strength if she must continue to contend with her troubles. She must leave Tayrb tomorrow. She must first, though, plan some way of avoiding the Police at the gate. She was wonderfully, miraculously lucky, she realized, in having been able to enter the city from the river and on the crowded quay to escape their notice.

Bulinga liked the darkness of the room.

She could feel that at last she was dropping off to sleep. Did one ever really register the exact moment when one fell asleep? She couldn't remember ever having done so. But it would be interesting to know what it was like—just awake one moment and asleep the next.

It would be a drowsy wakefulness, of course. . . .

It would be nice if death were like that.

. . . just before one was asleep; wakefulness would be so drowsy. . . .

That scraping noise!

It was right in the room!

Pressing herself into the bed beneath her, hardly breathing, Bulinga moved her head, carefully, so that she could see the window.

A blackness, blacker than the black surrounding it

Someone was climbing in! Was astride the window sill!

Living blackness blotted out the faint saffron of the street brazier's light!

From the street there were more shouts and th

figure swung into the room with a recurrence of the grating discordance which had first startled Bulinga.

In two swift strides he was beside her as, wildly frightened, she started up and grabbed for the bundle beside her whether as a weapon or to prevent robbery he hadn't the slightest idea—then the hand of the man was across her mouth and that flat hard firm vise of flesh on her face terrified her so that she could not move.

She heard the fierceness of "If you scream I'll brain you, d'you hear? The Police are after me."

But she couldn't breathe.

Choking, gasping, she pulled at the hand, tried to nod her head so that he would know of her acquiescence, and remembered the darkness and the futility of a nod.

The hand withdrew a little, though: the man's voice said again, urgently, "You keep quiet, or I'll brain you!" and Bulinga, physically and mentally unbalanced, trembling, dragged herself up farther in bed and held the cover to her.

Below in the street was an ugly cacophony, shouting, a rattling of dagger hilts on doors and shuttered windows. If he were found with her, she also might be recognized and that would be terrible. The cursing and yelling, below, continued.

Had there been some light she would have been less afraid.

It was too dark, she could not see him!

Without warning of any kind at all his fingers were suddenly upon her, unexpected, groping, unpleasantly heavy upon her face and arms, and in an indignation the strength of which almost vanquished her fright, she realized that he was feeling her—to gauge her appearance and age, to assess her by touch!

The fingers felt her nose, her lips, and blundered into her hair, then paused, and twice explored the length of it, as though it were unexpected.

In one swift movement Bulinga slid from the bed, pushed her feet into the easily fitting sandals and swept the dress over her head and down about her. As she fumbled for the belt the hands came to her and grasped her and pulled her to the window, to the light. The hands grasping her had strength she could not withstand.

She saw the flash of teeth.

"So you are a girl," said the voice with a musing mockery in the tone of it. "Let me see you more. You feel like a very pretty girl."

Bulinga, cold with terror, raised her eyes from the strong black-haired hand to the face of Prince Dedn.

27

"Bulinga!" he said. "It was undoubtedly fate which led me here." He laughed. "Even the Religious Police have their uses it would seem. You must accept this meeting as a sign from the gods, and make no further misguided attempts to escape."

"But I did escape!" Bulinga pointed out.

"To what end?" he asked. "Only to fall again to my hand."

Bulinga found her fingers and palms were clammy with moist heat.

"I may believe in such a fate if *you* escape the Police," she said. "Do you not realize you will be caught if you stay here?"

"I will take you at your word," he said.

She didn't fathom his meaning. She knew he had moved for the tall bulk of him was not now where it had been. She looked about in some alarm. Then his hand was on her shoulder again and he was looking down from the dark room at the Police, an undecided knot, farther along the street.

"What do you think you can do?" mocked Bulinga, resenting the hand on her shoulder.

The Prince did not reply and Bulinga flushed with anger.

He was listening, but always he ignored her except when it suited him to speak to her.

The shouting had diminished. The Religious Police had decided to search systematically each of the houses. Only two were left on guard in the street.

The beats of Bulinga's heart lurched suddenly into an irregular rhythm which was painful in its intensity.

If she were found here—her hearing told her the inn had already been entered—they would accuse her of harboring and abetting a fugitive from justice—the whiteness of her hair would be discovered—it might even be revealed that she had escaped from their Temple in Nipsirc—that she had been the cause of the riots there! She could not continue indefinitely to enjoy miraculous escapes. And all this new danger had been brought to her by the sudden reappearance of this man who had brought danger to her many times previously. She had been, she told herself, secure and comfortable before he fastened on her again.

Prince Dedn's eyes glinted as he watched the street. She caught the curl of his lips as he spoke.

"Now," he said softly.

A little cry of alarm and protest broke from Bulinga. She was caught up, tossed under one of his arms, tucked there like a bale of goods.

He could not be strong enough!

She would fall!

She was swung into clear space, it seemed. Even his nearness, his hold of her, did not detract from that impression.

Using as foot- and handholds the thick staples of the furnace pipe which here hugged the wall, he lowered himself, and her.

She saw the dark rounded knobs of the street surface rise to meet her; she was placed on her feet; she staggered, his arm righted her, his hand held her wrist.

His grip of her was irresistible.

"Come on, run," he commanded, and she was dragged over the uneven cobbles towards where, a short distance away, another street crossed theirs and the hard angles of the corners deterred the light of the braziers.

Behind them a shout!

The shout swelled and was repeated, other yells replied to it; there was the thud of heavily slammed doors and the determined running of many feet in pursuit.

Bulinga was even grateful for Dedn's grip, for he dragged her on to a speed swifter than any she could ever have attained unaided.

The sounds of the pursuit resounded from the cobbles and the walls on either side.

Dedn had shouted something back to them, a laughing challenge with contempt spicing the laughter, and more furious threats and curses answered him. Bulinga wondered how he had the audacity, and the breath, to insult them so.

Bulinga and the Prince reached the corner. They were well ahead of the Police. Glimpsing three streets leading away Bulinga for a moment imagined that the Police would not know which she and the Prince had taken. Then she saw that of course they would separate.

She raced along beside Dedn. She was harder, stronger than the Princess who had left Grood one night—so very long ago. Though rough cobbles were not the ideal path for racing feet, she was keeping level with him. Or, the thought struck her, was he holding himself in? But she could run well, and she was taking strength from the hand which clasped hers. His grip had slipped to there. They ran hand in hand, and she knew his strength assisted her.

After a third turning, he pulled her to a stop.

Bulinga leaned against the wall. They were in a very

narrow alley. There was no sound, but they could not afford to rest. There was tomorrow to think of. Somewhere they must find shelter, find somewhere to lie hidden.

There was very little light where they stood. It was not easy to see him.

"Have we thrown them off?" she asked.

He came closer.

"Are you surprised?" he laughed down at her. "Perhaps you will trust to me, in future. You should. Slave girl, I tell you this, I rarely fail. Though I won't tell you all I have been doing to upset the oligarch of Nipsic since the recital might bore you——"

"Oh! I've left my cloak—and my bundle!"

"Your bundle! Oh, I have that," and he swung it up and pressed it upon her. "I knew you must have that, as you are never without it. But your cloak . . . No. I haven't that. Would you like me to go back for it. Or can you accept another in its place?"

Bulinga was too tired to argue with him.

Surely he couldn't be right in that her fate and his were to run side by side.

She shook her head.

All thinking must wait. They were in danger, still.

"Where have you brought me?" she asked.

He took her arm and walked her slowly along the long alley.

The winding narrowness oppressed her. The walls towered, seeming to slant to each other so that far above only a sliver of navy sky could be seen. And the walls were slimy, and stank. In the murky doorways crouched figures whose eyes gleamed warily and whose rag-covered arms groped quietly to knife hilts.

She supposed he knew where he took her.

They passed a group of men squatting in the street beneath a brazier. The men played some game, intently. One of them growled a warning as Bulinga's sleeve brushed his head. She was alarmed, but he was apparently more interested in the game and the gold he wagered glimmered in his palm. Dedn spoke. She did not catch his phrase. There was no reply from the men, but it would seem that whatever he said had satisfied them.

It seemed important that she must show her displeasure.

"You are placing me in danger by bringing me here," she said.

"The Police dare not follow us here."

"That, of course, is a reason, but are we safe from those who live here? And must we not stay till the Police have forgotten us? Is there a gate from the city, near?"

"You ask more questions than the Police do! What you need, my girl, is sleep. Bear with me. Sleep's not far away. There is an inn near here."

"An inn! In this squalid, noisome slum! Oh, I don't doubt there is an inn! But how can I sleep in such filth, and among such scum as live here?"

His silent laughter annoyed her.

"Your bed will be clean enough. And you are in no danger from the inhabitants. I know many here."

"And their women too?"

She felt his appreciation of that thrust, but didn't look at him.

"Some," he answered. "I have known Tayrb before, when I was not even a youth. There were people who thought me too wild. I learned all the lanes and alleys—and there are many who are still my friends. You need have no fear, you are quite safe with me, and I expect the inn will be satisfactory, it was so when I passed through here recently. We are not the only fugitives in Tayrb."

"You have been here long?" she asked.

"No," he replied. "I came tonight, to see someone."

"To look for me!" she said, surprised.

"No. You are a gift from the gods. From now on I keep you with me. We are now at the inn," he added.

The discordance of drunken singing reached them.

"Did you say you came here when you were young?"

"Yes, I did say so."

Prince Dedn kicked the door, it rattled and opened. There was light, there was drunken laughter, and about half of those within must have been singing to the accompaniment of a maimed ragged wretch successfully twanging a ghirza and drinking copiously at one and the same time.

"I can't imagine what sort of a child you must have been," Bulinga said.

The Prince gave a shout of laughter, and banged cataclysmically on the back of the door and used his foot to shut it.

Bulinga noted that in amusement.

He was right though.

The door was too filthy to be handled.

She lifted her skirts and preceded him.

A little man was coming down, peering at them, peering at her, and past her to Dedn.

"Prince Dedn!" he exclaimed. "You've come to stay? Shall I get her . . ."

"One night, Xob," said the Prince, holding up one finger.

The greasy little man was hobbling backwards up the stairs, much simple pleasure reflected on the wrinkled, seamed, scarred area which she knew to be his face.

At the top step he turned and yelled:

"Come and see who's here!"

"What did you say?" yelled back a woman's voice.

"I said come and see who's here!"

There was a curse which sounded violently unfeminine, and, with slow deliberation, someone approached along the badly lit passage.

She was still some way from them when she ceased listening to sounds behind her, and faced them.

She gave a start of surprise.

"Your Dignity! Prince Dedn!" she cried.

She reached to the wall and lifted from its shelf the lamp which stood there.

The innwoman was only thirty or thereabouts but her face was bleared with the accumulation of years of paint and powder which she had never washed off but repaired when it became stale. She had been raddled since she was eighteen or younger. She was not fat, but her plumpness was coarse: that she had been born with lovely feet was seen when she picked up her voluminous skirts.

She threw Dedn a glance both material and coquettish.

"Oh! It's you! You're becoming almost an inmate! It won't be more than a score of days since you were here last. But I suppose you'll come just whenever you want to. Come through, and your latest lady too!"

Dedn clasped Bulinga's hand and dragged her up the last step.

The odorous smoke of the badly burning braziers drifted in layers, so that it was hard to see within the long room. On the thick uneven pillars the plaster was often broken and fallen away exposing the cone-shaped bricks; where the plaster was intact it bore superimposed writings, incised initials, and drawings, mostly pornographic. The room was full. Every bench and table bore its load of men and pots and jars. Near at hand a nearly comely woman, whose hips were out of all proportion, swayed and joggled—belly-dancing for the entertainment of those immediately about her, though some quite close at hand ignored the exhibition and either stared dumbly and hopelessly into the emptiness of the pot before them, or, backs turned, discussed animatedly the matter—whatever that was— which was momentarily of supreme importance to them.

There was little jollity, though some laughter.

Although there was, probably, not one group which would have refused him a welcome. Prince Dedn eased himself round individuals and groups to a small table at which two men sat.

Neither looked at him until he had pulled from under the table a coarse stool which he sat upon.

"You take your pleasure seriously, Emalf," the Prince said.

"Dedn!" smiled Emalf. "Well! Now everyone of moment is here. Both of us. Will you tell me you too are a refugee?"

"What else! But why are you here? In Nipsirc I was told you were living the life of a gentleman."

"You were told the truth," Emalf waved a hand; "are not gentlemen from Nipsirc and Tayrb, and now Dejanira, all within this room! By the Serpent's Blood! I'd been five minutes a gentleman when the rioting broke out. I saw at once that when it was all over Nipsirc would be no place for an ex-trader. I dislike being harried. Some day several of these Police will be sent to the Moon by me. But I thought your person would have been sacrosanct!"

"No."

The Prince lounged lazily back to permit the clearing of several flagons from the table.

The other man at the table, a grizzled low-browed man, richly dressed, with much grey in his thin beard, picked at the ring in his left ear.

"The High One, Your Dignity, surely does not know of your present condition!"

"None better, Paltan. None better. Were I dead my demise would be by his express command."

"He will surely rue it," the man said hotly. "So to treat a Prince of the Good Islands!"

"He is drunk, with power," stated Emalf.

"He would not be drunk with other than that," laughed the Prince. "Will that sluggard never bring something drinkable?"

Emalf looked about.

"He comes now. So you are a refugee. It will be good for you, Prince Dedn. I doubt if you've ever tasted the life of the hunted. At least you know all the boltholes."

"Ah, drink," said the Prince. He lifted the pot placed before him, and tasted it. "Yes. That will do. They know me better than to give me poor quality.

Tell me, Emalf, have you ever traded in a place called Grood?"

"I know it well. Why? Do you propose to fly there? I would never advise it."

"Pestilential?"

"It would, of course, be so. Do they have many princesses there?"

"Several, and that reminds me of something—just a moment though, there is an extra plate here. You have a friend with you! It would be certainly a woman. Have you met many princesses from Grood, Prince?"

"One only," laughed the Prince.

Emalf stared. Almost his mouth hung open. He collected himself, and his head shook slowly, quaintly woebegone.

"I should have known," he said with a sadness not entirely assumed. "The most beautiful girls always come within your orbit."

"Then you shouldn't be so surprised," the Prince briskly told him.

" 'When anything happens, it is unbelievable to someone,' " quoted Emalf. "You see I have not neglected my studies of the Holy Books."

"You should be in the Church, Emalf. In fact the more I think of it the more I like the idea, for you. You are too handsome to be running loose."

Emalf grinned.

"Your concern for my moral welfare is flattering, my Prince. Should I deduce it to be suspect?"

"There you go again. A suspicious mind. All priests are so equipped I have found. Make a new ambition, now, my friend. I recommend the Church."

Emalf laughed.

"Not me. Even if I can quote like a priest. I can quote what the High One should know. A text he should re-read often. Though it is a quotation he would not think appropriate to himself."

" 'Beware the trader who extols too glibly!' " suggested Dedn.

"No, no. 'The man on high can fall among, as well

as fall upon, those beneath him.' One day that will fit the case." He motioned towards the doorway. "What happens over there?"

A brawl had started, near the door. Not only a brawl, a commotion. There were lewd invitations shouted.

Bulinga could not retreat from the room. There were men behind her now.

In the crook of one arm she carried her green bundle, for she felt that to have left it in the room above would have been to lose it.

The cries about her became more vociferous and with strained eyes she searched the room behind the crowd. She became angrily desperate. An auburn-haired ruffian, a young and large man, grasped at her as she forced herself past him and pulled her down to his lap. Bulinga struggled. She was still held. With a whooping laugh he pulled her close and turned her face to his, trying to kiss her.

She nearly fell to the floor as her assailant was dragged up, and felled with a blow behind the ear.

A voice from farther back said:

"You pick such beauties, Prince," and laughed.

"I pick them for myself," the Prince said, meaningly, and the incident was over.

Dedn took her arm.

Bulinga unclasped his fingers. She trembled with anger and hate of him that he should have allowed her to be in such a position that scum could molest her. Then Emalf came within her vision and she swept forward.

"Emalf! You here!"

Emalf stood.

"Your Tranquilness . . ." He stopped. What else could he say? He had thought of her, often. Were two stormy meetings, both in one evening, basis for concord at a later meeting?

Words broke from Bulinga. She laughed excitedly, words tumbling through her brain to her lips and jamming there because of their number.

Emalf waited.

Dedn took the chair vacated by Paltan, who had joined another table. .

Dedn looked from one to the other.

He rubbed two fingers across his chin, thoughtfully.

"Tranquilness," Emalf said, there being here a pause in Bulinga's *résumé* of her adventures, "I am truly astounded. I never even entertained the idea that you would get this far and, yet here you are, with your aim achieved."

"Do you live here now, Emalf?" she inquired.

"Not here, no."

"Oh, I didn't mean right here, in this place. I meant in Tayrb!"

"For the moment, yes, Princess. I . . ."

"But I had forgotten. You are not now a trader!"

"No, but . . ."

"I suppose you were in Nipsirc? Are you being hunted by the Police?"

"Not really, but I . . ."

"I suppose your friend Carpen would protect you!"

"Carpen would protect no one. Nor would I think to ask him to."

Emalf, in these surroundings, appeared to be more than ever aristocratic. She could have thought him the Prince's social equal. It was queer that they should be so friendly. And yet not. It was Emalf's grace and bearing that had at first drawn her attention to him away back in Grood. She knew now that all outlanders were not like him. He still stood out from them, and above them. In fact he didn't seem to belong to this part of the world. He was different.

Her fingers went to the little pangolin at her throat.

He was all she wished Gatil to be. Emalf was older of course. He must be about thirty. Perhaps in years to come Gatil would acquire such grace and manners. She must remember Emalf, use him as a model for Gatil to emulate.

From his dagger scabbard, the Prince handed her a small knife and chopsticks of polished ivory.

"But you . . . ?" she asked.

"I shall use the inn's."

"If you can remain here four more days, I could, I believe, smuggle you both to the coast," offered Emalf. "I have business which holds me for that time."

"That is attractive," agreed Dedn. "I make a good trader, do I not, Emalf?"

"An excellent trader, Your Dignity, but I still remember that when you traveled with me, you insisted on retaining all the profit from your endeavors."

"That is why you know each other, then!" Bulinga said in the voice always used by those who have made a profound discovery.

"Yes, the Prince—er—holidayed with me for forty-two days," agreed Emalf. "As a trader he would go far."

"And you wished me farther," laughed Dedn.

Emalf let that rest. He turned to Bulinga.

"You do go to the coast, I suppose?"

"I am taking her with me," Dedn assured him.

"And my offer?"

"That is perfectly all right," said Bulinga, "and I am not going back with the Prince, at all. But I should have to live here! Must you wait four days, Emalf?"

"Unquestionably. Tonight I live here. I have to meet five traders in the city of Datames. They wish to purchase my most valuable article gained from my last trip. Indeed, almost invaluable it is. Probably the first and only male cat ever to leave Grood. It was that which attacked you, that first night."

"Oh, Emalf!" cried Bulinga, her eyes laughing. "It was the lord Rughted's cat, and a very specially valuable beast. Oh, I'm very, very tired. I think I must go up to bed. I enjoyed meeting you again."

She stood. She looked towards the door, then to Dedn.

"You will be unmolested. They all know, now, you are mine," the Prince assured her.

She climbed between the rugs.

There was a soft under-rug. It did not reach up to

her neck. There was a hole in it which was aggra
vated by her knees. The dark mass of rug seemed
always about to fall on her face. It was good seeing
Emalf again. She liked him. She tugged upwards the
under-rug so that its comparative smoothness protected her face from the heavy prickly menace of the
other.

She fell asleep immediately.

28

Through streets whose narrowness and windings op
pressed and suffocated, under arches dripping with
damp, up and down slimed steps, past deep sunk
archaic doorways whose dank darkness almost con
cealed the watchful forms crouching there—and at al
times in and through a crowd, slow moving and quick
talking, colorfully, wonderfully and variously clothed
and odorous of sweat and dirt and strong pungen
perfumes which came suddenly to one's nostrils and
spiced them and left them with the movement of the
crowd. Through all this Dedn and Bulinga moved to
leave Tayrb and a community which was the home
and the harbor of all for whom an orthodox life wa
poison, now lately added to by the newest of such
classes.

There was no gate, no Police Post to pass. No
Police came to this part of Tayrb and no Police would
have left it had they come.

Here, almost abruptly, Tayrb ended.

There were no villages merging into the country
side.

Beyond the wall were only heaps of stones, then bare treeless hillside.

Bulinga, uneasy in the crowd, was relieved when the uneven cobbles became more and more uneven, when the streets showed patches bare of cobbles, and became an earthen track fringed by ruins. The nearer the gate the fewer the people.

At the untended gateway the cobbles were big, uneven, split. Walking was not like walking. It was climbing on the flat, and Bulinga stumbled, twice, then slipped and was caught, for at once his arm was around her and he was asking "Are you all right?"

His unnecessary solicitude, his readiness to touch her, irritated her.

She stopped and faced him.

"As the circumstances in which you met me have now altered radically, I intend to forget all that has passed between us and to treat you merely as a traveling companion."

She stepped from the large flat stone to the dust of the road and started off along the track which led the sight away over the green and brown and golden land to a horizon whose blue distance revealed nothing and promised everything.

"How kind of you," said Dedn. "Have you perhaps forgotten I bought you with real money?"

Bulinga made the effort and controlled her impatience and irritation.

"As the circumstances in which you met me have . . ."

"Oh, I know what you mean, but still, morally, legally and indisputably you are my concubine, a possession of mine and a possession with which I do not intend to part. So much for your theories, or do you believe that, apart from the fine legal point, you are not, morally, mine?"

He stooped, picked up a small flat pebble and sent it skimming, ricocheting along the track.

"I suppose it is because you are still fanatically

yearning to mother that Gatil boy that you are, as yet, immune to my qualities."

"How do you know of Gatil?" asked Bulinga, regarding him in astonishment.

"You told me. In the palace garden in Nipsirc, sweet slave, when you were stopped from climbing the wall, sweet slave."

"Do not call me that!"

"Never yet have I met the woman I could not sway to my will."

"There is one with you now."

"You have seen so little of me. Now if I strive . . . Is that bundle heavy for you? Let me carry it. I'll treat it very carefully."

"I shall carry it myself, thank you."

"Let me know when you tire. We leave the road here."

He went ahead.

Bulinga followed him down a dip almost knee-high in bracken and, at first wondering at the cessation of conversation and soon contented that it was so, across an undulating stretch of turquoise grass stippled with small flowers.

He marched in front of her, steadily, not looking round, apparently knowing where he made for, stepping aside from small hollows, always choosing the easier path.

Clouds, almost as transparent as rice paper scraped to an exquisite thinness, seemed to have been pasted to the blue board of the sky, although inexpertly, so that their edges frayed and furled out.

Everywhere up the slopes of the hills were trees like sun-hazy green fountains.

They were making good headway.

He strode purposefully, there was no meandering, there was no conversation to slow their steps, and so far she had kept to his timing. She was still just behind him, and finding it easy. That would teach him his vaunted strength was—well, other people could do as he did.

The grass was alive with green and gold and glinting insects. Large wildflowers flaunted their complicated shapes and vivid colors and hot heady scents.

Flowers, tall in the tall grass, flowers never outside the line of vision, brushed the edge of the cloak of bleached shark's skin worn by Dedn, bent beneath the edge of Bulinga's pink dress and sprang up again inside it to brush her legs and her knees and even her thighs. Flowers worked, tickling, inside her sandals.

There were flowers on the few trees, blossom, mostly white, but high from the ground.

Unable to contain herself amidst such a natural wealth, Bulinga began to pick the flowers and even ran some distance aside when she saw one she couldn't possibly miss.

He lounged after her through the thick flowers and grass when she ran to pick some beauty she had seen, and he handed to her a bunch of white blossom which he had taken from a branch too high above her head for her to reach.

"Oh, thank you," said Bulinga breathlessly, and stood still for a moment while she arranged her booty in her hair, in the neck of her dress, in her belt and in the creases of her bundle.

Dedn was sitting, tolerantly regarding her.

"If you're hiding from the Police, you've certainly achieved your object. No one would think you anything but a small flowering bush."

Bulinga burst out laughing.

"Does it look silly? But, really, have you ever seen so many flowers all together? I just couldn't help picking them! Oh! A stream, a tiny one, down there. I'm so hot and I feel as though I might boil up any minute."

She slipped from her sandals, ran barefoot over the slope loosening her weight of flowers.

Dedn carried her bundle.

Between the flowered banks she paddled till she reached a place where it drowned her calves and the pink dress had to be held up and caught in a knot just above her knees. Then she stopped and cupped the water into her hands and laved her face with its trickling coldness.

Dedn watched her, the pearly glow of her limbs beneath the water, their length and shapeliness as she waded, the long slim grace of her feet.

When she came out the edge of her dress was wet and she shook it a little and caught up her bundle and her sandals under her arm.

There was a cloud shadow, tremulously lovely, passing over the ground just as they reached the trees which were now seen to top a moss-sided bank hanging high over a pool. Sitting, Bulinga and Dedn were undisturbed.

There were bushes on which grew berries.

Bulinga insisted they pick some, though Dedn assured her that shelter was no more than a small distance away and the berries were therefore unnecessary. Besides he wasn't sure they were ripe.

She gave a small cry as the length of her hair was caught among thorns, and then gasped as she felt his arm around her and his fingers, heavy and firm and competent, brown in the white softness of her hair as he disentangled it for her. For a moment the strength of his proximity almost overpowered her, then she murmured thanks and sat on the ground and offered him berries.

She hastily pushed a handful of berries on him, crammed several into her mouth and, head averted from him, stared down into the water.

She was sure she was blushing.

Had he noticed? Or might he think it was just the effect of wind and sun?

It was so ridiculous but his nearness had made her tremble. She was almost sure he had meant to perturb her. And of course he had also known perfectly well that she could disentangle her hair herself. And even if he had been so gallant as to do it for her he needn't have put his arm round her. Her dress was so thin that all his thoughts, certain kinds of thoughts, had communicated themselves to her from flesh to flesh.

Bulinga bit her lip and continued to outstare the high-banked oval eye of the pool.

What a queer thing water was! Bulinga watched the thick fishnet of light on the fusing green and blue and turquoise flakes and layers of the water. A continuous movement was on this pool, sequins were always gathering and flashing up to the sky and dispersing and disappearing. The pool made an eternal soft wooing sound. The surface shifted and lapped and murmured gurglingly and the green and blue and turquoise sheets continually changed their places, one with the other, so that sometimes the eye was almost dazzled by the movement as the blue took the place of the green and another strand of the gold net which the sun had superimposed on the water shimmered in between them.

The rich color scurried away again and again as Bulinga dropped little stones into it.

Dedn, smiling a little, saw the hot color fade from her cheeks and a rapt look come into her eyes.

"What are you thinking of, Bulinga?" he asked, his voice low and caressing.

"I'm looking at my reflection," she answered. "It's my face, inside out, and all broken with little lines of water."

He rose.

"Come on, child. It's time we were moving again."

Bulinga found she and Dedn were running, swiftly, near the bend in the road where she slid a little in the gravel and his hand flew out, protectingly, to steady her, through the knee-tickling grasses at the verge of the road, laughing, jumping over dips and holes, blundering through the tough coarse clumps of meadow ferns, dodging between briars and breathlessly down a green thick high-grassed slope where the drops of dew, still unvaporized in their thick green hiding places, were catapulted and spattered back onto themselves, over the lower curve of the road and over a grassy expanse to the small black trees which steadily neared them, the wind singing past their faces and small and shrill and exultant through their loose strands of hair.

A glory of white and silver-gray cumulus clouds was in the sky.

Then they were under the trees whose great roots snaked over the ground half embedded in the dun earth and Dedn was laughing down at her, the black liveness of his eyes exploring without reserve the curve of her throat and the wind-tangled sweep of her hair as she laughed up at him.

"Now to the other ridge," she cried, and at once had swung forward over grass warm and ankle deep, unable to match him though his pace was effortless, down the slope of a hill and up another till they had come to a ridge from whose height could be seen a large plain stretching to mauve distant mountains.

And flat, beyond the mountains, seen through a gap, was a line of unusual blue.

Land in the distance couldn't be like that.

She clutched his arm and pointed.

"Beyond the hills, in that gap, what is it?"

"That is the sea."

"The sea!"

The sea!

She made to plunge down the slope but his arm held her.

"There is no hurry. It is far away. But look at it well, while you can. You won't see it again till Edrigir is reached."

She stayed.

"Where is Edrigir?"

He waved away north—to the right, and she strained her eyes though there was nothing to be seen.

The sea, she gasped to herself.

She felt that the end of her journeyings was in sight.

But to reach there she must be practical.

She looked to him, for leadership.

The slant of the ridge was steep but rugged and easily negotiable; knit with rocks and tough grass. Dawn blue flowers had grown everywhere among that grass.

An extraordinarily lithe stream coiled through the plain. From here it was such a fragilely thin and twisting stream that it seemed possible it had once been blown into its innumerable coilings by a strong wind.

"We go down here?" asked Bulinga.

"Yes, come on," he replied.

Bulinga shook free his hand and scrambled down the cliffside, determined to descend so swiftly and competently that he could not possibly offer any help.

At the bottom she slid and his hand steadied her.

She turned to him, but as he seemed to expect her to speak she maintained a silence.

They walked briskly, the warmth at least of his nearness comforting her for the afternoon was growing chilly.

The sky, she thought, looked almost as if it were gold, which she could see between the massive purple clouds, but, shifting her focus, she realized that this gold was no more than the reflection of the sun against the purple cloud edges.

A heliotrope shadow fell behind each grass blade, each fallen leaf; every gnarling of the tree trunks, every vein in the soft smooth *eau de nil* leaves, was outlined in gold.

The sun set.

The sky of evening was an effervescent welter of red and gold and orange and yellow and fiery cloud; gnats, caught into the light, like points of flame swung and dithered before those clouds so like enormous fires; the sun, a large salamander, climbed down slowly between the clouds, flared and died.

Night came.

A small hostile chill wind skirled into being.

Bulinga shivered.

It was an involuntary action, and at once she felt something placed about her shoulders. It was Dedn's white shark's-skin cloak taking the place of the marten she no longer possessed.

Round her, under the cloak, his arm was a heavy bare protective band of warmth.

Now, when there was less light, the richness of the sky was dull, under its purple, with a sullen color which was an almost yellow. In the sky stars had been pricked in breathless numbers, showers of points, a white delicacy thrown haphazardly into glinting existence, unmatched in size and irregularly placed. A breeze filtered down between them, fanning their light and causing their twinkling, and came to the earth and became larger and contemptuously tossed at the trees and swooped into a madness in the grass through which it swirled and slorled and ruthlessly forced the weight of its way.

Bulinga's hair was ice blue beneath the palpitating flicker of the huge white and blue stars.

Dedn held her close and the softness of her did not fight against the new curve of his arm.

A moth, which seemed no more than the wraith of a moth, flowed past, passed in less than a moment, flowing on the curve of the wind.

Through the dark wild lonely chilliness of the night Dedn guided her between the grass and high rocks, through the gusting gurgling ominous moan of the wind, past hollow logs in whose phosphorescent interiors were blue cobwebs sapphired with dew, under trees whose foliage struggled sonorously to refuse passage to the wind—a battle of immortals who cared nothing and knew nothing of the humans who passed beneath them. Dedn guided Bulinga to a group of trees whose bulks were thick about the timber walls of a hut.

"This is where we stay the night," he said. "Tomorrow we will go on to Edrigir over the plain." And the wide band of gold on his arm gleamed as he pointed in the direction of Edrigir.

Secure in the circle of his arm, without protest Bulinga accompanied him into the hut.

29

Men, with weapons, stood within the doorway and Bulinga clutched at Dedn's arm and Dedn laughed.

He pushed her gently to the thick black fur one of the soldiers hastily spread before the charcoal fire.

"The lord Hylun?" the Prince asked.

"He has not yet returned, Your Dignity," a soldier said. He paused. "He is long overdue."

Dedn seated himself beside Bulinga.

"These Religious curs become more and more of a nuisance," he said. "My own horse disappeared from where I left him. No," he went on in answer to the look on the soldier's face. "It could not have strayed. It was taken. But I don't grudge the High One an occasional horse. It is a little victory. What sort of banquet have you prepared me? Do I smell fish?"

"Yes, Your Dignity," answered a man from the corner. "They are almost cleaned and will soon grill. The stream you showed us is populated by trout of a most unusual size. And there are flat cakes Hilp has baked."

"Good. There has been no one seen about here?"

"No, Your Dignity," replied another soldier. "We have seen no one and no one could have seen us. We have been most careful."

"Someone is not being careful now," remarked the Prince.

All looked at him, questioningly—then all heard the erratic beat made by a galloping horse.

The door was thrown open and, carrying drawn swords, three of the men ran out.

Dedn smiled at her.

"It will be Hylun," he assured her. "No one else would gallop to here. Only he knows we are here."

Bulinga smiled in answer.

She was now warm. And comfortable.

There were trout spread on a rough-made wire grating above the fire, the pile of flat cakes near her made one's teeth water and there were here so many men within a small hut that she need have no fear of Dedn's intentions. Besides she was gaining a new respect for him. He was obviously liked and admired. He fitted, naturally. He spoke to the men without descending to their level and without emphasizing his level. She saw that he could rule men.

She liked him like this, a soldier braving the forces of the Religious Police and the plans of the High One.

He sat, contemplating the trout, and, one would say, oblivious of the horse stampings and jinglings and hoarse loud whispers, all noises which entered the hut through the half-open door.

There was a flurry of legs and dark brown cloak and the lord Hylun was on one knee beside him.

"Alone?" said Dedn pleasantly.

The lord Hylun glanced quickly at her; wondering she supposed, if he could speak freely before her.

"The—the party follows me. But there is this I considered I should bring to you quickly."

The Prince took from him the slim roll of silk and broke the seal.

"Get your cloak off, man, and give yourself rest; there'll be no peace here soon," he said and unrolled the silk to read it.

Bulinga eyed the trout.

The soldier Hilp re-entered, dashed to the fire and turned the fish.

Bulinga smiled at him and received in return a boyish grin.

"You are hungry, Ladyness?"

She nodded, vigorously.

With scale-silvered fingers he broke the trout in two, placed each half on a flat cake from the pile and handed them to her.

Dedn held one palm out and continued reading.

"Yes, Your Dignity," said Hilp and placed a generous portion for him.

Bulinga looked round the small log-walled room.

She wondered if he'd had the hut built. It was new and clean, or seemed to be so. And what a delightful idea to have a little gurgling stream running over the grass-grown floor, over in the corner where Hilp was.

They were all inside now. Eating. Except Hilp who buried himself in the corner, cleaning trout, stacks of them, and stopping now and then to stir a mixture in his helmet which was held upright beside him by its long spike stuck into the ground.

Dedn removed from his lips a small bone which had escaped Hilp's fingers.

"You'll have a companion soon," he said.

Hylun had risen—and was leaving the hut, so too were the soldiers. Hilp brought two huge leaves, one bearing several cleansed and flour-wrapped fish, the other a pile of shaped but uncooked cakes. He placed them near the fire and followed the others from the hut.

The door was pulled shut.

"Who is coming?" asked Bulinga.

"A lady I knew in Nipsirc. I don't think you know her."

Bulinga placed the remains of her fish, there was little left, on the large stone which protruded from the fireplace. She wiped her fingers on the grass of the floor. Her eyes never left his.

"Do I not? What is her name?"

"Lelahla."

She sprang to her feet and strode to the wall and back and looked down at him in fury.

The strength of her objection amazed her almost as much as it amazed Dedn. He still sat looking up at her.

Her eyes blazed down at him.

"Why was I not told this was expected?" she demanded.

Dedn looked up at her, cool amusement entered his eyes and Bulinga's fury made her tremble.

"My sweet slave, believe me your annoyance that we are not to be alone is fully shared by me. But," he spread his fingers, "how was I to know I was to meet you in Tayrb, and bring you back with me? I did not know you were there. They were entirely other matters which led me so fortuitously to your bedroom in the inn. But never let it upset you, this visit of Lelahla. In any case I could not be a party to the idyll you expected between us this night."

"You are spoiled to all decency," Bulinga told him hotly. "There cannot in all the stretches of land here and beyond the water be anyone more vain. Is it for nothing I have said all I have ever said to you! You insult me with your continual and repeated innuendos. I have over and over again told you that never will I permit you to touch me."

Dedn's long arm grasped her ankle and pulled her down.

"Sit there, my beauty," he commanded, "and listen to me, now. Until this day, my sweet slave, I thought your scruples sincere. Perhaps they were, once."

"Your own lecherous nature misleads you. To you I am a slave, and nothing more. I have today, as always, refused your attentions. Today I have given no single sign, nor said one word that could make you believe so . . ."

Dedn picked up one of the cleaned fish from the leaf it lay upon and swung it idly by its tail.

"That will not do, Bulinga. You are not talking to some callow easily-imposed-on youth from the traders stalls of Nipsirc. Understand me now, my slave Prin-

:ess, I am Dedn, Prince of the House which rules all
:hese lands, despite, let me add, our funeral-faced
friend the High One, and I am not to be imposed upon.
My experience is wide, and varied, and I have forgotten
:o count my women, though I will admit I've never had
one so beautiful as you."

He deftly caught her hand as it swung to his face
and held it down among the long grasses.

"No, no," he laughed. "You do not treat me like
that either. Let be, my sweetling. By the Scales, I tell
you I understand! There is no need for your fury! Had
I known I was to find you I . . . But there'll be other
nights."

Bulinga stopped railing at him.

Hurt entered her like the swift unexpected thrust of
a dagger blade.

He was like that. She had known. She should have
remembered. All this day, while she had thought of
nothing but the fact that they were companions, fugitives together, he had been noting how she allowed him
to touch her—even coolly measuring for how long—
and what were her reactions, and drawing self-satisfied
inferences.

Dedn's head turned towards the door as he saw from
her face that Lelahla had come.

He sprang to his feet and took her hands, held her at
arm's length and admired her.

"It is such a small room, but we will soon transform
it," Lelahla's husky voice intoned, comfortingly. She
withdrew her hands and turned about as her two maids
and her litter bearers and attendants crushed through
the narrow doorway bearing loads of draperies, furs,
cushions, rugs, huge candles in holders, coil after coil
of thick silken cords with enormous tassels, for festoon-
ing, and a great mirror swinging in an ornate stand,
and centered in each of the bright panes of glass a
carved, gilded and enamelled rosette.

The soldier Hilp frantically leaped for the corner and
retrieved his helmet and other things and Lelahla from
where she stood directed the garnishing of the little hut.

Dedn had said no word.

Bulinga marveled, almost enviously, at Lelahla's
dress.

Diaphanous drapery fell from her shoulders, and
above that from a jeweled topknot high on her head.
Her throat was bare of ornament and her bodice was a
low piece of thin gathered stuff. A short skirt of lam-
bent golden cloth reached not even to her knees and
from below that were full trousers of a semi-transpar-
ent, rather stiff black material striped with black rib-
bon. These shameless trousers were caught to the ankle
with slim black bows.

As there were now rugs and masses of cushions covering the grass Lelahla had stepped out of her green
and gold sandals and her bare feet twinkled round the
room as she tugged hangings and ornaments into place
and considered possible better arrangements of the huge
colored candles. She trod the cushions carelessly, sink-
ing into them, and each of her nails, on hands and feet,
was painted a different gleaming color.

Now the litter bearers and the soldiers and the attendants had gone.

Lelahla turned to the Prince, spreading out her
hands, pleased with herself and her work.

"I . . ." began the Prince, and stopped.

Lelahla had twisted about as her maids entered bearing wide ribboned trays.

Odds and ends, ivory hairbrushes and hand-mirrors,
little caskets from which escaped ropes of jewels,
dishes of ornamental imitation fruit and flowers, knick-
knacks and bijouterie were spattered by a lavish hand
about the room.

And the maids again left.

The lady Lelahla swooped to a pile of cushions, the
view she gave of her back cleverly deliberate, Bulinga
was certain. Then—there was the lady Lelahla spread
out, in a most languorous pose, atop and among the
adeptly shaded cushions, looking across at them from
perfectly green eyes and, so quiet was it after all the
turmoil, almost convincing the two who watched her

...at the room had always been like this and that she ...ad always been here, waiting for them, waiting to welcome them to comfort and . . .

Bulinga pulled herself together with an effort.

"Dedn! Your Dignity!" Lelahla hummed. "I am ...eased you are with me again. It has been most boring ...ithout you. So you found her again! I am glad. It ...ust have been convenient to you when in Tayrb, but ...ow we are rejoined she won't be needed. What shall ...e do with the child? Sit down, my dear," she said to ...ulinga, her kindness momentary and uninterested.

Bulinga saw that Lelahla's attitude contained not a ...ot of professional jealousy. She was sincerely incapa...le of believing that any other woman could be desir...ble to a man if she, herself, were available.

"Yes, sit down, you must be tired," said Dedn, and ...ulinga found herself exhaustedly sitting beside him ...n the cushions. She felt like a child, staying up with ...vo adults long after her proper bedtime. They had so ...uch obvious vitality. She had none.

"You have traveled all the way from Nipsirc?" ...elahla asked her with what Bulinga considered sheer ...upidity.

"Yes," said Bulinga tiredly.

"Poor Bulinga." Dedn caressed the fingers of her ...and which was near him. "You've had a wearing day ...ut you won't be needed tonight."

Bulinga snatched away her fingers and regarded him ...ith hate and loathing.

The platelike leaf of wet fish was near to hand. She ...aught it up, saw the surprise in his eyes and threw it ... hard as she could.

It missed him.

They both stood.

"Oh, but you are contemptible," Bulinga told him. ...er voice, husky with emotion as she began to speak, ...ecame cold and restrained and all the ancient Kings of ...vo royal lines looked out from her eyes.

"Often I wished," she said slowly, "to have you at

my father's court to see you slowly flayed. But now—
would not. You are too contemptible."

Without the advice of Lelahla's shocked gasp B
linga knew she had said too much—then the star
anger died from his eyes and punctiliously he took th
half step back which was her due but which he ha
never accorded her.

"I regret that I must leave you here," he said. "B
my men will remain with you."

There was no expression—not in his voice nor i
his face nor in any line of him.

Silent, Bulinga watched him part Lelahla's curtain
and they fell into place again behind him.

Bulinga's hand stirred, fingers loose, a movemen
which meant nothing and yet seemed to her to expre
appreciation of finality.

Lelahla's voice said something—but Bulinga didn
hear.

The door opened again. The curtains swung apart.

But it was the lord Hylun who stood there.

"His Dignity Prince Dedn," said Hylun, evenly, "d
sires me to present his regrets that he may not stay, b
this night he must be in the city of Datames. I am
ensure your safe escort to Edrigir."

30

Bulinga leaned against the tree trunk.

The lord Hylun and Hilp were darknesses in dar
ness.

Hylun was nearer to her. He stood, quite close, l
side her.

In his hands Dedn's white shark's-skin cloak waved in the breeze like a waist-high wraith.

"Your Tranquilness, I was expressly instructed by His Dignity to ensure that his cloak reached you. The night is a chill one. These breezes from the sea, Tranquilness, are treacherous."

"Thank you. I will take the cloak," said Bulinga.

She moved from the tree and permitted the long cloak to be fitted about her and fastened in front.

"Why do you so address me?" she asked.

"His Dignity Prince Dedn advised me that you were so entitled. I have only four men, Tranquilness, His Dignity having need of a man with him. It will therefore be difficult for us to attend you with anything approaching the requirements of your rank." He paused, and said lamely, "The other men at the moment are assisting the lady Lelahla's people to repack."

"Yes. Yes, of course," agreed Bulinga.

"The man Hilp, here, Your Tranquilness, will be your personal guard and servant until I can get the whole party moving."

"Thank you," said Bulinga.

He left. She knew he had bowed. Hylun was one who would omit none of the niceties, even in the darkness.

So she was alone, with Hilp of course, and she could hardly see him.

She had been rent by emotion, pulled down almost to the dregs of living. Now, when it was all over, he had commanded his men to treat her as the Princess she was.

She had at last convinced him. She was free! Not, she hastily told herself, not that she had ever, even for a moment, considered herself to be his slave, but he had. And now he didn't.

Well. That was good.

He could have his Lelahla. He could have anyone else he set his eyes on. It was no matter to her, though she did think it was rather disgraceful that he should be so—so animal in his desires.

Viewed as a companion, as an associate in adventure, she could see he would be attractive. He was strong and courageous, he made light of dangers which to a lesser man would be overpowering. That side of him she liked.

And he could be kind, even.

He need not have sent his cloak to her. It was a sacrifice, for a cloak was a thing necessary to everyone.

Anyway that was something done and finished with.

She need worry no longer about him, and moreover she was bound on the last stage of her journey to Edrigir on the coast. In Edrigir she could get a ship, a ship to take her wherever she willed.

She straightened her shoulders against the tree and smiled happily at the stars.

"Hilp," she said.

"Yes, Your Tranquilness."

"Are there any of those cakes left?"

"Yes, Your Tranquilness."

"Could—could I have some?"

"Yes, Your Tranquilness."

"And, Hilp . . ."

"Yes, Your Tranquilness."

"I suppose there aren't any trout cooked, are there?"

"Yes, Your Tranquilness. Shall I bring you some?"

"Yes, please."

"Yes, Your Tranquilness."

She heard him move away to the hut.

How nice it was to be "Tranquilness" again.

The stars were so beautiful up there in the sky.

She wished the sea could be seen from here. It would be so wonderful—that day when she would stand by the sea. Her mother had told her of the sea—but it was apparently something not to be visualized. She could only imagine it as a great deal of water, and a great deal of water was hard to imagine when all that had been seen together in one place was a pool twenty or so feet from side to side.

Bulinga had nothing to guide her as to the hut's direction; there was no sign of a light.

Undoubtedly Hilp had been pressed into service at the hut. All the lord Hylun's endeavors to free him would have no effect. She could imagine the turmoil there, packing everything under the direction of Leahla.

She would go back to them.

Bulinga lifted her bundle and moved cautiously clear of the trees. She remembered there had been upjutting roots but she seemed to have maneuvered these successfully for her sandaled feet met no obstructions.

Away from the trees it seemed to be lighter, sufficiently so for her to move more easily and with a more rapid gait.

Bulinga wandered on for a few minutes.

Her feet carried her down the slope.

She turned and hurried on; she must really hurry or they would not find her.

In a moment she stopped.

Here was no slope!

She was lost! She must keep calm and endeavor to return to the trees.

She turned and ran as hard as she could, her breath hurting, her eyes smarting, and rhythmically gnawing at her that never-to-be-assuaged mortification—the consciousness of having been a fool.

Bulinga stopped running, paused a moment, and walked on.

She stopped again and shook her head sadly.

And not only had she no least idea of where to go but she thought it more than possible that her absence had not yet been discovered by those at the hut.

She stopped herself thinking of them. Nothing was to be gained from visualizing the anxiety of the lord Hylun, or the distress of Hilp, or the indifference of Lelahla.

Bulinga swung her bundle over her shoulder.

If she could find shelter of some kind she would like to sleep. Her fingers fondled the pangolin at her throat. Soon she might reach a copse or even bushes amongst which she would crawl and feel safer than if she merely lay down here, out in the open. And tomorrow if they hadn't found her she would make her way to the coast. It wasn't too far away. That was a comforting thought.

Bulinga allowed herself many rests during the long night; cold comfortless rests. Twice among bracken there was a boulder against which to lean, and although fears of meeting animals kept coming to her she met none, although once something large moved among tall grasses behind her but moved away in the direction opposite to that she was taking.

When dawn came she lay down, wrapped in the cloak she was so grateful for, and slept, and after a while the wind awoke her and she struggled up, stiff and tired, and hungry so that memory of Hilp's cakes was a torture, and she saw, nearer than they had been yesterday, the mountains beyond which lay the sea.

The stark grasses bowed to the wind which screamed through their matted clumps. Slowly, over the waste of the plain, a red and yellow speck approached. It came nearer and nearer, winding and zig-zagging over the dreary russet dunes, sometimes out of sight but always approaching, steadily. Soon the yellow horse and its red-clad rider were beside her. The horse's long mane was chalk-colored with dust.

"Ai!" the rider called her a greeting. "Are you alone among the dunes?"

"Can you tell me the way to Edrigir?" Bulinga shouted in return.

"Follow the land's curve to the forward of you, and past the seven tall trees."

Bulinga thanked him, and the man, a trapper of small game, she guessed, seeing the pelts hanging at his saddle, wheeled his horse and disappeared again among the dunes to her right.

Bulinga trudged on doggedly. She floundered into a big puddle and emerged dripping and cursing, wet to the thighs.

A fine mist of drizzle, an undertone to the rain, had come down like an intangible colorless screen. In the distance the mountains lay like great wretched monsters attempting to crouch to the earth and to ignore the miserable weather.

Bulinga walked, bending her head to force herself against the wind, and all the time she felt the drum of the rain against her into the hardly resisting almost absorbent surface of her cloak. It had long ago become soaked and now adhered to her legs in clinging wrinkles. Her bare ankles stung where the rain splashed and spat and slashed viciously at them; puddles started up right beneath her feet and she splashed into them before she realized they were there, and the water between her toes squelched at every step.

Bulinga looked up and there were tall trees. Seven of them.

Bulinga went up to them and saw that the plain fell beyond them—that they were, in fact, on the brink of a dip.

She began to scramble down, wet clay transferring itself in layers to her dress, when voices made her pause and she saw with a start of alarm and caution that there were people in the valley.

A party of men, all wearing substantial brown cloaks, were standing round in a circle listening to the orders of a fat man foreshortened to Bulinga's sight. Another, a more spare man, less readily discernible, stood beside him.

At the same instant that her sight gave her all this the sound of her slithering had been heard. She turned swiftly upward again through the gray drizzle but men sprang after her, and she was jerked and dragged roughly down the slope again, through the ranks of the ruffianly Police, to the fat man who even advanced a little to meet her.

"Were you spying? Or are you merely a vagabond?" he asked her, his tone, almost deceptively, indulgent.

Bulinga looked up at him and found time to be insulted at the swiftness of his recognition, for at this third meeting there was mud on her face and in her hair, her dress was the draggled dress of a wandering slattern, and in spite of the ruthless grip of the Police she still held not only her limp green bundle but a dilapidated truss of vegetation—twigs and stems and tangled leaves, all bearing berries which she had meant to eat when she had her greatest need.

"My dear young lady," said Stapo, "what a pleasant surprise! It is a pleasant surprise, is it not, my dear young lady? So very, unexpected. What a long way you have traveled, have you not? My men, I think you may release this young woman's arms. She is not—er—likely to run away, at the moment. Come and meet the others, my dear."

It was amazing, Bulinga thought, that, no matter how gaily and widely his mouth smiled, his eyes could never change from that hard black flatness.

Then Bulinga realized that behind Stapo stood Carpen—and there was another figure. It *must* be Gatil. But he was farther back, the man who must be Gatil, and—but that moment Carpen spoke to him and he went several steps away to speak to some of the Police.

Stapo pushed her towards Carpen.

"Look what we have here," said Stapo. "This I may permit myself to think a good omen. Eh?"

"So it is you," said Carpen soberly. His mouth twisted. "A good omen! It is possible that you may be right, but if I were addicted to a belief in such inanities I would prefer to consider your captive an indication of failure."

"Failure! We cannot fail!"

"So do I believe. I was but pointing out to you, apparently not to your comprehension, that for you success does not follow possession of this young woman."

"I see. Yes. Now that is something I hadn't thought. I was so very pleased, my dear," he said, turning to Bulinga, "to meet you again," and he even bowed.

Abruptly he turned back to Carpen.

"What then do you suggest? Shall I have her killed?"

Carpen's face showed no emotion. He shrugged, and

adjusted the cloak which was too wide at his shoulders and had slipped from him.

"Do as you will. It is not my custom to obscure my mind with unnecessary thoughts. We have our duty to the High One. Our instructions were explicit."

"Then shall I let her go?"

Bulinga looked at Carpen with scorn. It was vexing that he paid no attention to her.

"For whatever action you take the responsibility is yours. This only will I say. I do not believe her to be worth the trouble involved in guarding her till she may be brought before the High One for sentence, even were he interested in her fate. Moreover I much doubt if he would be interested even in hearing she had fallen to your hands. And what is more she cannot now be virginal. To expect that is to be a fool."

Tired and dispirited though she was, and intent more on discovering where Gatil was, Bulinga heard the last phrases.

She started forward.

"I . . ." she began—and her wits came back to her and she stopped.

But Stapo had heard enough.

"Are you so?" he said smoothly. "Now I, my dear young lady, have a larger experience than my friend Carpen, and I am disposed to believe you."

He looked at the back of Carpen who had moved away.

"Ah. The rain has stopped. In a little while, you will see, the Sun will show his face—and there it is. Perhaps that anyway I may take as a good omen. You have cost me much, my dear, one way and another, and I think, I really believe, I can turn this meeting to good account. Ha, Gatil. Come over here."

It *was* Gatil.

Bulinga stood, demurely, waiting for the light she would see in his eyes when they met hers.

Then she remembered her appearance and—but what could she do? Other than to brush the mud-caked hair from her forehead.

He looked at her.

There was no light in his eyes—they were dull.

"I want you to make yourself personally responsible for the safe custody of this young lady," Stapo told him. . . .

Bulinga's mouth trembled.

Gatil had looked away!

But his eyes came back now—and—and he *did* know her.

His eyes were wide open.

"Oh, why must he look like that?" Bulinga demanded of herself.

Wrinkles crossed her brow as her hurt deepened. Her head shook a little in dismay. He seemed not to care.

". . . I have a use for her. In Tayrb," Stapo was saying. "They will pay much for her and she has slipped from me before. True, *not* before I made a quite profitable transaction, but she is an adventurous young lady. Watch her. Make sure you keep her with us. I myself will watch as well as I can. But we must be off."

"Biltan," he called, as he moved away.

"Biltan! The cylinders are dry? Good. Carpen, my friend. We are on the move. Or, at least, we ought to be."

Gatil watched him go. Then:

"Princess Bulinga!" he said. "He knows you?"

"Oh, Gatil! Gatil! I knew we would meet again."

He brightened.

"You know, you are quite dirty," he said. "I wouldn't have known you."

Bulinga smiled.

"And I had to pretend not to know you in front of Stapo. He's a swine. Does my uncle know you are here?"

She nodded.

"Oh. I wonder what I'd better do?"

The wrinkles had come in Bulinga's brow again. Deep inside her something moaned "Oh, Gatil!"

"Anyway I'd better do as Stapo says, so come on." He gripped her arm and began to walk, and Bulinga, quite numbly, went with him.

"It's difficult to know what to do," Gatil said. "You don't want to go to Tayrb, do you? I'm glad we're out of that hollow. It's been foul there for the last two hours. We stayed there for the night and all got wet. It was a stupid place to pick for camping. And Stapo and my uncle have both been swine about it all. And we're all thirsty too for the water-jars were broken when three of the Police fell on them. But we'll get a drink soon when we reach the river, it's just over there. Are you thirsty? Though I don't know how we're supposed to cross it. I suppose you saw I'm in the Police now. My uncle Carpen had that arranged. I didn't want to be, didn't like the idea at all, but it's not bad, because I'm an officer, quite a good officer too, and all I have to do is tell them what Stapo says they have to do, though I wish he weren't so swinishly oily when he tells me things. One of these days I'll tick him off, that is if I don't lose my temper first. I've a very hot temper. Did you know? And if he does make me lose it, he'll soon rue it."

"Poor Gatil," thought Bulinga. "He's such a baby in some ways."

She wished she were less tired. But this bundle was heavy—and awkward.

She looked about, not really interested to observe that there were approximately fifty Police, all rough-seeming men, though most of them weren't big. They kept in a rough formation of three parties, moving in no particular order, but merely each party behind its officer.

The sun was drying the mud, not only beneath her feet but on her.

She rubbed off lumps of it from her arms and dress but that made more of a mess because it just wasn't dry enough yet.

Now, ahead, she could see the river he'd mentioned

—a gray sheet, bluer in the middle, and it must be quite wide. Gatil would get his drink soon, poor boy.

Another thought, a more cheering one. She would be able to have some sort of wash, be able to clean herself a little.

Gatil talked on.

Wouldn't Dedn laugh to see her bedraggled like this? She smiled as she thought of him, leaning back, laughing, and then he would do something about it. Not at once, perhaps. He would do it as and when he pleased. But he was so competent.

It was unfortunate that she had no other dress— yet there were ways of surmounting all difficulties and she believed she could deal with this one. She had Dedn's cloak. If she walked right into the water, slipped her dress down and off, and washed it as well as herself, she could dry it in the sun as they walked, just wearing the cloak of course, and when it was dry, well—put it on! Perhaps she could ask Gatil to carry her bundle while she saw to it that the dress was dried properly all over.

But she was hungry.

She was very hungry.

She looked at the twigs still in her hand and threw them from her in disgust.

31

The rope across the river swayed and swung and dipped and came up again wet and shining, streams trailing from it to drop whitely into the water and be whirled away.

It was a very broad river but shallow here, where,

as could be seen, cattle in droves were accustomed to
cross.

Bulinga sat on the bank and munched at a loaf of
rather dry bread. Beside her she had a little heap of
enormous faelberries, and spread out before her the
pink dress lay in the sun and dried. Washing hadn't
improved its color, for the clay stains had been hard
to move. The pink was now very patchy.

Men shouted and ran about, for the most part to
no end that she could see, and those at each end of
the rope made a fuss of holding it. It was all rather
reminiscent of boys in Grood playing in a streaming
gutter.

Gatil's party had waded across with the help of
the rope. The rest were still on the other side, making
a raft from bales of brushwood and rushes. They
could take all day over it and she still would be uninterested. This was a heavenly rest. She was bathed
and clean, her hair would soon be dry—so would her
dress—she had food—and she had Gatil with her—
not exactly with her but not far away, and he'd said
he would soon be back with her and would explain
what was happening.

Wading up to the armpits through the river had
been fun, except that clothes were rather in the way.
She hadn't felt safe. Twice her feet had slipped and
once she had screamed when she was sure a fish had
nibbled at her—still, with the rope to hold to and all
those men about there was little expectation of being
swept away.

Bulinga squashed a whole faelberry into her mouth,
pulled away the stalk and looked up to see Gatil at
her side. She was unable to do more than nod and
pat the earth with her hand.

"They are making a raft," Gatil told her.

Bulinga tried with her eyes to express a polite interest.

"It will take them a while yet, but they will manage
it all right. Isn't the weather good?" Gatil went on.

She nodded.

In a moment she would have the stone free of the flesh then she could push it out, with her tongue, to her fingers and be able to answer him. These were enormous faelberries.

"I didn't think the weather would be so good today. I thought it might rain all day," said Gatil.

Bulinga made agreement noises and waved to the faelberries.

She meant it as an invitation to have one, but either he didn't understand the wave or disliked the look of them or never ate faelberries.

"I'm glad it's not going to rain all day," said Gatil.

Bulinga's eyes rolled sideways in annoyance at him.

To have at such a time a whole mouthful impossible to dispose of without waste was bad enough, but to have to hear all this about the weather was to add a burden to the day.

The stone came out and she threw it into the river and wiped her finger tips in the grass.

"Why must they make a raft? Is it for Stapo?"

"Well, yes, in a way, but that's not really the reason; you see we must keep the cylinders dry."

"What cylinders?" Bulinda asked, turning over the faelberries to make sure they were ripe all over.

Gatil's feet shuffled a little.

"Well, we're not supposed to tell anyone but they're the gas cylinders."

"Oh, I see," said Bulinga. She broke the last piece of crust in two and offered him half.

He took it without a word. She looked much better when cleaned up, he decided, almost as beautiful as he'd thought when he'd seen her first in Grood. But there was a difference, somewhere. Anyway she didn't appeal to him so much now. Though, of course, he could see she was still much attracted to him.

He chewed the bread stolidly.

He was inclined to forget she was a princess. He still felt that he should make some use of her feeling for him; by the Yolk, he might yet, but for two things. He hadn't been very successful before and it made him feel a fool when he was with her. Also there had been a rather important discussion between the three officers, himself and his uncle and Stapo, while Bulinga and the men were wading the river, and he had been given to understand by Carpen that he must behave with circumspection. Stapo, the swine, had intimated, in that jolly tone he couldn't bear at all, that if Bulinga were permitted to escape or if anything untoward happened to her before Edrigir was vanquished, then he, Stapo, would take action—with the aid of the Police.

"Stapo says he is taking you to the new Temple in Tayrb," he blurted out.

"Yes," said Bulinga.

"You—you don't mind?"

"I'm not going."

"But he will make you go."

Bulinga placed a hand on his, and then took it away.

"Gatil, he cannot make me. I know he will try, or at least that this is what he plans. But before now he has planned—and yet as you see I am here and not in the Temple of Nipsirc."

"Yes," agreed Gatil. "But . . ."

"So I am not really worried about what he plans. I think he is a fat slug. And I am not afraid of him. Besides . . ."

"Besides what?" he asked after a moment, when she went no further.

"Besides I have some friends who would soon get me away from there. And deal rather hardly with Stapo too. They probably will in any case."

Gatil smiled to himself.

He didn't place much faith in that sort of talk. He was himself too addicted to it to be taken in.

Bulinga placed her hand over his again.

"Oh, Gatil," she said, leaning close to him, "I am so glad to have found you again. Ever since I left you that morning with your uncle Carpen, whom I cannot like, I have thought of you and planned against the time when we should meet again, for I was quite certain we should, and you see I am right. I cannot be-

lieve that we have been so brought together just for
the sport of the Little Gods of Things and Places.
And as that is so, you can see why I do not fear Stapo
and Tayrb. You see, don't you? Once your uncle
Carpen would have been a menace to me, but he i
no longer interested in me, nor would the High One be
He was a thin-souled, mean-spirited man and I an
glad Dedn hit him in the face with the ring. Perhaps
I should tell you, too, that I think your other uncle
Vathok, has been eaten."

"Has he?" said Gatil, almost politely, his mind still
trying to understand some of the other things she had
said.

"Yes. I don't think they would have let him get
away."

He nodded.

Blast Stapo to Hell and all his threats! Why
shouldn't a man who had a lovely princess in love with
him make love to her when he wanted to?

She was very desirable. Very different from the girl
he knew in Nipsirc; and even that one in Ulkerie
who'd wanted to have him marry her, wasn't so at
tractive as this one. Now that she was washed h
could see she was really beautiful.

He glanced down.

He pretended to be thinking and kept his eyelid
lowered. That way he could steal looks at her nake
leg which the white cloak thing wasn't completely hid
ing.

He looked across at the other end of the long rope
The raft was still building.

He looked about him.

His own men were mostly watching him. At leas
they were looking his way. He could do nothing now
But wild schemes were revolving about in his brain
Not schemes, desires. They were not yet formed int
plans. Yet surely he could do something. He almos
groaned at the growing intensity of the wish. She ex
uded a sort of scent which aggravated him.

He would do it. In Edrigir he would find the means

and in the meantime he must go all out to fan her desire of him.

Her eyes looking at him were a pure purple. Her hair, dry now, was white and soft and radiant. Great Yolk, but she was beautiful! Her chin—her cheeks were beautiful and rosy and soft yet with a firmness. And those lips!

Gatil's tongue slipped out and ran wetly over his own lips.

He had to look away. He must not let her see what emotions were in his eyes.

Bulinga saw that he was looking across the river. She too looked there.

The raft was being launched. Two men were between it and the stretched rope. Others waded in to help guide it. Stapo, helped by many hands, took his place on the raft.

Deep enjoyment of a ludicrous sight bubbled far inside Bulinga's eyes as she turned, smiling, to Gatil.

"What are they so careful of?" she asked. "Stapo, or the cylinders? They must surely be valuable, and why carry them about the country?"

Gatil gathered all the knowledge in his mind. He could impress her, here.

"They are a very special weapon with which we have already utterly conquered the court and city of Gabebal. They were found within the Temple in Nipsirc. They are very very ancient. Oh, eons old. But if they are allowed to become wet they are of no use. We have only two with us. We dare not let them get wet."

Bulinga's hand withdrew from his.

She remembered Gabebal.

What hellish things were these that could produce the scenes she had met in Gabebal? That awful, strangely pitiful death that had filled all the rooms of the palace.

There rose in her mind a vision of the dead Queen —her wonderful eyes blank and cold.

"How—did you do it?" she asked, in a small voice.

"There is nothing more simple," he said enthusiastically. "We simply throw the cylinders to the floor
We have to run out like anything then for a—a vapor
a sort of frothing steam comes out and goes every
where—and kills everyone—in a moment. But yo
can't see it after the first moment, you see, and al
the people just do nothing, but we don't—we keep a
fold of our clothes, which we have made wet, over
our mouth and nostrils, and it gets in a little to us
but not dangerously. But, of course, all the other people don't know to do that so they are killed."

Bulinga's lips were tight. She swallowed.

"That is what you did in Gabebal."

"Oh yes. Just like that. We took all the children
away before it got to them. Some of them died later
but we got most of them to Nipsirc where there was
a special observance in the Great Temple and the
High One thanked the Sun for them all, so that they
could all be brought up, from now on, in the True
Religion."

"And that is what you're going to do in Edrigir?"

Gatil preened himself.

"Yes. We'll soon have them understand that we
won't accept from them any excuses or—or anything
like that. Either they surrender to us and accept the
New Religion and a governing body which will ensure
decent living—or else we wipe them out."

Bulinga looked sideways at him.

This was appalling—it was vile!

Surely he could see the viciousness of it all! But he
couldn't, of course, otherwise he wouldn't talk so
glibly.

"She's quite beautiful and very attractive and she'll
belong to me before the end of this trip anyway,"
boasted Gatil to himself. "Even when she was dirty
and soaked in mud she managed to look a beauty!"

He convinced himself that he had always known
that.

"The Group Leader Stapo is almost across to us,"
said a voice in Gatil's ear.

He looked up at Biltan.

"Eh! Is he? All right. I knew. I'm coming."

He got up on his feet.

Bulinga wondered why she had never noticed be-
ore that his feet were so big. She averted her face
from them and ignored his downstretched hands. She
could get up by herself.

32

"It is appropriate," observed Stapo, "that we stop, for
our meal, in the Temple."

"But it is a *ruined* Temple," pointed out Gatil.

"Yes, my dear boy. At the moment it is. But we
will deal with that in the near future. That will be
your province, friend Carpen, and I suppose you will
desire to keep this boy of yours here with you."

Carpen swung back his cloak.

"That is not what I had intended. If you are going
to Tayrb and I am remaining here I would expect that
our third officer would be required to proceed with
all reasonable speed to the High One. He will be
awaiting a report."

"So he will. And he will get it. I'll send Biltan."

Carpen eyed Stapo with distaste.

Bulinga found in herself some admiration for Stapo.

Carpen produced his knife and chopsticks, as three
of the Police bore dishes towards them.

"Here is food, you may stop biting your nails now,
Gatil."

"Ah! Real dishes!" smiled Stapo. "Where have we
obtained these?"

"From the house we passed some miles back," explained the soldier.

"Fine," enthused Stapo. "Food is so much more satisfactory from a dish. I was afraid we would not again experience that delight until we had taken Edrigir."

Bulinga accepted her share without comment.

Stapo shoveled food into himself, expertly achieving perfectly articulate speech at exactly the same time.

"This delightful young lady had better remain here, under guard of course. Now I wonder who? I must have with me every possible man, for in the event of a complete capitulation, and we have some reason to expect that, we shall have to station men practically everywhere. Of course we will recruit at once for a local Police Force, but that will take time." He turned to Bulinga. "You are rather a nuisance, my dear girl."

"Then let me go."

He ponderously shook his head.

"Nonsense, you would not have me do that. Gatil, my boy, I believe you are the answer. Yes. But that is just what we will do."

He looked round at them, in actuality to observe their appearance, but when he saw their faces he laughed outright.

"My friend Carpen. You will agree that I frequently alter my ideas to line them with yours. Yes, you need not speak. I know. You do not advise me to leave them alone together. Well, I won't. I shall take her with me. She shall, moreover, travel with my party from now on. I want her near me. It rather seems that I am the one most to be trusted."

"It is you who want her," Carpen told him. "I clearly advised that she be not brought."

"It is a responsibility I gladly accept," burbled Stapo. "It will be a pleasure to have her smiling face among my followers. They are not noted for beauty but for other, more mundane, qualities. Well, that is settled. And now I may eat in peace. This trailing about over the country may suit you two, being ex-traders of course you like this life. But I am a city bird. And I find my appetite unwontedly good. Much of this kind of life and I should be eating much too much, and would become fat."

Quite pleased, Bulinga also bent to the enjoyment of her food. She mustn't let them know that Gatil had told her so much. "Praise to the Great Serpent and to all the Little Gods of Things and Places," Bulinga murmured, "that they had my feet led so that I could be with these gutter people, and please, Oh Immortals, make me an adequate instrument. See that I cannot fail, oh God! Guide my hand!"

She carefully spilled the water from her gourd.

"It is to be hoped you will never be in need of water," observed Carpen. "If that time comes you should remember the water you have wasted."

Bulinga flushed.

She wasn't at all sure he had really thought her to be wasting it.

She rose and walked past the piles of debris to the door, where she turned—to see Stapo's head bent, listening to Carpen. Her lips tightened.

Gatil was close behind her.

"Gatil!" she said quietly.

He was at her side at once.

"I get so thirsty, walking," she explained. "Is there a vessel of some sort in which I could carry water with me?"

"Yes, Princess, there is. One of the men has a lidded gourd. I believe he obtained it in Gabebal. I will get it for you."

Bulinga smiled at him and as he went from her the smile became almost a little fiendish.

"Dear Gatil," she murmured. "He is so useful, sometimes. And he would very probably be pleased that I am about to put Stapo in a false position. I shall most certainly walk close to Stapo. I wonder where he is carrying the cylinders. I expect I can find out."

Outside in the roadway there were three untidy groups of men. Bulinga was enumerating to herself all the villainous qualities catalogued in their features when she found her arm taken by Stapo.

"Come with me, my dear young lady," he said affably, "and while we are sauntering so to the city tell me why I was never apprised of the fact that you are the Princess Royal of Grood. Dear me. Perhaps you would not mind first telling me where *is* Grood? You see, I haven't traveled very much. As I said some time ago, I am sure it was today, I prefer city life."

"Oh! Did you not know that?" said Bulinga in sweet surprise. "I cannot understand why. Your friend Carpen knew, has known since he first met me, in a village outside Grood. Surely he had mentioned that when he was so busily engaged in installing me in your Temple in Nipsirc!"

Stapo stopped and swung her to face him.

He smiled, and Bulinga noted that this time his eyes, too, smiled.

"My very dear Princess," he said. "My *very* dear Princess. I am astonished. I have been guilty of the grossest stupidity. I have underrated you. But then, I believe I'm in some measure to be excused. Had I known just who you are, I should have taken more thought. Biltan! Just stand beside this lady for a moment until I return."

"Yes, Estimable Leader."

Gatil came rushing up, carrying a gourd mounted in silver bands.

"I have filled it," he said. "The top is larger than it seems. These catches loosen it. I must leave you. Somehow, in Edrigir, I will arrange things."

"Thank you so much, Gatil," she said. "I expect you will."

Gatil's own feet got in his way and recovering from his stumble he rushed away.

"Do you find him an engaging youth?" inquired Stapo's voice. "I must say I don't. But not everyone has a like taste, of course. You seem to be somewhat burdened, my dear Princess. Cannot I have these

hings carried for you? There is your—er—bundle—
and that *thing,* whatever it is."

"I have carried my bundle for weeks now, thank
ou," said Bulinga, "and this thing is a parting present
rom Gatil."

"How touching! Nevertheless we will have them
carried for you, now that I am aware of your rank.
I cannot supply much of courtesy but that is easily
done."

"I do not wish to lose them," she stated flatly.

"Nor shall you, nor shall you, my dear—sorry, my
dear Princess. You. You will march behind this lady
and carry for her her bundle and this thing."

Bulinga tried a little harder.

"He may carry the bundle," she smiled. "*I* will
carry this."

There was a moment's silence between them.

"Very well," Stapo agreed, and Bulinga's heart sang.

She found it almost impossible not to smile broadly.
She took her place, and without further waiting Stapo
waved a hand and the party moved off.

Bulinga gave herself up to enjoying her first sight of
Edrigir.

With Stapo, and Biltan, she was in front, and as
they trod the weed-surrounded flagstones of the roadway she decided she was well pleased with how things
had happened. She would have an unequaled view
of Edrigir, entering it like this. She had been afraid
it would be seen by her in joggets, between the heads
and shoulders of large men surrounding her.

Why this street should be so ruinous she could not
guess and she was not going to ask Stapo. Even had
she reason to suppose he knew the answer she would
not open a conversation with him. Although . . .
Should she? It might tend to disarm any suspicion. He
could not have guessed she carried water. He must
think this thing purely a useless ornament, which indeed it could be taken to be, being spherical and so
banded with silver.

She was very pleased with herself.

"Is Edrigir a large city?" she asked.

"By no means," answered Stapo readily. His wall
was rather a waddle, and it affected his speech. He
was inclined to wheeze now.

"It is not even a large trading town, for merchandise
to and from the islands is dealt with at other ports.
No. Edrigir is an outpost, if I may so put it, of Dejanira.
It consists principally of a palace, a jail converted
from an old palace and which we will find much use
for, and of course numerous houses of varying degrees
of nobility. And the harbor, I believe, is small, only
meant for smallish ships built for speed more than to
carry much. All this is from hearsay. But I do not
expect to enjoy my short stay here. Our mutual friend,
Carpen, may not either, but neither would he like
other places so this will suit him as well as anywhere
would."

Bulinga had stopped listening to him. They were
now much nearer the stone wall which surrounded
the city. They were so near to the stone wall that
little could be seen of Edrigir.

The Police were being watched with interest by the
few workmen who were about, but no one said anything, shouted to them or seemed to be aware of the
danger such a body of men might represent.

They were not even halted at the city gate.

The three Edrigirian soldiers on duty there, standing
beside exceedingly long-handled spears, wore resplendent uniforms of silver and green with fine triple lines
of gold near the foot of their jacket skirts. The soldiers
stood still.

The Religious Police marched into Edrigir.

Stapo's chuckles annoyed Bulinga. She held her gourd
to her. She simply must find out where Stapo carried
the cylinders, for surely he was carrying them now, so
near his objective.

"Why are there so few people?" she heard herself
ask.

"Part of my strategy," chuckled Stapo.

"You arranged it so!" gasped Bulinga.

"I arranged, my dear Princess, that we arrive at the time of the afternoon meal. Now don't talk to me, my dear, I have much to consider."

"There is more than you think, to consider," thought Bulinga.

She let herself lag a little so that she could more easily eye him up and down.

She didn't know what she was looking for. She had no knowledge as to the size of these cylinders. They surely couldn't be of metal or damp and wetness would mean nothing to them. Perhaps they were clay? Of course! Clay! And clay was brittle. It wasn't surprising that the cylinders were so carefully tended. They couldn't even be carried in a bag unless they were packed carefully in teased wool or moss or grass. And if they were required quickly . . . Of course! He must have them one in each hand!

Bulinga looked to his hands. They were hidden in his sleeves.

Almost she offered him a drink from her gourd—to see what he would do.

Bulinga stared unseeingly at the high glittering railing-topped walls which the marching party were passing.

She must hurry. She must do something.

She pretended to slip and fell against Stapo—who reeled and immediately Biltan's arms went round him and held him.

Stapo stopped.

Bulinga's eyes glinted. She knew now.

"Are you tired, my dear girl?" he asked.

"I lost my balance," she replied, and wailed inwardly as she heard herself add inanely: "carrying this, I suppose. It's becoming heavy," she added quickly: "but I can surely carry a little thing like this even when I am tired."

"Hand it to the man behind you," commanded Stapo. "And walk farther from me. Hand it to that man."

"But I can easily carry it."

"I wish you to be near me. . . ."

"Well, I can walk a little behind you. I will not risk losing it, and I will carry my own bundle, too. You are as aware as I am that your men are not fully to be trusted."

"My very dear young lady—my dear Princess," Stapo said, "what are you saying? Listen, girl. All our lives are in danger. More so than you realize. Do not come so close to me again. Carry your trash, if you must, put that thing in your bundle, but keep away from me." His voice lost its irritable urgency and became again smooth, urbane and oily. "Now, my dear, we will continue on our way. But what I said was important. Do not forget it."

The party moved again.

Those behind had clustered forward at the sudden stop. Now, Bulinga discovered, there was a greater distance between them and their leader Stapo.

Bulinga smiled.

She was at least three paces behind Stapo. He couldn't see her. She could smile triumphant smiles without fear.

Then she realized—she should have thought it all out before, she decided—of course Stapo was irritable! He could easily be carrying his own death in his own hands! And the death of all with him. Even hers.

But she possessed water. Had not Gatil stated that they held wet clothing over their faces to save themselves? Was that why they wore these brown cloaks? Were they to hide sodden clothing and not just to hide the eight-rayed sun? Was Stapo's waddle, and Biltan's surely uncomfortable gait, and the unsoldierly walk of all of them due to wet clothing?

And Gatil had not told her!

The boy must be a fool! Surely he could have thought to tell her . . . ! And Stapo had said nothing—but then he needn't—he could wrap a wet fold over her face quickly enough, a fold of his own clothing! Too, Gatil had been very ready to give her a gourd of water.

Yes, everything fitted into place.

Bulinga felt a little lightheaded. She looked round, behind her. The others were farther than ever behind.

Bulinga laughed out loud.

Biltan looked round at her, scandalized.

Bulinga sobered.

She must keep all her wits about her. And she mustn't get too far behind, too far away from Stapo. If she were near enough she could perhaps carry out her plan.

New fear entered Bulinga.

Her thoughts were becoming so muddled.

If she could do nothing it might mean her death, and of course the death of Edrigir. What if Stapo did not carry the cylinders so? Would they not become damp in his hands, from sweat, if not from the damp of his clothing? Oh, if only she knew something—definite!

She heard Biltan speak.

"This is the palace entrance."

He put out an arm and steadied Stapo. Stapo stopped.

Bulinga caught up with him.

Reluctantly the men behind caught up.

The road had widened.

Carpen was coming forward.

There was no one to be seen but the Police party. Bulinga felt desolate. She was alone with dangerous men carrying a terrible awesome weapon. What possible hope had she? How could she do as she had planned! She hugged to her her bundle and the spherical silver-mounted gourd. If only it had a handle it would be easier to carry it.

Gatil was coming forward now.

They all stood in a knot, a formless knot.

Gatil smiled at her and without thinking she smiled, wanly, back at him.

"We are behind the palace," Stapo said.

Bulinga's knees trembled, and oblivious of everything, except that her legs would not support her, Bulinga sat on the paving, tucked her legs under her, placed her belongings on the flags beside her and drew deep breaths.

"We enter by the gate yonder," Stapo continued, "and are then in the palace grounds. We four and the Princess keep together, the men follow and they must follow in reasonable order—not like a rabble." He paused and wiped his brow with his sleeved arm.

"I am not often of a mind, friend Carpen, to envy men of a thinner mold, but I do today. Do you, by any chance, believe you might be better fitted to carry these ever-to-be-cursed cylinders?"

Carpen stood stiffly. He replied stiffly:

"The High One deputed to you the duty. If you feel that the courage you can muster is not sufficient to permit us a certain end—if you believe your nimbleness is . . ."

"Oh, all right," Stapo interrupted. "All right. Me it shall be. Wipe my face, Biltan."

Bulinga watched this operation, fascinated.

She must be right. Her deductions must be correct.

"The men will wait outside. They will not object to that," Stapo said with a touch of humor. "One of us must get quickly out to them so that they can mask." He straightened his shoulders. "We all go together. I have altered our reason for requesting entrance. It is not good, but it is better than demanding entrance in the name of the High One. We shall say we have been sent to bring this—er—lady to safety."

"I do not like lies," Carpen stated bluntly.

"Hell take you, man, we must get entrance!"

"Then let us use the formula the High One himself commanded us to use."

"We will use the formula I have outlined," Stapo snarled. "I will tell the lies if you cannot. Leave all the speaking to me. *We must get inside.* We go now into the palace grounds. We follow round the road inside, to the front. We have come this way because we are strangers. That is our excuse if we are asked. As their guard here is purely ornamental it is at the front, at the main entrance, so we should meet no one before we come to the palace door. Atlan's Lights! One of you take these things from that silly girl. We cannot claim help for a princess carrying bundles!"

Dumbly Bulinga saw her belongings snatched up. She tried to cry out, to protest, but no voice came to her.

The fingers of both hands went to the pangolin at her throat.

"Oh, mother," she moaned in her mind, "oh, mother, get help for me!"

33

"It is not a very likely story," pronounced the chamberlain, "and that gives to it some degree of probability. We have had various reports of the churchman to whom you refer as the High One. I would not have expected . . ." The grave old man stopped. "I will admit you," he said slowly. He looked past them down the wide pale green steps to where on the paved space were drawn up in formation the three troops of the Religious Police.

"You have an adequate escort," he said.

Stapo bowed.

"They are not only an escort. When we leave you, they go to other duties."

"Yes. Yes. Quite so. They must remain there."

He looked behind him, turned back to them again.

"I must see if the audience chamber is in order. All must be according to precedent."

He strode away abruptly.

"All is as it should be," Stapo said confidently.

"They are ridiculous here in their insistence on alway following precedent. We shall soon be inside. We nee not haste."

"It is a good practice, a following of precedent,' Carpen said.

"It is the practice of fools," said Stapo cheerfully.

Carpen went closer to Stapo. Carpen's voic thrummed with restrained anger.

"Stapo. Why I should have been commanded to accompany you on this task I know not. I presume tha the High One knew the qualities we both possess, and considered that such qualities were necessary to the success of the venture. But we are not suited to be so harnessed together. In my reports . . ."

"Stop talking or there will be no reports . . ." ordered Stapo. "He returns."

"Follow me," said the chamberlain.

Stapo bowed and followed close behind him, Bulinga received an unceremonious push from Biltan and stumbled along. Her mind, everything of her was dead but her body, and soon it too would be dead. She had now no possible weapon and unless Stapo saved her she would surely die, with Edrigir.

Unseeingly she crossed the pillared hall in Stapo's wake.

Unseeingly she passed the two pools as the others had passed them. She did not see them as pools. The huge saucered leaves of the lilies permitted no sight of water—but the next two pools were bare to the sight.

She was beside them before she realized that this was water. At once she sprang the two steps to Stapo and using all her weight and strength—her arms round him—she lurched into the first pool carrying him with her. Stapo's fists rose in the air above him. For a moment he tried to keep the cylinders dry. Bulinga's action was so sudden, so unexpected that it did not at once occur to him to throw them clear—it did occur to Bulinga. She clawed at his arms and dragged him into the water. She had not the strength to hold him.

He struggled from her grip, and, sobbing in fear and exultation, and then despair because she thought that after all she had failed, Bulinga dragged her soaking form over the narrow parapet and sank to the tiles of the hall floor. Billows of smoke surged and belched to the ceiling of the hall and the water bubbled alarmingly. Carpen started forward—paused—and rushed from the hall. Gatil lay prone on the floor covering every part of his head with his damp undercloak.

Stapo climbed out.

He stood, soaked dripping, a loathsome, wet, slug-like figure, his face the mirror of a hate so malignant that Bulinga crouched back against the parapet of the pool and held her hands out before her to ward him off.

The chamberlain seemed unperturbed.

His hand, which was held out before him, turned over and in response to this signal the hall became quite full of armed men. The points of long spears kept Stapo from Bulinga. Gatil had not moved. He still lay face down. But that he breathed could be seen.

The chamberlain spoke to one of those near to him, who left hurriedly on the ordered errand. The chamberlain crossed to where Bulinga sat on the parapet of the pool.

He bowed.

"It was an admirable action, lady. I have sent for those who will attend you. I trust your exertion, and immersion, have done no more than wet you."

Bulinga found it easy to smile at him.

"It is all right now. I was afraid when I saw the bubbles and the smoke!"

"I assure you that your action completely nullified the intended action of the gases. What you witnessed was a harmless concomitant."

"I am so glad."

He bowed.

Two ladies were now behind him.

Bulinga stood erect, and water poured from her.

The years with her mother, all the effect of that

training, now came to her aid. Bulinga completely ig
nored the state in which she was, she even barel
noticed the clothing of the ladies.

"These ladies will conduct you to where you ma
repair any possible damage to your appearace. I shoul
like to beg that you will return here soon, that I ma
conduct you before our ruler. We had arranged an im
mediate trial of those assassins. If you so wish it i
within my power to delay all until your return."

Bulinga bent her head in acknowledgement.

"Thank you. Yes. I would prefer to be there. Hav
you command of the men who were left outside?"

"We are, Estimable Lady, in full command of th
situation."

"One of the men will be carrying a green bundle
which contains the few possessions I have."

"It will be sent to you at once."

34

The chamberlain withdrew and left her alone with the
soldier.

The soldier's bow was a deep obeisance and when
his back straightened again his face was a brick red—
only partly because of the unusually long time he had
remained bent.

"Princess—Your Tranquilness," he began, and
stopped.

He tried again.

"Your Tranquilness, being on duty last night I was
requested to bring a message to you."

Bulinga looked her interest.

Then as no more seemed to be forthcoming:

"Yes?" she said, interrogatively.

"From the prison," he blurted.

"Oh."

Bulinga knew at once from whom the message came.

"From a prisoner?" she said.

"Yes'm. Yes, Your Tranquilness. He . . . said you'd
e interested."

"What is the message?" asked Bulinga.

The young soldier drew a deep breath.

"It's a man named Gatil, he . . ."

"He wishes to see me?"

"Yes, Princess, Your Tranquilness."

"You can escort me there?"

"Yes. That is, would you want to? He's only a
risoner—and, I beg your pardon, Princess, I mean,
our Tranquilness, but shouldn't you have an officer?"

"An officer? Is an officer necessary?"

This was asking him too much. He was at a loss.

"I shall come with you at once. Will I be able to
ass the guards? I mean, do I not require any permit?"

"Well, I know them as'll be there."

"I see. Yes. Will you lead on?"

"Now?"

"Yes."

"Yes, Princess."

He turned about as if on a parade ground.

The guards at the steps, and at the gate, and outside
he gate, all saluted at her appearance. Bulinga felt
rather certain her soldier enjoyed the salutes more than
she did—and to her they were gratifying. For so long
she had had perforce to do without such civilities.

This walk would give her some view of the city
which she had not yet explored.

She wondered where the prison was. If it were near
the sea she might see that, too.

After all, why shouldn't she go to see Gatil?—
poor Gatil?

It couldn't be very nice, in the prisons, and she
knew that he wasn't very brave. How surprised he
must have been when she had ruined all their plans.

This must be the prison then. She stood back whi
the soldier spoke to those at the bleak but not ug
doorway.

She would not have been surprised had Gatil no
hated her.

Yet he had asked for her to come and see him.
had been her action which had placed him in prison—
she surely owed it to him at least to go and visit him

Preceded by her soldier and followed by anothe
Bulinga was bowed into a narrow corridor.

It seemed that Gatil was steadier in his affection
than were some other people. Gatil's character wa
definitely weak, and she had now no yearning of an
kind for him, but in spite of all she had done, and from
his point of view she must certainly have behave
very badly to him, he had yet asked to see her. An
His Dignity Prince Dedn, now back at a friendly cour
with scores of girls around him, seemed to have no
further use for one who had accompanied him throug
dangers at the mere suggestion of which the other
would all probably have fainted. But that very com
panionship seemed finally to have bored him—h
whose interest in any woman, as she had known, was
always purely selfish and easily sated. He had turned
to newer and gayer companions—companions too who
were probably more easily tempted—she was treated
with cold respect, as a stranger.

"There is a step here, almost in darkness, Your
Tranquilness," the soldier ahead of her warned.

"Thank you." Bulinga negotiated the step without
the slightest trouble, and resumed her line of thought,
keeping close to the soldiers, for though the plain
stone passage was clean and smelled clean and fresh,
the few windows along its length were narrow and
admitted little light.

Gatil should not mind being incarcerated in one of
these rooms past which she was now being led. But
after all—and even she didn't know—what were they
going to do with him, and Stapo, and all the Police?
If they didn't kill them, they might ship them to the

ad Islands of Rutas-Mu. She had heard that was done
o prisoners.

No longer did she very much wish to go to Rutas-
Mu. Since she'd learned that Dedn was Prince of
Dejanira. If *only* she could get to Atlan easily—Atlan
was a much more attractive proposition to her than
was Dejanira. As it always had been. Of course, Alona,
who was such a nice friendly girl, would be there when
her father's term of office here was over—but no, she
couldn't bear to be at Prince Dedn's court, even if, as
Alona said, he was rarely there.

This time left to her to be with him at the court of
Edrigir would be bad enough, even though she was
being lauded so gratifyingly for doing what, after all,
had been unnecessary because the Edrigirians had
been prepared for Stapo's coming.

"This is the room, Your Tranquilness," said the first
soldier.

"Oh, thank you," said Bulinga, brought up short
before a closed door.

The soldier unlocked the door, and called: "Hey!
Prisoner! Come out."

Gatil emerged, very shamefaced, and Bulinga and he
were escorted to a large empty room containing a
bench and nothing else whatsoever.

The soldier left them reminding Bulinga to call if
she wanted anything, and excused himself for leaving
her but he had business elsewhere at the moment—a
more important visitation was being held elsewhere in
the prisons.

"Thank you," said Bulinga, and waited for the other
soldier to go too. He didn't. He leaned against the door
post.

Gatil looked from her to the soldier.

"But I don't mind," he told her. "I can say it all.
He won't go."

"Oh, Gatil," said Bulinga, "I really am truly sorry
to see you here, but I—what did you want to see me
about?"

"It's awful here," Gatil whined. "Why did you have

to push Stapo in the water, Bulinga? I know he's bee[n]
deserving it for ages, ever since he told me that—an[d]
before that, anyway, too—but you know I told yo[u]
that water was the very thing to spoil those cylinde[rs]
and stop them working. And why have they given yo[u]
all those new things you're wearing now and not eve[n]
put you in prison or anything? It's as the High On[e]
said—one law for the rich and another for the poo[r,]
you being a princess and everything. It's not fair, [I]
mean I didn't want to be in the Police, you know tha[t]
don't you, Bulinga, and it was my uncle and that fou[l]
swine Stapo who made me help to kill people i[n]
Gabebal. You *do* know that, *don't* you, Bulinga?"

"Oh, Gatil," Bulinga said helplessly.

She looked at the soldier, it all seemed so muc[h]
more sordid with him there.

"You needn't wait," she said to him. "I shall be al[l]
right alone."

"It—it's regulation, Your Tranquilness."

"Well, they can hold me responsible. But you ma[y]
go away and do something else."

He shuffled his feet.

Princesses were all very well. And how could he tell
her he couldn't leave? He'd better hurry to the under
officer at once.

"Yes'm. Shall I lock the door?"

"Whatever for? I should be unable to get out!"

She watched him, until the door closed behind him,
then she turned back to Gatil.

She regarded him silently. All her muscles were
slack and sore in concert with his helplessness.

It was all her fault he was here, and what he said
about his not being responsible for the dreadful things
the others had planned was really quite true. . . . But
it wasn't as if he had been suborned against his every
impulse. He was only sorry because he'd been caught.
Still, he was only a boy, mentally anyway. And he had
been brought up with no ethics.

"What do they intend to do with you?" she asked.

"I don't know. Kill me, or worse still, ship me out

o Rutas-Mu. They do that, you know, it's a dreadful
>unishment, with all those other swine." Gatil's voice
quavered and his lips twitched.

"Oh, Bulinga, I'm not afraid to die, but the rest of
my life on those Islands would be too awful to bear.
There are terrible monsters. I just couldn't bear it. I'm
not born for that sort of thing, I wasn't made for it, I
mean, and . . . Oh, Bulinga, can't you do something?
I have done lots of things for you, you know, Bulinga.
I've been so miserable," he went on, staring despon-
dently at the floor. "They brought me water but I was
so unhappy I didn't even have the heart to wash."

"I can see that," said Bulinga.

"Yes, I know . . . and I feel simply foul. I'm sure
there're rats or something foul like that in my cell.
They never bother to keep prisons clean—Bulinga, you
can do something, can't you? I mean, of course you
can, you're well in with these beastly people and I'm
sure it would be quite easy for *you* . . ."

"I—I don't know," said Bulinga. "I don't know
what to do—and, Gatil, I'm pretty sure I can't do anything . . ."

Gatil tried to put his arms round her.

"Bulinga, we could get away together—they haven't
captured my uncle, and I think I know where he probably is—or we could just go off together, if you don't
want to meet my uncle again and I don't very much
either . . ." Wild ideas of adventure, of cutting free
from all the restrictions and ties his uncle had forced
on him, whirled into Gatil's desires.

"No, don't," said Bulinga, pulling herself from him.

"But, Bulinga, you know you can help me, and it's
no use pretending you don't love me—you've shown
me that clearly enough and often enough . . ."

His unattractive arms entwined themselves self-
confidently about her.

Bulinga, furious, with herself as well as with him,
struggled determinedly.

Gatil, puzzled, annoyed, held her. He tried to kiss
her but Bulinga jerked her head away.

"Stop it! Gatil!" she said. "Leave me alone at once!"

The door opened, and an instant later Bulinga found herself released so hurriedly that she almost fell over.

Bulinga was inclined to resent Prince Dedn's interference in the affair. He had no right to go knocking down her companions when he had no further interest in her.

"Get up, you little cur," Dedn said.

Bulinga moodily eyed the pair of them. Gatil lay whimpering. Dedn stood over him, an almost aggravatingly splendid figure of angered masculinity, thought Bulinga. It was not in Dedn to have compassion on one who had roused anger in him—particularly while the anger was still there—although Gatil had been doing no more than Dedn had done often enough. Gatil was even probably very much the sort of person Dedn had been when a boy—although Gatil had less intelligence and much less courage.

Dedn turned and bowed to Bulinga, evidently feeling that this should be done. The bow was so perfunctory as to be almost unrecognizable as one—and his eyes did not meet hers.

"How did you come to be here, Your Tranquilness?" he asked. His head was still turned towards Gatil.

"I came at my own desire to meet this—prisoner," Bulinga answered coldly, and unequivocally.

Prince Dedn's bow was this time exaggerated.

"I apologize for my interruption. But as I was passing through with another prisoner whom I had been interrogating I heard you call out, and, of course, was fortunate in being able to rescue you from the advances of this prisoner. Perhaps now you wish to be escorted back to the palace?"

"A soldier brought me here. He will do as an escort," Bulinga said coldly.

"He cannot now be spared." Dedn's voice was as cold.

"Then I shall return without an escort." She paused. "Thank you."

"I see."

There was a long pause.

Gatil got himself up from the floor.

"And what shall I do with—this person?" asked the Prince, the effort of restraint quite obvious.

Bulinga opened the door.

"Oh, put him in the bear pits. And jump in after him," she flared, and slammed the door behind her.

His Dignity Prince Dedn rubbed his chin thoughtfully.

Gatil cowered back against the wall from the cold eyes which glinted at him.

"I . . ." he whispered and stopped.

"Bear pits, eh. Well!" Dedn laughed.

To Gatil his laugh sounded demoniacal.

35

She knew she'd turned the wrong way when she left the prison, but she was so glad she had.

This was the sea.

And she had seen right along the marketing street too and it was most interesting.

But this, the sea, was the important thing.

Bulinga looked at it.

She felt a little flat. She tried to work up an enthusiasm about the sea but she could not help thinking with one part of her mind that she should have been more coldly polite to Dedn instead of losing her temper, and with another that she must have seemed so ridiculous—believing herself at all interested in Gatil.

Now she felt unclean. She had profaned her mind by giving it over to adoration of him. And there was yet another thought which was connected somehow with the other two. But Bulinga felt she must do something about the sea while she was here.

A small wind was blowing her skirts against her and there was a peculiar virility to the tang of it. It must be the smell of the sea.

She walked carefully over the planking—some of which was insecurely pegged down and wobbled as she trod on it—till she reached the end of this peculiar continuation of the road jutting out into all the water.

Bulinga ignored the men. She knew she was an object of interest to them. There was no other woman there. They were interesting to her. Bare to the thighs and mostly not wearing any sort of jacket, they went about their work with agility.

At the end of the jetty she looked down into a boat.

A man, bending over some bales, straightened his back and looked up. And he smiled.

"Princess!" said Emalf. "Is Prince Dedn there with you?"

"Oh no," Bulinga said, very definitely. "I am alone."

"Then I will come up to you."

Bulinga watched him critically and decided that he was just as agile as the other men.

"I meet you in the most surprising places," said Emalf.

"But you knew I was coming to Edrigir!"

"Yes. But not to the end of the jetty. Have you really no escort? But surely Prince Dedn has not permitted you to come here alone!"

"Prince Dedn has no jurisdiction over actions of mine."

"Did you come here alone?"

"You mean here, where I am standing?"

"No. To Edrigir, from where I saw you last?"

"Not—really. But I did come with Prince Dedn. I would have you know I am quite accustomed to traveling alone."

"Come over here and sit down."

He led her to a long low crate which had carried or been intended to carry objects of pottery. But the packing of coarse dried bracken had not safeguarded the pottery, broken shreds of which lay about.

Emalf scraped these aside with his foot and cleared a space for Bulinga.

"You are indeed much traveled, Princess. And now you are here. I was most pleased in Tayrb, but that I should meet you in such an inn and in the company of Prince Dedn too was surprising. May I know how you became acquainted?"

"We met in Nipsirc," Bulinga said, circumspectly. ..

"Before the rioting?"

"Oh yes."

"I am glad you both escaped from there. But, indeed, I see quite fully that such happenings could not be expected to entrap either of you. I should have liked to meet you there, I . . ."

"Well," said Bulinga, "you almost did."

"Did I?"

Emalf rested his chin in his hand, and looked at her. That he admired her was conspicuous.

"I find it difficult to know whether to tell you," she said, laughing. "It does not present me in too good a light. Tell me, Emalf," she inquired, ingeniously, "do I seem to you to be grown from the Princess of Grood whom you first met?"

"Undoubtedly."

He looked far out to sea, then brought his eyes back to her.

"You do not need me to tell you, Princess, that you are a beautiful woman. I knew that in Grood. I do not know whether I am correct in assuring you that your beauty has increased and yet I believe that is so. And no one could have traveled so, no one with your beauty could have so traveled without being subject to —to much in the way of adventure—of one sort and another. It is that which has changed you, I have no doubt."

"In what have I changed, friend Emalf?"

"It is not easy to put into words, Princess. You see," he picked up a piece of pottery large and curved and with his fingers which were, Bulinga noted, long and slim, he broke off piece after piece.

"What do I see?" Bulinga pressed him.

"I suppose you had always the seeds of this your unconventionality, and they have been fed, those seeds. I have heard of no other princess who would sit here, upon a broken crate at the end of a sailors' jetty, and talk, with a trader, and yet—and yet because of her quality lose no"—he searched for a word—was obviously unable to find it and finished—"lose no shred of her quality."

Bulinga watched the little bits of burnt clay fall one after the other from his fingers, watched them fall between the planking, listened, between the noises which beset the jetty, until the little plop told her each bit had entered the water.

"Where would I now be," she wondered, "had I accepted this man's offer—the offer he extended—when I stole his horse?"

"Are those ships?" she asked him. "See, those small specks—far out."

"Yes, Princess—those are ships. They are those which this morning unloaded a cargo of soldiers. They go for more. They are far out. You see well, Princess."

"You pay me far too many compliments, Emalf."

He stood.

"Do I offend you by doing so? I assure you I would not wish to do so. I," he laughed, "I find it impossible not to compliment you."

"There—you do so again," she said, her eyes laughing.

"But you do not dislike it!"

"Oh no. I think it is just that I am not much accustomed to such a conversation."

Bulinga watched the far-out specks, well aware that the man was studying her profile.

"Of what are you thinking, Emalf?" she asked, softly.

"Of your fairness, Princess. I was thinking it made you—somehow lovely. It is not the fairness of this end of the world. And I think too of what the King Rugul, your father, had told me. In all these lands, lady, there is not your like. You knew your mother was of Atlan?"

Bulinga's fingers went to her pangolin.

"Yes."

She turned to him.

"Emalf. You are very much traveled. Have—do you know Atlan—more than by hearsay?"

He shook his head.

"No—yet have I seen much of many Atlanteans. I come from a countryside greatly to the west of here. To the northwest, just a little east of the confines of Atlan proper."

Bulinga did not speak. She did not know quite what to say, and this was not a moment for just any words.

Atlan.

Emalf brought it suddenly closer.

Bulinga clasped her fingers about one knee, and searched the horizon till she again found the far-out specks which were ships. She was, she knew, looking in the wrong direction—but Atlan *was* far away; Atlan was beyond seas similar to this.

"Is it possible to sail—by sea—to—to there—Emalf?"

"Yes, Princess."

Emalf stood and tossed over the side of the jetty the remains of the bowl he had held.

"Yes. But it is a long long way away. Only twice, I believe, has it been reached that way."

He waited—then asked:

"That is your aim?"

Bulinga nodded.

She turned to him.

"Is it possible for me?"

He shook his head.

"You ask too much of me, Princess. How could know?"

He hooked his thumbs in the loops of his sash an allowed his mind to wander idly. He, too, had ha dreams of such a sailing—although it was a land nea Atlan that was his target.

"When I met you first," he said slowly, "Dejanira was your aim."

"Do you believe I should remain satisfied with that?"

"I—would not dare Those who control our fate by such, or any other, advice. . . . Dejanira is so—easily within your grasp, Princess."

"Just across the water," said Bulinga.

"Yes. Just across the water. Moreover you have the personal friendship of him who is its next ruler."

She turned to him.

"Prince Dedn!"

He nodded.

His Dignity.

So he was Dejanira's next ruler.

"Will you not tell me," asked Emalf, "by what mischance I missed meeting you in Nipsirc?"

"I was being carried off, against my will, to the Temple. I saw you arrive—with your train—and called to you for help. It was of no avail. But you had heard, I think."

Emalf sat again.

"Yes. I heard. So that was it." He became silent.

His eyes moved sideways and thus he regarded her intently, to the best of his ability.

"A man can be many times a fool in the space of a short life," he murmured, soundlessly, to himself. "Yet, how was I to know? Even now I am a fool. True, I have some riches—though to me a lot, to others little; what else have I that I may offer? And I have had men call me wise. Am I only wise in the ambitions of my folly?"

36

There was a deep darkness on the center of the river which flowed through the gardens, but tiny lanterns, no more than an inch in roundness, were spittering and twinkling everywhere on its banks—among the bushes along its entire slow-winding length.

"But I cannot talk to you all night," Bulinga protested. "I shall become hoarse."

"This *is* so serious. Is it not?" complained the man with her. And Bulinga wondered how he had come to be there. He was so unlike Dedn. True he was tall and dark. . . .

"What do they in Grood?" Alona desired to know. "It has a most delicious sound. Grood!" She savored the sound of it and Bulinga had to admit that said so, in her voice, it brought a measure of nostalgia.

"They are proud of their gardens. Which are very formal. I was taught that this formality was in reaction against the wildness of the great forest which hems us round, and indeed their gardens have a beauty, if you like formality."

"Then you must like flowers, Your Tranquilness. What are your favorites, Princess, or do you have varieties we have not heard of?"

"Oh! Magnolias," Bulinga said without hesitation.

"But Groodians *must* do more than tend to the beautifying of life," persisted one.

The Groodian life put so could not but make Bulinga laugh.

"Oh—they eat," she managed to say.

The little party laughed.

"But I do mean it so," Bulinga told them. "It is a institution more than a thing which is done. Grood not famous for its culture but for its cats."

"Oh yes. It was in my mind to ask you that. Sixteen there are, alive in Dejanira, all females and ten of them olding. I think we must persuade our Prince to rai Grood when our little work here is completed. We mus have cats in plenty from Grood. Yes. That's wha Grood is famed for. Cats!"

"*And* princesses!" said the other man, his eyes en deavoring to ensnare hers. "Devils take your cats, Par nil. Tell me, please, Your Tranquilness, does Grood produce nothing but females of the *very* highest order? For, and I appeal to all to support me, that is wha would seem to be so."

Bulinga laughed, politely, and then as a glimpse smote her of her last view of Rugul's court, her laugh became real merriment.

"There are probably ogres there too," offered Alona. "There are, are there not, Your Tranquilness, huge ones, with teeth so!" and she hung two fingers from her mouth so drolly like a tusked Arvela that again laughter broke Bulinga's smile, and she had perforce to present the Arvela to her small audience.

"All this," Bulinga told herself, "*is* that for which I left Grood, and I am indeed proved right in what I did."

And of Prince Dedn there had been not even a momentary sight until the moment she held aloft a magnolia bloom, to be the guerdon of he who told the most improbable short tale.

Then she saw him, clear in the light, only a few steps from her, kissing a girl whom she knew to be his cousin Frellis.

She watched Dedn, fascinated. It was a long kiss, a practiced kiss, and she didn't like Frellis; she searched for some definite reason and clamped on the manner in which a curl of hair had been trained by Frellis to encircle a beauty spot on her cheek.

"The guerdon! Judgement. We demand judgement,"

from voices close to her brought her back to the matter
in hand.

"But I wasn't listening," she apologized.

"There is nothing for it, then, but that they must all
be told again."

"Life in Edrigir is a terrible thing," moaned someone.

Bulinga felt the bloom plucked from her fingers. She
looked round and discovered herself face to face with
Dedn.

Everyone else drifted discreetly away.

Alona raced past to the river with four of his officers
in hot pursuit of her. She stopped and waved. Prince
Dedn waved, Alona raced away again and Dedn seated
himself on the small table beside Bulinga.

"Sit down, my dear Tranquilness," he said, "while I
try to think of somewhere to keep this bloom I have
earned."

"But you didn't," expostulated Bulinga. "And, anyway, I'm not at all certain you should call me your dear
Tranquilness."

"I agree it is unorthodox. But I'm frequently the
inaugurator of new titles. I like that one."

"I suppose I must thank you for all those flowers
you sent to my room."

"Yes. It's generally expected. You should appreciate
them. They were most expensive. The price of magnolias, in the market street this morning, reached un-
precedented heights."

"Then I shall sell all mine tomorrow," said Bulinga.
"I have masses of them."

"You disappoint me. I really expected you would
wear mine next to your heart."

"That was Frellis, your cousin, wasn't it?" she said
naïvely.

"Yes, Your Tranquilness," he agreed, politely.

"Are you going to marry her?"

There was a moment before he answered. Bulinga
was not looking at him, and his eyes searched her face
for some clue to her feelings.

"Marry her! By the Moon, Bulinga, you astound me. Must I marry every girl I kiss?"

"What have you done with poor Lelahla?"

The Prince laughed.

"This conversation, my dear Tranquilness, answers to no rules. Ladies like Lelahla do not officially exist in this particular society. As you seem anxious I expect I should tell you that the lord Hylun successfully, eventually, maneuvered her in the direction he wished her to take. When I caught up with them I was —rather anxious—to discover that you were not with them. I know now why. What induced you to wander away?"

Bulinga ignored the question. She was trying to work towards a decision. Why was he so cold, almost ignoring her when he arrived here? What should she make of that disgraceful exhibition in the prison this morning—of his magnolias, which were lovely?

Also, he had to search more often for words, in the present conversation he seemed to some degree less self-possessed than was usual to him.

"You are very beautiful, Bulinga, beautiful when you walk, beautiful when you talk, beautiful when you are not listening, but most beautiful when you are angry."

"Are you trying to anger me now?"

"I am living still in the past," he assured her. "At the hut, to be precise."

"But I've often been angry with you!"

He laughed.

"Never as tempestuously nor as alluringly as then."

Bulinga felt she must drag the conversation to safe surfaces.

"Where is she now?" she asked.

"Lelahla? She is in Edrigir."

"I might have guessed," Bulinga said lightly.

"And has sent me a note intimating that she wishes to have nothing whatever to do with me."

"It is an invitation."

"It is an invitation I shall have to ignore for the

moment. Forgive me if I recall memories you would prefer to abandon, but that remark shows you to be considerably unlike the lady I met in Nipsirc. It is not so much that you have more poise as that it is a different poise. I think you may have learned it from me."

"You," Bulinga retorted, "are in no whit different from the person I first met in Nipsirc. I still find you overbearing and utterly unprincipled. Do you mind if we walk along the river bank? I have wanted to see it and have been unable."

The Prince rose and bowed.

It was right that he should bow, others in the same circumstances would. But from him she felt it to be ironical, or did she feel so only because she had grown to know him, so well, but from another angle?

And here, this evening, while she was yet fresh from a circle of admirers—not all utterly sincere she feared, but only with her because she was the fashion—he was more attractive to her than she would like him to know.

The embroidered cloth of his sleeve was harsh against the bareness of her flesh and she glanced up at him, from the ends of her eyes, wonderingly.

The wind, rising, caught her hair and thrust it at Dedn's face.

She wished she had not suggested the river.

All interest in the river had left her. She felt that her senses had been deluded, had been lulled—as by false promises.

Through the darkness, between the trees in whose foliage the globes of light passed the corners of her vision like slits of lightning, his arm guided her, she felt it hard and warm about her.

There was in him some superlatively vital quality, leashed yet, which clamped her to him as they moved, over lawns ivory and ebony, through dark avenues where groups of guests were few.

They were just beyond the edge of a disc of light.

"Dedn," faltered Bulinga and her fingers plucked tentatively at his sleeve.

Dedn's arms were around her.

A languor caught and drained her to a helplessness which she found it impossible to refuse. The dark blur of his face approached: her being melted to his and she felt herself disembodied. It was awful and yet wonderful.

Dedn released her.

"Oh, Dedn," she whispered.

"Bulinga," Dedn's words said, "you do believe me now. Don't you . . . ?"

"Believe what?" she asked, drowsily. She lay in his arms, against him, quite happily stupefied.

"Believe, my Bulinga, that I want you more than anything else in the world. That I must and will have you, that . . ."

She drew herself away—and left him—and was immediately in the darkness beneath the trees—and she ran.

Bulinga awoke to the rending of the night by a shouting and a trumpeting in the courtyard below.

She ran to the cold balcony.

Sleep had left her at once. There was a terrible urgency in the trumpeting, a hoarse brassiness which tore some emotion from deep within her and sent it clattering and echoing against the unresponsive heavens.

Wild oil flares lit the scene below her.

Armed men, armed in dulled metal and night-sombered color, stood about.

Slaves ran, carrying accoutrements, obeying hurried commands.

A black mastodon, whose tusks and toenails gleamed white, pranced into the central space of beaten earth. Its great jagged ears were flipped back to its long head; the eyes glittered with a roguish, dangerous excitement: again and again the sound of its trumpeting swelled awe-inspiringly over the court.

Slaves, a half score of them, clambered over the beast to harness its vast bulk; a tasseled caparisoning was buckled into place over the high-ridged back.

Its hugely long pink and black trunk coiling, it waited with excited impatience for the ride to start. The light of the flares glinted along the long length of the coarse red hairs that streamed in the breeze from its shoulders and cheeks and in a broad line down the elongated snout.

Torches were handed up to the slaves on its back, and soldiers, four of them, mounted, fitting themselves into the slitted folds of the caparisoning, testing their precarious positions before they accepted the torches which were held to them. The flames fleered out like rusty streamers on the breeze. The smoke obscured the stars.

Someone accompanied by a great bowing of attendants and clamorous excitement came out from the shadow of the palace, from far to the left of where Bulinga stood.

It was, she could see, Prince Dedn.

He climbed up the dropped swaying ladder till he reached the broad-walled saddle atop the animal's back; and the capable coolness of his action, the quick grace with which he reached his place, were breathtaking in their ease and effortlessness.

He kicked its side carelessly; the crowd of slaves and his own attendants in the courtyard sprang aside; and the huge grotesquely lovely animal, blacker than the sky and more alive than the torches whose flames fleered and streamed out behind it, galloped from that place.

Bulinga watched him leave. She watched until the lights no longer flared along the broad streets but were but a glow far away. She watched the torches of the soldiers who marched out after their general. Watched till the streets were empty—and the shutters of the houses became closed and dark again.

She waited just a little longer.

She had not noticed how cold the night was.

The bed where she had lain was cold now, too, and

she drew her feet up to her to warm them, settling th
heaped covers about her in crumpled layers, then bury
ing her face into the crook of her arm she cried hersel
to sleep.

37

How wet the sea looked.

It sprang up on the rocks like a hungry monster, it
threw spray quivering hugely high—and, baffled, but
not calmed, it drew itself back and again hurled itself,
its gray liquid weight, forward—again and always
again—and the tempestuous beat of the spray caught
Bulinga's flesh and its salt spice was on her tongue and
in her eyes and wet on her face and in her hair.

Emalf drummed the point of his longer dagger rhythmically on the rock.

He pushed another bundle of brushwood into the
fire and the light flickered and glanced over the darkness, conquering it exultantly; springing out, falling,
jumping and springing again.

Bulinga leaned back and clasped her knees glowing
in the warmth and the light.

The sea spray fell in salted froth and sizzled in the
fire, and the fire crackled and spat and the thrum and
boom and swish swash of the sea and the thudding of
the waves on the rocks; all continued in a lulling restful yet threatening beat.

Somewhere about them, near, loosed yet not directed
at them—was all the strength of the ocean. A raw
naked force. A tremendous unbearable strength which
because it touched them not engendered in Bulinga a
throbbing uncanny pride.

The sky seemed all about them, even down among he rocks between them.

She watched the light play on Emalf's face.

Shadows fled back and forward across it giving unlikely emphasis to the height of the cheekbones, the lean clearness of his jaw, the square boss of his chin.

She discovered, almost with a shock, that he was fair. She had never noticed this before.

He idly pulled closer to him one of the twigs; the thin trail of smoke from its glowing end caused Bulinga to flinch. With the edge of the knife he sliced off the glowing end and swept it aside.

"It is very late, lady," he said.

"Yes," agreed Bulinga. "Yet there is no reason, other than that, for leaving here. Surely that is a small reason."

Emalf smiled.

For upwards of an hour there had been no speech between them.

Before this only with men had he enjoyed such a silence.

He had not expected it to happen this evening.

"Yet I believe we should go," he said. "The desert, too, is like that. Sitting late, like this, with a fire, either in the desert or by the sea, induces a hypnotism which is hard to upset. Yet we cannot stay here always. And I feel that you should have sleep. You have been out all day in the boat with me. Sea air is heavy. I have been surprised you are not asleep now."

"There was a time that I felt drowsy, but that is gone. I have no need for sleep nor do I feel that I shall sleep tonight. It won't be ordinary sleep if I do."

Neither moved.

"Oh look!" cried Bulinga.

She pointed, excitedly.

Emalf smiled.

"Shooting stars."

"Are they really falling?"

"Oh yes. But I believe they are smaller than they appear to be. Such showers are often seen at night. The sailors say they tell of a coming battle in which man will be killed."

"Oh."

Then:

"Emalf, do you believe such things are a sign from Those who control our fate?"

Emalf wiped his dagger point clean of earth and slipped it back in its long sheath.

"It is possible. But I have no fixed belief regarding omens, portents and auguries, Bulinga. Yet it is true that sometimes, in a most unlikely manner, soothsayers and omen-mad old women are proved correct."

"There could be a battle tonight, Emalf."

"Yes, of course."

"I know so little of battles," mused Bulinga. "Have you been in any, Emalf?"

Emalf tossed more stick to the fire.

"Once only, in my own country. That was many years ago, and I was little more than a boy."

"Were—many killed?"

"Yes."

"Are—princes and generals killed much, Emalf? Is it especially dangerous for men in such positions?"

"You are thinking of Prince Dedn!"

She nodded.

After a moment he said:

"I do not know. It could be so. But I could say either way was the truth and still be wrong."

"They have been gone three days."

Emalf said nothing.

Bulinga stood and took the two steps to the edge of the great rock on which they were.

The spray spluttered about her. The rhythmic boom of the seas almost deadened her mind.

Emalf watched her. He tensed himself, ready to grasp at her should she slip, and relaxed and sat back on his heels as she turned to him, came back and stood beside him, looking down.

"These have been three wonderful days, Emalf. You are a good friend to me. I never thought it would be

but I had no mind to sit about the court. These
ree days each of which I have spent all on the wild
ater with you will always remain in my mind. I am
rry tomorrow cannot be like them."

Emalf smiled.

"There are other days in the year, Princess. But
deed I regret tomorrow. I am expecting to have to
tend to business then. Yet it may turn out not to be
. In that case should I send to you?"

"Oh yes. I would be very sorry, if you did not." She
aused. "I have learned to love the sea." She paused,
gain, then: "While I stood there a moment ago, you
ere ready, were you not, if it should have happened
iat I fell? But indeed you need not have entertained
nxiety. The sea will never harm me. Do you receive
i your mind vivid impressions such as that? From
here they come or by what force engendered I do not
now, but my mother, I think, could have told me. She
new much. But I shall never come to harm from
vater."

She laughed gaily.

"It is something I am pleased to learn. Now I can
ake risks which, otherwise, would frighten me."

"If you really have no fear for the sea, it will not
iarm you. Confidence is a great matter. Yet, I think
must teach you to swim. Confidence should be forti-
ied by competence."

"The day after tomorrow then," said Bulinga.

Emalf stood.

"Nothing will be allowed to postpone such a meet-
ng, and I think you will be quick to learn if you have
a love of the water."

She nodded.

"As I have said, Emalf, you are a good friend to
me."

He shook his head.

"Now, yes. But I have not always."

"You mean in Grood? The night I wished you to
take me away? Perhaps you were. I—have wondered.
I believe you always were."

She discovered they were walking down the roug̣
path away from the edge. She had not noticed he ẉ
leading her. Yet it was late. They should be returnin̩
In Grood she could not have been out alone with ̣
man, and he a trader too, at such an hour, at aṇ
hour. Here in Edrigir no one had said—or was thḁ
only because she was a princess and it was no ṛ
sponsibility of theirs what she should do?

Yet how could she be expected to subscribe to pet̀
conventions, she whose life had, since leaving Grooḍ
forced her to discard one convention after another?

These would not be the first days she had speṇ
alone with a man. Though these were the most enjoy̩
able.

Were they?

There had been a day—between Tayrb and a hut—
a day, an entire day, alone with Dedn.

He was, now—where she had no idea.

Bulinga's breath caught suddenly as she remembere̩
the falling stars. Was there really destined to be ̣
battle, tonight?

She tried to visualize it. She could see masses ọ
men, bearing weapons. What she had seen of the riot̀
in Nipsirc helped her imagination. In the center of ị
all she placed Dedn—high astride the ridged back ọ
the enormous mastodon. What a beast that was! Surel̦
except from thrown spears and stones a man was safệ
in such a position! And things thrown rarely reacheḍ
their mark when the mark could move. That must bệ
so. She could not think otherwise. Nevertheless, shệ
could and must implore aid and protection for hiṃ
She did not want him killed.

The pangolin at her throat comforted her, as alwayṣ

"Tranquilness," said Emalf.

She looked round at him.

"I made you free of my name," she said softly.

"Yes," he said softly, "and I have used it, today, tọ
taste the feel of it on my lips. Perhaps you forgeṭ
though what I am—a trader—while you are a prin-

ess. Can such a friendship last? I would give much for
to do so—but I fear to do what might split it."

"I do not think you can, Emalf. And am I a princess? Am I not merely a woman, or should I say a girl,
or indeed you know I am little more than that. There
are times when I believe I must be hundreds of years
old, others when I am just, let us say, upwards of eighty
and others when I feel very young. Tonight I am of no
age at all, and that is because of the sea, and because
of my friendship with you. And Grood is far away.
These people treat me hospitably, and I cannot repay
them. I do not expect they would ever require repay-
ment, but in any case I could not do it. My wealth
consists of about forty gold parings—and a few little
items of jewelry bought in Grood, and some things
from the Temple—which I suppose are mine now.
Do you think a girl can remain a princess, long, without wealth?"

"You can marry."

"Yes. I can marry."

He allowed the little silence to continue while his
mind searched out the words he wanted.

"I do not think," he said, "you would experience
any difficulty in obtaining a husband who was rich and
of high rank. You are a most beautiful woman, Bulinga. Never have I seen anyone more beautiful. Often I
dare not look at you because of your beauty." He
shook his head. He was talking more to himself than
to her. "And that is not all. We have said little to one
another, out there in the boat I hired, yet I know you
to be strongly favored by the Little Gods of Things and
Places. Unscathed you have come a long way, and all
the facets of your character become more polished so
that as with a fine jewel the depths are more easily
seen. Do you know that I love you, Bulinga, Princess?
Only on such a night as this could I tell you, only in
the dark, but now that I have told you I find it easier
to continue the theme. These last three days have been
heaven to me, a heaven I had no thought could exist.
I think I have loved you since that night in Grood,

and the thoughts and ambitions of that night make m
writhe inwardly in shame. But no matter what hap
pens, I know I shall always love you. It is impossibl
for me to stop."

His voice died away and he glanced aside at her.

She walked easily, confidently, beside him.

Her lips were parted, and leaning forward a little h
could see there was a rapt look in her eyes.

He waited.

"Of what are you thinking, Bulinga?" he aske
hesitantly.

Bulinga started.

"I am sorry," she said. "Did you say something? I
have been thinking of Prince Dedn."

38

Bulinga faced Emalf and gave him her hands to hold.

"They have been, oh, *so* lovely, these three days
with you," she said. "Get rid of your business, quickly,
Emalf, I want more of such life."

"It will be my ambition to give you much of it," he
said.

She thought he said it a little grimly, but when she
looked at him there was a smile on his face.

"I shall go back from here to the palace alone."

"It would be no inconvenience to me to escort you,"
he said. "It would not only be a pleasure to me; you
would honor me by accepting my presence."

Bulinga laughed.

"You have been honored enough for one day,
Emalf, and there is no need to be so portentous. You
told me tonight there are many days in the year. You

ll be sickened of my companionship if, as you say
u will, you get a boat of your own. Is it to be a big
e?"

"Big enough," he said enigmatically.

"Then there will be no end to the bother I make
r you," she sighed. "But now I am more tired than I
ought. And I shall come to no harm between here
d the palace. And the chamberlain, that fine old
an, will have a servant there to admit me and see to
y wants. So, good night, Emalf. You will send me a
essage about—your boat?"

He nodded.

So she turned and left him.

He stood still, looking after her.

He leaned against the wall, quiet and still, and
atched till the slim white figure was out of his sight.
nce he thought she was about to turn and wave.

He walked slowly to his lodging near the jetty.

He had taken barely thirty steps when the noise
om upwards of a thousand throats ravaged the quiet
f the night.

After that first tremendous ragged shout there was
e bare moment of a silence, hardly long enough in
me to be called a silence, then utter pandemonium
roke out.

Doors were opening, curtains pushed aside, shutters
anged to the wall away from windows and voice after
oice endeavored to intercept him, to ask him more
han he knew.

He knew one thing only. Once before he had heard
uch a shout, and he knew all it portended.

The city of Edrigir was being attacked.

Had she time to reach the palace?

He felt that she had, but until he reached the palace
ates he did not stop. There he saw no sign of her and
new she was safe within.

Bands of armed citizens, yawning, half clothed, in
no shape to fight off invaders, rushed past him.

The palace gates were being barricaded. Someone in
the palace knew what to do, and there would be

soldiers, servants, slaves—men in plenty there.
would be of more use near the jetty for men could
round the coast too.

He sheathed his black knife and ran at top spe
down the long slope.

There were other men, and women, and boys, wa
ing by the jetty. The city walls were low here b
jutted well into the water. There would, without doul
be an attempted entry here. There could be no gener
worth his pay in command of this invading army or t
first rush would have been here, at the shore, Ema
thought.

He approached a tall burly man holding a long ste
bar, and told him his thought.

"Oh, Emalf. You think so? You must be right if yc
agree with me, and where can such an army com
from, one place only—Tayrb. And it will be no arm
either, for no such thing exists, as I have been tellin
these—people. It is the scum of Tayrb we have t
beat off and that will be no problem."

"They will outnumber us five to one," interjected
small man with a straggling gray beard.

"There will be more than from Tayrb," Emalf said
"Nipsirc—and maybe other towns. All their Police ar
the scum of the cities, or very nearly so. And what wil
raise such an army for them? The promise of loot an
ravagery! Whatever the odds we must beat them off."

"That is what we will do," said the big man.

Two women emitted little squeals and rushed away

"Do you run to hide the crockery?" shouted a man,
and many laughed.

"Do not laugh. It is a wise thing," growled the man
with the steel bar. "There are daughters, too, to be
hidden."

"Look!" came a shout.

"Yes. They come now, wading about the walls,"
said Emalf.

"There are always soldiers there, now they can earn
their keep. We will wait here for those who get

rough. There will be some. This night has just be-
un."

"If only the army was here."

"And Prince Dedn."

"We will do this without them," said Bartin. "The
rince has plainly been outmarched. What do you say,
malf?"

"I don't know of course. But it seems so. I would
uess they watched him go, to Tayrb I think he went,
hough no one was told. Bartin, we should be nearer
he walls."

"No. We stay here. There are others nearer the
valls. There will be those who come to us, soon
nough, and we'll be more fresh for less running madly
bout. Let me see. Tayrb is not three days away. They
night be on their way back by now."

"Yes. We must hold them. They come now, my
riend. The end of the wall is darker. They must have
aken a longer road to here and gone right around our
rmy . . ."

"And our army," laughed a man, "won't know and
vill have gone off to Nipsirc or Datames or farther
inland or will stay and enjoy themselves in Tayrb!"

But Emalf didn't think so.

He had more wit than, in this quarter of the town,
to claim a personal knowledge of the Prince, but he
knew Dedn well enough, had even suffered at his
hands often enough for him to learn what the Prince
was likely to do. And though it seemed he had been
outwitted here Emalf was ready to wager it was only
a matter of timing. He would be here. Perhaps a little
late. He prayed the Little Gods to let it not be too
late. The army had left men here, but they were out-
numbered and . . .

A discordant exuberance had been suddenly added
to the already deafening yelling.

"They come," said Bartin quietly.

Great fires were suddenly lit on each of the sea wall
ends and by their light could be seen a straggling but
growing mass of figures surging along the beach.

There were thousands of them!

And as he ceremoniously kissed his blade an checked his position with a quick glance to left and right, Emalf divined what that other massed yell ha betokened.

The horde was through one of the city gates.

Two men ran at him.

He sliced the first man's face half away and parrie the thrust of the other—then he became one of man men fighting desperately, almost swallowed in a crow no one could have beaten back.

In the city there were streets still empty, but mos were rapidly filling. What were, at first, little hand-to hand battles quickly became a *mêlée* in which blade could only be used shortened and where the mo. trustworthy weapons were daggers or short lengths c heavy metal bar.

Hastily erected barricades were easily torn asid and doors battered in with barricade material. Afte that there were screams, for most men had gone to th walls at the first, but a household axe can be a dread ful thing in the hands of a determined woman, even i the hands of a fear-crazed woman, and the Nipsir scum found their first entry into the houses a mistake Besides, there were shops to loot, and the liquor ware houses near the prison, and it was there most of th crowd were led. This, too, was an error, for many troops seemed to have been billeted there.

The palace was still inviolate.

The city gates had been taken and several parties o troops had fought through the horde and retreated to the palace.

The defenders marshalled all the troops from the walls and from the warehouses and prison and swept on the dock area, which was soon cleared, but as these troops attempted to drive up the hill, through the city towards the palace, they found themselves faced by a foe who had more than life to lose—there was loot to lose. And small parties of soldiers entering houses were met by overwhelming odds and thus many men were lost.

But in the streets the discipline of competent trained fighting men meant slaughter to the scum of Nipsirc.

Though the soldiery exacted terrible vengeance for the murder and rapine they had seen since they reached the streets, their upward march had another effect. They forced the mob back and back to the palace, practically concentrating its strength where it should never have been, and although the military efficiency of the defenders beat through the brutal force of invaders, one of the gates was lost.

The mob poured through the gap.

The mob in the town, either to cover their retreat or from mere accident, started a score of fires and a dreadful flare, a wild crackling and a gathering crescendo of screams rose to the blackness of the smoke which hung and refused to be dissipated by too light a wind from the sea.

There were few wounded left alive for long.

So crazed were those still defending their houses, so difficult was it to distinguish friend from enemy, that wounded who managed to crawl to houses were met by insanely furious householders if not by the brutality of Police in occupation.

A large proportion of the invaders thought it better to snatch what loot they could. This conception of their duty spread rapidly. There was a lull. Jealous combats, often between Police and Police, were fought over the half-clothed bodies of trembling women; men now fought bitterly against those who should have been with them, against anyone who invaded their looting area, against anyone who lived.

The attempt at the palace gates, to reclose the gap and cut off the enemy within, succeeded only for a few minutes and cost too many lives in officers and men, and again the mob poured in.

The flare over the town rose awfully and licked high and redly and maliciously from the roofs. Scraps of floating material whirled into the air and floated and

sank and spread the fire till it reached the trees abou
the palace.

The soldiers, the palace attendants and the yelling
excited slaves had twice now hunted down and exter-
minated those of the mob who had penetrated the
gate. But a swift, deadly, unexpected rush up the street
carried the gate at the side.

Howling, furious at the long delay, carrying torches
and brands lit in the great fire, the rabble rushed into
the palace grounds, a mob robbed of humanity by
anger, by plunder, and by blood-lust, surged against
the triple line of defenders and the line broke and little
knots of encircled defenders fought, and with terrible
effect, but were decimated.

Along one bank of the river the trees were in flames.
The smoke was acrid in the eyes and nostrils of those
on the river's farther side, and they watched burnt
timber being tossed into the water and used as rafts.
Then the rabble found the river to be shallow and
leaped in in swarms.

The leaders of the Religious Invasion entered after
their men.

Gradually, almost unbelievably, their commands to
the mob were accepted and obeyed; as concerted attack was hurled against the palace guard on the farther
bank, sheer weight forced the palace guard to retreat,
but its retreat was orderly.

The invaders' leaders screamed urgent and exultant
commands.

Carpen, his face a mask of blazing fanatical ecstasy,
led his group right up the wide steps and into the
palace and there poured in after them a close-packed
stampeding multitude.

No resistance inside the palace could be other than
gallant—but co-operation of group with group was
utterly impossible; the attackers preferred insane looting and rapine to fighting, the entire palace was open
to them and scenes the city had seen were re-enacted
in the palace, but the slaughter and pillage in the
palace were more wholesale, more horrible. Women

were dragged screaming, even maimed, from incredible hiding places. Palace slaves found alive died, and as they died the laughter of their murderers spread through the palace as the sport found favor in room after room.

And suddenly, without warning of the slightest, almost silently, there were long ordered lines of fully armed competently marshalled men behind the plundering despoiling rabble.

In a matter of moments the rabble were beaten and cowed. To them death became a swift irrevocability. A frenzy of terror shook the looting hordes, their weapons had been discarded, surrender bought them no respite from death, hundreds left by the windows, to drop and maim themselves on the paving, to find themselves looking up into the unmerciful faces of men with swords and axes—the outside walls of the building became black with crawling climbing fly-like figures trying to get away, to get to the roof, to get to safety, but there was no safety. Armed men bent over from the eaves and dealt with those who climbed.

In a small outbuilding in the grounds the remnant of terrified palace women—servants, ladies and slaves—supported each other and a pitifully few nobles and guards, almost all gravely wounded.

There was a silence over this last stand of the defenders, and because of the silence the returned army took some time to find them for the palace itself had engaged all their attention.

Bulinga stared out past the solitary nobleman who guarded the open portico. Alona and she, and the black slave girl who stood with them, bore weapons of a sort but with no expectation of benefiting from their possession.

Those who now faced the little party, those who now edged forward for the final slaying rush, were the fanatical core of the Police. They were about to exterminate the heathen—and the first few shouts from single, scouting soldiers disturbed them not at all.

They were moving forward, determinedly, quite

quietly, just about to break into the rush which inev
tably would have destroyed the palace remnant—whe
they found there were men of another army amon
them. The attack never reached the pavilion. Carpen'
men turned to the new attacker and Dedn's army nov
received practically the only objection to their pres
ence.

It was difficult for the last remnant in the pavilio:
to realize that the horror of the night was no longe
for them. The horror had descended upon them littl·
more than two hours before and yet it seemed to hav·
been raging for an eternity—in which time had beer
a non-existent factor. The relief was so sudden, s·
divine, that to believe it at once would have beer
damaging to the balance of mind. There were some
the power of whose wills could carry them no further.
But many of the defenders found that to abstain from
battle was impossible, they found their tired bodies
alive with new strength and hacking stubbornly, shoulder to shoulder with fresher troops.

At the doorway where Bulinga had been stationed
the solitary nobleman still stood on guard, stubbornly
refusing aid, he knew death had come to him already
—was with him now. The Police had recalled those of
themselves who had encircled the pavilion, recalled
them to this spot, so they in turn could make a last
stubborn fight. All these seemed to have a loyalty to
their Religion and their cause and not to be mere
vandals and scum like the army they had lost.

Bulinga caught sight of Carpen's face, as she was
being escorted past—no, through—the fighting which
was now broken from one mass of struggling men into
many small separated groups.

Then, almost at once, she saw approach them, along
the blackened burnt body-strewn loot-scattered avenue
which led to the pavilion, the great black mastodon of
the Prince—of His Dignity Prince Dedn—dancing
towards them over the bodies and between the fighters,
on its hugely high face a look of ineffable almost
human delight mingled with disdain.

Bulinga gasped, involuntarily, a queer excitement caught her as she saw Dedn high in the great saddle on its back.

His approach caused men to fall aside: the great beast was unusual to the mainland.

Only in one place, some three yards distant from where Bulinga stood, did the fighting continue. Carpen's hard core of men were still not beaten. In their turn these Police had no hope—but they were no less fanatical than before.

Carpen, his face cold but with an inner fire which Bulinga had never before seen to it, lifted his arm and said something to a man near him and Bulinga saw that he was pointing at Dedn.

The man was raising a sling—his gaze, with eager concentration, judging distance and direction.

Bulinga swooped forward, falling, outstretched—and caught the man's ankle, pulled and brought him down. Deflected only a fraction by her action the stone flew and a soldier beside Dedn fell lifeless from the mastodon's swaying back.

The eyes of Carpen and Bulinga met.

Recognition entered those of Carpen and with it the realization of all she had done. A glare of sudden insane venomous hatred lit him.

"Accursed pagan! Heathen, vile and evil! Even at this time you thwart me! Kill her, kill her, kill her!"

There were none to obey. Soldiers of Dedn's ringed him round even as the stone had sped on its way, but Carpen, face and figure and mind distorted by the sweeping furious hate of a fanatic, caught up a metal bar abandoned to the ground by one of his men, raised it and brought it down heavily upon Bulinga's back—then laid about himself wielding it as battle axe, until a thrown axe caught his neck, half severing head from shoulders.

Bulinga knew she was held by someone, being lifted up and up, and someone's face—a blur which became

recognizable as the face of Dedn—was bending dov
to her, anxiety in the darknesses which were his eye

"It's her, Your Dignity: the Princess."

"Yes, I know. Give her to me." That was Dedn
voice, she knew.

"Dedn, it's me, Bulinga," she murmured drowsily.

"Bulinga—you're all right? Where were you hurt?

"On my back—but it is all right—I feel quite a
right," she murmured again.

She lay against the firm unyielding comfortabl
warmth of his chest and his arms were protectivel
around her and she knew she was on top of th
mastodon—with him in its saddle.

"It is all over, Bulinga," Dedn's voice said, deep
and near to her ear, and she could sense all the gentle
ness in it and feel the way it moved up out of th
brownness of his chest against which she was so com
fortably pressed.

"We're going back to the palace now."

Bulinga's eyes were hard to keep open.

"Don't go away again," murmured Bulinga.

"I wonder if you have succumbed at last?" he
mused. "Surely if it were not so you wouldn't rest here
so contentedly."

Bulinga's eyes opened.

She knew he was only teasing her but a flicker of
resentment was roused in her. After all, what he said
was true at last and he knew it.

"Bulinga, I love you, so very much," he said, and
she realized that that note in his voice had not been
and still was not a note of teasing, but of a pleading to
her and yet at the same time a wry mockery of himself. "With you here, like this, I must tell you,
Bulinga. I have tried so hard, everything, to make myself attractive to you. I have teased you, cherished you,
bullied you—I have tried on you a dozen different
personalities and still you seem unimpressed, and tell
me that I am no different for you from the person you
met in Nipsirc. It was when I left you in the hut that I
realized that I loved you, and I thought you had

own me at last how much you loathed me. I arrived
Edrigir overwhelmingly relieved that you were safe
at determined to leave you as severely alone as you
ished me to do. And then—in the prison that day—
seemed to me—Bulinga, I have tried . . ."

"You tried everything but that which I might have
ccepted," Bulinga said bitterly.

"But that last night when you ran away from me I
was trying to ask you to marry me!"

"You are sure?" Bulinga gasped.

"Of course I am."

"But . . . oh, Dedn, I love you more than anyone
else in the whole world—more than anyone I have
ever known . . ."

She felt the astonishment of joy, in him.

There was a long pause.

"Dedn, I love you so much."

"Bulinga," Dedn said, and his voice trembled, "it is
inexplicable, but at this moment I feel almost afraid to
touch you."

"I want to stay here with you forever," Bulinga
murmured, drowsy again. "I'm so comfortable like
this. I can't believe Carpen hit me."

"Where did you say he hit you?" Dedn inquired
suddenly.

"On the back . . . but there's no need to sound so
worried. I feel so happy. Dedn, I love you. . . ."

His arm tightened around her.

Bulinga's eyes closed again. She leaned against him,
almost asleep.

She knew that the man in whose arms she was
allowing herself to be held was a libertine, and yet
not even in her mother's arms had she ever felt such
gentle protective strength about her as that of his arms
now; she was very tired, and a very pleasant languor
seemed to flow from him to encircle and enclose and
lull her. Surely nothing could hurt her with the arms of
such a man about her. Though how many other
women had lain in this very harbor, and thought these

same thoughts? No matter, he loved her so much. . .

Dedn carried her down from the mastodon and ga[v]
her into the arms of the waiting chamberlain.

His voice quivered.

"Be careful of her," he begged. "She is dead."

Emalf stood on the wet planking and watched t[h]
sturdy, high-masted vessel sail into port.

"Now that I have the ship for Atlan, she is almo[st]
certain to come with me," he said.

At the sound of his voice two men near him eye[d]
him curiously.

Emalf ignored them.

She looked to be all he'd been told of her, this littl[e]
ship.

He looked to the morning gray of the sky and th[e]
charcoal gray of the sea, the robust white of foam an[d]
surf.

"She won't mind a little weather today," he mused[.]

He began to walk up to the town.